Hell In The Choirstand

Titus Pollard Publishing

P.O. Box 1902

Clayton, NC 27528

Hell In The Choirstand© 2013 Titus David Pollard

ISBN-10: 1692214968

ISBN-13: 978-0-692-21496-1

First Printed April 2015

Printed in the United States of America

Hell In The Choirstand

By

Titus Pollard

ACKNOWLEDGEMENT / DEDICATION PAGE

I don't think it the least bit cliché when I first thank God, my Lord and Savior for this particular novel. I started HELL on January 4th, 2004. Eight rewrites and seven plot changes later, here it is! This novel exists because I truly waited on the Lord for the right story to be told!

I must thank my beautiful wife, Melissa, for her patience, criticism, and prayers. "I'm good honey, you go write," she would say. Thanks Honey! You are my gift.

To my mentor and my friend, Jacquelin Thomas (hey Bernard!), who encouraged, critiqued, prayed for me. Now I take my blessings and throw them like a boomerang at you – and a double blessing.

To my writer's group, New Vision: Jacquelin, Monique, Karen, Casandra, Suzetta, Sandra. *Plan your work. Work your plan.*

To my beta readers: Coach Mandy, my close friend Roger, Andra, Andrea, Barbara, Jackie, Tara and Lauren who critiqued my story from start to finish. Thanks for the encouragement and advice.

To my Pastor, Rev. Daniel Sanders, Springfield Baptist in Raleigh NC. Much of the storyline is because of your inspiration and ideas from your sermons.

To a group of fabulous musicians and ministers of music who may never see this: V. Michael McKay, Rev. Stephen Hurd, Kyle E. Kelley, Min. Roland Perry, Min. Ray Watkins, Moses Tyson, Malcolm Speed. Some of the drive to take my ministry to new levels came from conversations with each of you.

"You can have a great book, but people have to know you wrote it," says Stephen and Vicky Toth of Your Web Image, as they helped me tie up loose ends in my marketing plan!

Much appreciation goes to Professors Garcia, Dixon, and Sampson from my alma mater and HBCU, Lane College. I drew from and channeled your music history, theory and conducting classes for the *true stuff* ♫♪ in this book!

Thank You to any musician, choir director, pastor, singer who has been influenced in some way by my music, teaching videos, workshops, etc. I've learned as much from you as you have from me!

An Abridged History of the Society of Tyrus

By 9th century Byzantine tradition, music was thought to be submitted to the masses from "heavenly origin", in which the mortal composer would receive little (actually, no) financial acknowledgment. As musicians wanted recognition (payment) for their works, the general clergy saw this as the first step toward musical carnality – and the worldwide degradation of church music.

In the 17th century, the ideologist and musician **Archimedes Giannopoulos** (Archimedes interpreted as "master of thought"), wrote treatises which condemned the worship practices of the universal body called the Church. Just as Christians regard the Bible as the undisputed Word of the Living God (with its 150 Psalms divinely authored by David; shepherd boy, master musician and King), Giannopoulos claimed to have received direct orders from Satan to be a disciple and an imperial messenger of the musical underworld, commissioned to author dissertations on how singing and instruments may be used to conjure, "Methodical, profane responses to a Mythical Overseer." As these manuscripts were read, interpreted, critiqued and passed on, they fell into the hands of disinterested historians and musicians who failed to catalogue them and, eventually, lost track of their whereabouts.

Giannopoulos' original, anti-Christian manuscripts on musical history and theory were re-discovered and authenticated by the 20th century historian, curator, and Lutheran musician, **Phillip Western**, who founded the **Society of Tyrus in 1911.** Western began to incorporate his personal concoctions, spells, and other forms of witchcraft into Giannopoulos' demonic manuscripts, attempting to manipulate what he believed was a world of incredulous people passing themselves off as Christ-like. As an acclaimed authority on satanic music, Western used his written principles and formulas for exclusive membership in the Society. When asked about the motivation for his controversial campaign, Western would cite:

Pastors who could not prove their calling
Lack of a considerate journeyman salary
Overall disagreement with church (religious) dictates

Western began to spread his gospel as he traveled the United States and parts of the world. Many of his fellow musicians and singers considered him an infidel, but in spite of his dissenters, he amassed an increasing number of followers. To Western's amazement, this core group of fellow musicians convinced Western that they could organize under his leadership, develop the manuscripts into membership manuals, and conduct annual membership meetings where they would share their experiments in musical warfare. Before the culmination of their meetings, the brotherhood would vow to return to their various churches and worship centers, and incorporate the spells they had learned and developed into the church services for the purpose of confusing the people's belief in their God. This was the thriving measure of the Society of Tyrus.

The Society held the theory that music in any organized fashion is merely for art sake with no true spiritual value. For how could music enhance the worship of a being that the congregate does not truly have faith in?

Those considered for *The Society of Tyrus* are:

Classically educated in the Arts, particularly Music
Biblically knowledgeable
Highly skilled at improvisation
Must be in charge of or play at a congregation of 500 members or greater;

Must own themselves to the philosophy that they can rule congregations with their music; and
Fall under belief that they have been called by a higher being that was created to corrupt and confuse the "people of God"

As these self-willed, heretical musicians became familiar with the liberality and comradery of their Society, membership increased to the point that Tyrus' leadership saw a need to establish chapters in strategic areas, labeling them the Pentagrammatory. Among this group was the Gamma Γ chapter, established in the Detroit metro area and chartered in 1962, which encompassed the city of Olds.

The Gamma chapter exists to present-day, where the national Society recognizes this group of musicians for its exertion of demonic power.

This is where our story finds one member of the Society of Tyrus in particular, Renard Singleton, battling against the saintly Jeremiah David Day for domination of the music that will influence their personal lives, the life of Ezekiel Baptist Church, and the life of the Church Universal.

Prelude

In the 3rd Judicial Circuit Court
Wayne County, MI
June 20th, 1984
State of Michigan vs. Adrian Singleton, father of
Luciferious Singleton
Friend of Court (FOC) Support Hearing

I don't frequent courtrooms. Today happens to be my first visit. Arrays of God's creatures are jamming the courtroom. Here comes an assortment of stuffy types in bowties donning cracked leather satchels. They're beginning to swirl freely along the perimeter of the room like notes careening on sheet music.

They act like they own the place.

There must be some strange brand of humor floating around inside this room because all the legal types came in joking and whispering to the hodge-podge of city cops, sheriffs and detectives, who in return offered despicable smirks and giggles. I guess they can afford to goof off. It's a party to them probably because they're not defendants with cases pending.

Then there are those like me; everyday people having to scratch and search for available space on these frigid planks of greased hardwood. From my vantage point, I can compare obviously wealthy versus cash-deprived middle-aged men, and whether this same group of humans are healthy or drug-laden. Every man within reach of me appears to be a defendant to their individual predicament, so after the court clerk reads my name on the docket and I declare my presence, I'll pray that the court will be impartial, even merciful, to my situation.

The judge first disposes of child support cases where the father spent an evening or two on the top floor of the Municipal Building - a special guest of the taxpayers.

Perhaps they couldn't be trusted to appear on their own. Glad I'm not one of them.

"Adrian Singleton, case number #MCL23407," the clerk announces. The moment of reckoning is upon me.

Judge Rhonda Abbott is a fair-skinned woman who, by her demeanor, doesn't fit the usual human assumptions I give to stormy-eyed, bleach-blonde females. Now that I get a good look at her, I'm sure I heard someone call out her name as she brushed past me in the hallway a few minutes ago.

She extends a pleasant "Good Morning," and then immediately begins examining the documents in her hands. She gives me a disjointed look. "You named your baby what?"

I can't see the harm in letting a couple seconds roll by, because this woman's already got me on edge. "You've got it all wrong, Your Honor," I say as I shift my weight to steady my nervousness. "I had no part in naming our baby. I wasn't given a chance to."

"I see." Judge Abbott adjusts her rimless glasses, leans forward on the bench, and gives me the type of look that makes me feel like I'm lying, even though I know I'm testifying to the truth.

I swallow hard just to regain some composure. "You see, Your Honor, I know my baby's mother gave our son that name just to spite me. She's always angry."

"Really?"

Perspiration begins to roll down my forehead. "Yes ma'am. When she told me that I'd gotten her pregnant, I knew that I would do anything I could to take care of the baby, even though we don't get along."

O Lord. I have no confidence that she understands my explanation.

"Luciferious." She pauses, seeming to crinkle the court document between her hands. "Who in their right mind would name a child this?"

"My baby's mama told me the boy deserved that name because she said, 'The child's a seed from Satan.'"

There is a series of hollow vocal clatters coming from the courtroom audience. The judge smacks her gavel.

"Is the mother here?" Judge Abbott asks. She flicks through the pages of the court order. "A Miss Tracy Wilkes?"

She pauses but the courtroom remains silent.

"Well, I'll tell you what, Mr. Singleton, this court is baffled. The child's mother didn't think it important enough to show up for the child support hearing that benefits her baby?"

She didn't give me enough time for a response. I really don't think she was looking for one anyway.

"Besides," she continues, "I want to hear her explain this – Satanic - child's name. Firsthand. Do you have any idea where Miss Wilkes could be?"

"No, Your Honor."

"Mr. Singleton, before I even entertain a ruling on child support and visitation rights, I'm taking a personal liberty and setting a Name Change Proceeding in accordance with Statutes MCL 711.1 thru 711.3, to present evidence for changing the name of dependent child, one Luciferious Singleton, set thirty days from today. I would advise any and all parties that one Tracy Wilkes be located and convinced to appear at hearing per this order, or there will be a warrant issued for her arrest."

That kinda scares me. I'm really not into getting Tracy in trouble. She's making enough trouble without my help. "Why Your Honor?"

"Wouldn't you like to see this child have his name changed to something that might give him a more positive outlook for his future?"

"Yes ma'am." I'm in full agreement of what the judge wants to do, but inside of me there's an eerie feeling that no matter what my child's name becomes, he's already marked for life.

Verse 1 ♫

For we wrestle not against flesh and blood, but against principalities, against powers, against the rulers of the darkness of this world, against spiritual wickedness in high places. Ephesians 6:12 KJV

Most would've considered the city of Olds, Michigan, the worst place in America to stage a victorious musical battle. Who would've thought; a *musical battle*?

In mid-June, Olds' academically failing public schools were closed due to summer vacation. The city air had been Ajax clean for quite a while by then – no longer pungent from tanning leather, burning rubber and forging steel, which any laid-off factory worker would have preferred over the present spectacle of vacant warehouses and inactive assembly lines. Big Three Auto execs found retreat with their golden parachutes, nestling themselves away in Bloomfield Hills. The blue collars began clawing for the few non-automotive jobs floating around. Investors and brokers lusting after the same dividends that automotive stocks had afforded them, shifted their well-managed portfolios to less riskier investments.

The Lions deflated their pigskins and moved from the Silverdome, leaving it infested with cobwebs for five years until a group of European immigrant types stepped up and purchased the stadium for less than the median price of a four-bedroom Colonial.

Over the course of several years, Olds' local government either lacked restraint or common sense, concocting ways to strangle the city and its constituents of funds, honor and trust; which landed them in prison.

Parts of several congregations in Olds departed their right minds by listening to some of God's so-called elect, who plotted and schemed with promises in a future of financial prosperity, forcing the laity to have faith in ideas that were not and never would be. Many lost everything they had. Some even had the gall to blame the Lord for their misfortune, forgetting that their own greed shaped their outcome.

The city was a wretched, yet, in many ways, a symbolic example of how an urban metropolis could be reduced to a remnant of itself. No one but God the Omnipotent had the ability to breathe new life into such a skeletal city. In spite of the pitfalls that surrounded them, the citizens and inhabitants of Olds tried not to despair. In the history of the world God did, after all, fashion and rebirth a valley of dry bones.

So should Olds be considered a complication for the Almighty?

All God needed was one city, one church and a few people poised for His calling. Maybe a God-fearing musician could be fitted into the picture, for good measure.

Then, the battle of music could begin.

Jeremiah David Day counted on one hand the number of times he had been to Olds, but he wasn't lost. He had fallen into that manly habit of gassing up his vehicle, driving around and seeing how a city's streets connect. He wouldn't look at a map. He refused to cut on the GPS. He didn't call OnStar®.

And no, he wasn't going to stop, roll down his car window and ask for directions.

Jeremiah was slightly distracted as he listened to a radio announcer on Praise 102.7 giving details of an upcoming auction that was to take place in the city. After spouting off the date, time and venue for the auction, the announcer sounded comfortable in doing an editorial, petitioning prayer for the pastor and congregation of a church whose occupants appeared to have been forced out of their building for lack of payment and, from the sound of things, maybe even more.

"I want my listeners to understand something. The only way to the true and living God is through Jesus the Christ, and I don't care what Pastor Felix Timmons has preached, or what new religion he thinks he's found. This radio station will continue to pray for him and the entire congregation as they go through this trial of faith. We encourage you listeners to do the same. The announcer cleared his throat. "Now folks, excuse me, but I have to say this. I feel for what the church is going through, and I really am going to pray for them. But there's a lot of repentance needed when a pastor's heresy displaces a church body of five thousand people – all in the name of what he says he learned – from some Gospel music club."

Jeremiah flinched at a loud squelch the radio made. He figured there was a squabble going on at that radio station, judging by the background voices.

There was a silent pause before the DJ came back on air. "I may be fired for what I'm about to say, but while I have the microphone, I'll speak my conviction. Heresy and excommunication should be the first of the charges and punishments for this - pastor – and I use that term loosely," the jockey announced.

Gospel music club? Foreclosures? Heresy? Jeremiah began to wonder just what kind of city he had contracted himself to.

Verse 2 ♫

Before I formed thee in the belly I knew thee; and before thou camest out of the womb I sanctified thee, and I ordained thee a prophet unto the nations. Jeremiah 1:5 KJV

Jeremiah counted it a blessing that his girlfriend wasn't cruising around in the car with him. She would've been going on, fussing about his listening to the radio, talking to her, tapping out chord progressions on the dashboard and driving - all at the same time. He didn't need a reminder that multi-tasking while operating a vehicle was careless behavior, but recent opportunities to practice with an actual piano or organ had been few and far between.

Jeremiah toured the city in the same roundabout fashion as the previous week; viewing churches, hoping to meet and talk with any church folk that would make time to chat with him on the Lord's greatness. He couldn't seem to erase from his mind a particular church he'd driven by and stopped where a gentleman - he later learned was a deacon – had brushed him off like he was a penniless vagabond asking for a handout. Jeremiah winced at the thought of how that same righteous church officer would've treated an actual sinner with a dire need, because his treatment of Jeremiah was sub-par at best.

Jeremiah had since learned that off-putting personal responses were commonplace in Olds, whether they proclaimed Christianity or not. He thought that it could be a result of urban blight, or a lack of understanding what it meant to be Christ-like. Whatever the reason, Jeremiah didn't want any part of it.

That following Saturday evening he'd passed dozens of churches on dozens of blocks and he could've stopped at any one that appeared to be open, but angelic-like forces seemed to direct his lefts, rights and stops. His faith in God prevented him from believing in chance events, so it wasn't mysterious to him when his journey ended on Auburn Hills Road.

Ezekiel Missionary Baptist Church was planted on the outskirts of suburbia. Experience taught Jeremiah that churches rimming the perimeter of a city's main thoroughfare tended to be smaller in structure. Ezekiel, however, was a mega-church; a monstrosity on the edge of nowhere geographically specific with a welcome sign under the church's name spouting *The City's Best Kept Spiritual Secret.*

He decided to give more attention to the radio announcement of the church auction a bit later. The gate to Ezekiel Baptist's entrance was unlocked and open. Curiosity beckoned for him to take a look around.

On that evening, Ezekiel's church grounds appeared vacant. Jeremiah's plan, however, to investigate the campus in solitude was short-lived.

From the corner of a connected building approached a gentleman with a dark roasted complexion. As he came within a few feet of Jeremiah, he stopped. "Let me guess," he said, and then he smiled. He had a towering, athletic build that seemed in contrast to his somewhat serene manner. "You just happen to be in the neighborhood, huh?" He didn't seem to be bothered by Jeremiah's intrusion. He said he was walking the grounds, spending time in meditation, and that he wasn't aware that the front gate had been left unlocked. "So what brings you here?" he asked.

Jeremiah informed him that his new job brought him to Olds, and was searching for a church to attend the upcoming Sunday.

"New job," he said, "in what occupation?"

"I've accepted a teaching position at Olds Central High."

"Oh." The man turned and looked off into the distance. "We're talking about public school, right?"

"Yes." Jeremiah sensed the pessimism. The man probably asked himself why anyone would accept a teaching position in Old's public schools. The financial condition of the city had forced teachers to be in more of a Mosaic Exodus than an Abrahamic Promised Land entrance. "Have you ever done something that you can't really explain, but somehow you know that – you're being – led?"

The man smiled as if in contemplation. "I've been guilty of that. On several occasions."

"Can you tell me about this church?" Jeremiah asked, wanting to divert from that topic.

The gentleman started walking down the drive which was parallel to the length of the church. "C'mon, follow me."

As they conversed, Jeremiah received a tour of the church's hundred year old original structure, their current sanctuary and their future worship center – a concrete hull under construction.

"We're proud of our mission's department," he declared. "And I'm somewhat confident that a solid word comes from the pastor. Our church has outgrown its present structure even though it's only ten years old."

"An evolving congregation during a recession. Pretty amazing," Jeremiah said.

He continued to elaborate on some of the various church ministries; ones in which he must have believed added to Ezekiel's growth. "We're only lacking in one area," he said. His voice lowered, "Our music…"

Jeremiah heard the man, but refused to respond or do anything to stir a curiosity. He did hear the man, though.

"Daniel Trantham," the man declared as he held out his hand.

"Jeremiah Day," he responded, realizing that the two of them had talked, had even gone into detail over various subjects, without the benefit of a formal introduction. Jeremiah felt an ease with the gentleman, a comfort unlike any he had experienced since his arrival in the city.

As they continued to stroll along with Bro. Trantham doing most of the talking, Jeremiah's eyes did a faith walk inside the hull of the new edifice. He envisioned concrete clothing itself in carpet, the pews bolting themselves to the floor and a rostrum marching forward to center itself in the pulpit. Ezekiel's congregation was taking up every available seat just as the worship service began. Jeremiah even began to debate on whether he should picture himself at their organ. "And you built this building too small," Jeremiah alleged before he could chase the statement back into his mouth.

Trantham gave him a bizarre gaze. "So that's what you think about me and my congregation, huh?" he asked.

His blood suddenly ran cold. *Oh my God. I've been talking to the Pastor the whole time.*

Verse 3 ♫

*Be not thou envious against evil men, neither desire to be with
them. Proverbs 24:1 KJV*

Detroit. A Mecca for Gospel music. City natives and dedicated
cultural aficionados knew that the Temps and the Jacksons were not the
total musical makeup of that city. The saints couldn't get enough of the
Winans, the Clarks, Hammond or Franklin. The Motor City had been
baptized in church music, and Olds collected the drops of overflow.

Renard Singleton could lay some claim to a portion of the
fortune the city's tremendous musical heritage provided.

He had double-majored in music production and music
business from Arizona State University and had the added pleasure of
finding his bride, Kira Wakefield, while there. Although he matriculated
out in the heat of the western desert, it was the Midwest he loved and
Olds was his hometown.

He'd dreamed of being the heir apparent to his father, Adrian
Singleton, who was the consummate traveling musician, producer and
film scorer. Unlike his father, he would have the good sense not to mire
himself among governmental and business corruptors who manipulated
many of Michigan's prominent musicians straight into bankruptcy, and
the venues at which they played into foreclosure. He wanted no part of
that scene even if it could provide a duo of ultimate desires: unbridled
fame and immense fortune.

He desired employment in the music profession once he
graduated from college; but a job as a church musician? Not really his
first choice.

Yes. There's been countless times on TV when a secular artist
clutches their newly awarded Grammy, looked into the camera, and said
amidst tear-stained sobs, "I'd first like to give all thanks to God!"

Well, this was *not* the lineage of Renard Singleton.

Church wasn't on his mother's mind. Renard's maternal relationship had been strained right through to the point of breaking. Tracy Wilkes was found in the lone closet of their disheveled apartment with enough drug paraphernalia and chemical to choke a large farm animal. Renard was found there on that day, just outside of the closet, clothed in a twice-muddied diaper with an empty strained carrot baby food jar in his hand.

Church wasn't on his dad's mind, either. Now forcibly abandoned by his drug-ridden mother while still a toddler, Renard was taken up to be raised by a loving but tremendously preoccupied father, Adrian, who was a working musician very much caught up in the secular world.

It was safe to say that Renard wouldn't belong to the ever-growing American population of music artists claiming to have sprouted their roots in the church. No, he didn't blossom with the spiritual, only to leave its confines to seek after the world's trappings. The Singleton family attendance at church, any church, was a distant memory by the time Renard graced the Earth.

Yet somehow, like a wayfaring stranger, he ended up on the doorsteps of a musician-needy Ezekiel Chapel Missionary Baptist Church in 2010. The church considered it a blessing, a visitation from the Holy Spirit in answer to a prayer.

As for Renard, he didn't know how to consider it.

A group of selected church leaders auditioned him for the position as the church organist. They asked if he had received any formal training. That became his opportunity to put on a stellar performance. He claimed, "My training came from school, but my gift came from the Lord." He then hit a few vocal riffs, spouted off just enough church lingo to be dangerous and the church was outdone; they'd found the ultimate musician.

A few *Hallelujahs* and *Thank You, Jesus'* later, the pastor made a recommendation and the church hired him immediately.

Since that time, one hundred, eighty-two Sundays and some four hundred rehearsals have come and gone.

Renard did an ear deafening slap of his hand against the wooden cabinetry of the Hammond, and then stood up. "Come on and get the notes right!" He waved his arm. "Sopranos, if you can't do any better than that – shoot, I can make you sing the passage one person at a time. That way, I'll bet we find out who's singing off-key."

"I don't mean any harm," rebutted one of the ladies in the soprano section, "but some of these notes are just too high."

"I didn't ask you, or anybody else, for advice. Did I?" Renard coughed to clear his throat, and then massaged the shadow forming on his face.

Georgia Fisher, the choir's president, was a no-nonsense lady who claimed belief in two institutions: education in any form, and the Lord. She claimed to view the church as a community beacon that existed to fulfill the needs of a needy people. The blood of her savior was thicker than the blood of her kinfolk.

Whatever.

In one way, Renard feared Georgia. If his misdeeds ever produced a bad reflection on her blessed Ezekiel Baptist, she'd press the laity for a called meeting, state her case against him, and see to it that his personal items accompanied him out of the building.

Georgia stood, leaning back on the wooden partition that separated the choir stand from the pulpit. She spoke in a whispered tone, "Renard, the song really is high. Give us a chance to work our way up to the notes."

"This song isn't high. It's what happens when the singers get lazy." He met Georgia's eyes with a glare, reading her calculated moves, knowing that she was working through a well-known routine. "I know what I'm doing," he told her. "Stay out of this."

Georgia angled her gaze from his direction towards the choir members. "He doesn't mean it like it sounds. It's his tone. It's extremely harsh. And I'm being nice when I call it just that."

Renard swelled up on the inside. Georgia had to have known that he heard every word that came out of her mouth. He shot back, "Oh no, I mean it *exactly* like I said it."

One of the tenors fidgeted up to the front of his seat with an enraged look on his face. "We're adults here, and you better start recognizing us as such!" he screamed while slamming his hymnal shut.

A few choir members held up the all-to-famous, Baptist church forefinger and began hastening out of the choir stand in two different directions.

Georgia used the partition to stand erect. "Just stop, everybody!" She faced Renard, her head hung as in a state of embarrassment. "You're a Christian leader that should lead in a Christian way."

Renard smelled the dissension in the air, laughing to himself at the thought of being called a *Christian*. "Is there anything else you feel you need to say before we sing the notes correct this next time?"

One of the altos startled Renard as she stood up and pointed a finger at him, her eyes wide and mouth parted. "You can demand respect from me when you start giving it. Don't think you're frightening anyone by trying to out talk them. I'm no child," she shouted as she dropped back onto her seat, shuffling an armful of lyric sheets.

Renard, angered from the choir's response to what he thought should have been a normal choir rehearsal, spun around and stamped back to the organ. He made a swift decision not to address their comments any farther. "I'm not going to be here all evening. So we might as well continue." He raised his arms in a conducting position. "Let me hear the part again. *Correct* this time."

After some brief murmuring, the choir members opened their music, fell into place, and resumed rehearsal.

When Renard gave a signal, the choir rose slowly from out of their seats. He played the chords leading up to the phrase from the *Milton Brunson and Tommie's* song:

♫♪*Burdens are too much, for me to bear. There is no way I can live without you.*♫

The choir ran through the phrase a second time with fewer difficulties. Renard gave a director's signal for the choir to hold the last chord. When his hand dropped, the choir collapsed out of exhaustion. He thought, for a moment, about how he would phrase his next comment, but he was broiling in anger that the singing wasn't to his liking. "How do y'all call yourselves a choir and let these little phrases kill you? Good god."

Just as those last words spewed out of his mouth, Renard could hear a voice crackling on at the far end of the choir stand. "Uh, brother musician, are we working on the solo part this evening? I'd like to try it, if you don't mind." Mavis Crenshaw, *Miss Congeniality* of the choir, flipped through the pages of her choir notebook, clearing her throat.

Renard wondered how she had the courage to even suggest an attempt at such a feat. He swallowed, wishing to himself that her singing was as fine as she looked. "Sister Mavis, you try every solo part that comes available."

Mavis raised an eyebrow. "And?"

"And . . . you couldn't hold a tune if God himself poured it in you. Get serious. I need somebody that can sing the solo and not waste everyone's time imagining themselves with it." He turned his back to her. "Anybody else?"

Moments passed.

"Tamla, why don't you come and try the song?" Renard asked.

"Okay," she said, faintly.

Tamla Horton was a musical dream. Most of the women envied her talent and looks; many of the men – including Renard - worshipped her for the same. The older saints shied away from her because of things they'd heard she was involved in. He guessed they found it difficult to bear witness to her singing because of her lifestyle, since she was better known for having her legs open than for her melodious voice. That didn't matter. As long as she kept her voice in form, Renard cared less about the frequency of her sexual conquests.

Tamla strutted out of the alto section.

There were whispers coming from the choir stand, and eyes rolling in heads. Then, there were more whispers. Tamla seemed to be undaunted by their reactions.

Renard played a short introduction on the organ as Tamla took the mike, drew a breath, and sang:

♪*You know I can't make it on my own, on my own. . .*♪

She gave a faultless ad lib, drawing closer to the choir's entrance for background. The song progressed, and the choir became more comfortable as they carried their vocal drive to the vamp:

♫*I have tried it over, and over. 'Cause there is no other way, is no other way; is no other way. There is no-o-o-o way I can live without you.*♫

When the choir and the soloist reached the finale of the song, they slumped into their seats, some gripping their heads or chests while others looked around in disgust as though they weren't fazed by the physical exertion of the singing.

"I guess that's all for now. It's a cryin' shame that this is the best sound I can get out of you right now. Like that

little singing would kill you," Renard fussily told them. "I'd
hate to see how you'd react if we had to rehearse an entire
concert. Just pitiful."

One of the tenors spoke out. Since he wasn't
important to Renard, he'd never paid attention to the guy's
name. "It doesn't matter how you think we did." He
scratched his graying, thinning scalp. "Well . . . maybe it
matters some. For the notes and how it sounds. But it's the
Lord who looks at the heart," he said with an obvious hint of
contempt.

Renard grunted loud enough to be heard by whoever
might be listening. "So you say. The Lord just may look at
the heart. It's the listener's ears that I worry about when you
sing." With a rush, he dismissed choir rehearsal before
someone else decided to throw out an insult.

At his home later that evening, Renard grew dizzy
from watching Kira as she ran about the house wiping,
dusting, and chatting something indiscernible. He couldn't
bear the commotion.

He retreated upstairs to his home office because he
wanted time to wind down from the humor and disruptions
that choir rehearsal always brought about. He found comfort
in studying his favorite membership book, *The Edicts of
Tyrus Society*:

> *Feel assured that human fallacies show up in
> public displays of ignorance, tyranny, jealousy and
> violence. There is no savior or god for this! Carry out
> your role in The Society as instigator for foolish
> human actions, and your assignment will be tranquil.
> AΩ*

Verse 4 ♫

So then because thou art lukewarm, and neither hot nor cold, I will spue thee out of my mouth. Revelation 3:16 *KJV*

A couple days later, Renard had settled himself behind the doors of Sound Shocker Studios, where the walls were lined with posters of the hardest of hard rockers; Mollie Hatchet, AC/DC and others, coupled with gangs of the gangsta rappers - Monsta, SlimThug and so on. Not quite the atmosphere for the Messianic faithful. It wasn't intended to be.

Inside the studio, the sound booth's coating of charcoal ebony paint and matching acoustical carpet established a tabula rasa ambience meant to enhance musical awareness and deaden unwanted sound waves. This was the atmosphere Renard craved, his preferred space for creativity.

It must've worked.

Eighteen hours and one hundred fifty-six takes later, a rap tune, *Mythical Messiah,* was birthed from the shadows.

"Don't you think the track could use a bit more reverb?" Renard Singleton reached across the mixing board to adjust the midrange and bass, and then he listened to a few more bars of the song. "It's missing something. Another lyric line or something on the chorus, I think."

"Dude, I don't get you. Still trying to mess with perfection," said Fredrico Knight, Renard's childhood friend and music engineer. "You tweak the mess out of every song you write. This track don't need no more punch. Leave it alone."

Fredrico had done well for himself. He had taken a red brick, dilapidated building and turned it into one of the most formidable music production studios in the area. Given his personal history as the product of a convicted, drug-dealing dad and a mother who birthed six and raised none, Fredrico deserved the gold for battling personal odds and coming out on top. Even at twenty-one years young, he was still hood rat enough to know how to add freshness to a hip-hop or R & B cut.

"What's your take on the bridge?" Renard asked. They had agreed on inserting a *Judas Priest* sampling to his composition.

"Ingenious! And aw man, the way we weaved *I Rule My Destiny, It's Mine* into the chorus. It's just seamless. I'm telling you we've got a hit. Have you given thought to marketing this cut?"

"I want to release it as a single in the Digital Underground first. Buy an ad in XXL. Maybe another artist will pick it up and nurse it to another level."

Fredrico rubbed his buzz cut from front to back, then back to front. "Yeah. Sounds like a plan. But-."

"But what?" Renard gave him a motionless gaze.

"Re'Re' I've wanted to say for some time . . . when are you gonna kill this under-the-table, behind the scenes work with your craft?"

Renard glanced up, alerted by the change in Fredrico's voice. "There's only so much exposure I can do right now. You know that."

"That's what I mean. I mean . . . you're still at this church right? Ezekiel?"

"Yeah. And I'm trying to keep *that* gig."

"Doesn't mixing this music with church songs and stuff, like, get all messed up in your head?"

"Okay Socrates! You're imagining things. Nah man. I'm straight."

Fredrico stood up, walked around to the back of his studio recliner, leaned forward. "On the real. Wouldn't it be easier to swear your allegiance to either your secular work or whatever you're doin' in the church?"

"What? I've been up all night working on this cut. You ever known me to put this much into a *church* song?" He cussed. "If this doesn't show you where my allegiance is, I don't know what can."

Fredrico pulled the computer mouse closer and clicked it a couple times. For a few seconds, he stared at his computer screen, and then made a motion for Renard to remove one of the portable hard drives that contained a copy of their recorded tracks. "I'd be scared. My dad's in prison and we ain't gonna talk about my sorry mama. G'ma raised me. That's cool. But while I was in her house, her rules meant going to church whether I liked it or not. And she had this thing – she was serious about her church. But hey. It don't mean nothin' but Benjamins to me."

As Renard packed the hard drive into his shoulder case, he wondered where Fredrico's sudden concern for his church attendance came from. He tried to keep his irritation with the subject from showing. "What about church?" he asked.

"I'm not saying I'm perfect. I'm far from that. But I've been wanting to say something to you about these songs, man. Things *happen* to you when you mix this stuff with that God-thing."

Renard pushed away from the mix board and laughed. "Ooo! Now you gettin' creepy on me."

"Look man. I don't go to church and I got no bones about it. And I don't see myself going no time soon. And G'ma ain't around to tell me different. I'm too old for any of my kin to think they'll whip my butt if I don't find myself in church. So I don't figure myself to be a hypocrite. But you on the other hand . . ."

"Oh, but I am, huh? I'm the hypocrite?"

Fredrico swung his chair around to a desk drawer, opened it, and pulled out a pale green Gideon Bible.

"What you planning to do with that thing?" Renard asked.

Fredrico lifted the Bible in the air. "I don't go to church. Not trying to go. But this," he shook the book in Renard's face, "I fear it and all it stands for. I sometimes tend to believe it brings me good fortune. That's why I keep it handy."

Renard grunted.

"Well, okay," Fredrico said, "maybe hypocrite isn't the right word for you. Is it possible you consider yourself an Atheist? Maybe an Agnostic?"

Renard stood up, snatched the Bible out of his hand, dropped it on the floor and stomped on it, grinding it into the concrete. He rifled Fredrico a determined stare. "The god your G'ma was so insistent for you to have faith in, is the one I don't believe exists."

Fredrico raised his hands in a form of surrender. "Hey! God knows, I've warned you. So do you, dude."

"That's exactly what you should let me do." Renard hopped up and side-stepped, avoiding a rack of equipment, trying to get some distance between him and Fredrico. "I got this."

When he made it home in the early morning hours with his eyes bloodshot and his body shockingly nervous from the consumption of endless energy drinks, Renard did a mental replay of his conversation with Fredrico.

He was no hypocrite.

Hypocrites. Humans with a reputation for talking a great game but acting totally opposite. Renard refused to be that way. He'd never been asked about some faith in a god, but if the day ever came around, he would have no problem telling it. The Jesus stuff? To Renard, it was hype, a fantasy thought up to give people a reason to hope, and the people who attended Ezekiel were no different. For him, that church was a means to his mission, and hypocritical Christians were too simple-minded to comprehend him or his plan.

Membership in the Society of Tyrus had enlightened his understanding that church was a venue to get paid for a display of artistry. Nothing else. The service itself held no significant meaning for him, and he wouldn't sway because of some Christian's senseless belief and opinion.

After taking moments to purge his mind of any specific topic, he began reading and meditating on a passage from his *Edicts* Manual:

> *Address members in the Society by the secret word – LACRIMA – for it is known that water reveals a perfected reflection of self. At designated times in the calendar each of The Society's members must vow to empty themselves of food, but never water. It is through water – the Lacrima – that one may reflect upon thoughts and actions. AΩ*

Verse 5 ♫

. . . Stir up the gift of God which is in thee by the putting on of hands. II Timothy 1:6b

Close to ninety members and visitors congregated in Ezekiel's current sanctuary for their weekly, Tuesday evening Bible study that's led by Pastor Trantham except when an occasional engagement commits him elsewhere. Jeremiah found him to be sound in his Biblical explanations and pleasant when answering questions that came from the floor.

After the study that evening, Jeremiah took an opportunity to view the construction progress of the new sanctuary. The carpeting had been tacked down. The pews, still in bubble wrap, had been delivered. Electric wiring for chandeliers and sconces was poking out from the sheetrock, swinging in place.

After spending a few moments there, he strolled back by way of the connector, a forty foot walkway which seamlessly blended the present building with the future sanctuary. That hall had been transformed into a pictorial timeline of the church, complete with artistic renditions of past pastors, deacon boards, church mothers, and various choirs. When he finished admiring the artwork and got to the end of the connector, he peered into the current sanctuary and found it completely empty of Bible study participants.

Over in the corner at the edge of the choir stand sat the Hammond A-100 organ with its Leslie® speaker. The instrument seemed to be silently whining, begging to be played. There was Jeremiah's opportunity to lay hands on an actual keyboard and not have to pretend like he did when he was driving.

He walked over and stepped up into the pulpit area, placed His Bible and study book down beside him on the organ bench, and pulled on the organ switches.

START switch first. He could hear the buzzing of the internal motor. It was working fine so far. Then he flipped the RUN switch. The buzzing slowed and began to hum like a finely tuned auto engine. He released the START. Ready.

I've gone this far. Now what do I play? Praise and Worship? Hymn? Traditional? Contemporary?

He always favored the key of C-sharp or D-flat depending on what musician he was talking to - and took off on *My Soul Loves Jesus.*

In a matter of moments, his experience became angelic. The feel of the organ's action and the notes careening through the air as he shifted the speaker's half-moon switch from CHORALE to TREMOLO was . . . satisfaction to an overdue longing.

"I didn't know you played." The voice seemed to trail off into a distance.

Jeremiah was shaken from his world, so much so that he knocked books off the organ bench. "Huh?" He didn't immediately see anyone.

"I think you conveniently left that piece of information out when we first talked. I didn't know you played." At some point unbeknownst to Jeremiah, Pastor Trantham had entered the sanctuary.

Jeremiah recovered quickly from the unexpected surprise. "Oh, I'm sorry."

Pastor Trantham walked closer. "Don't be. I actually thought I was hearing things. It sounded like a CD player was left on or someone from the audio ministry had come in without me knowing it. And then I come in here to find that it's you."

"It has been a while since I played an instrument. Over a month at least."

"How long have you played?"

"All my life, or close to it."

Pastor Trantham squeezed his bottom lip and formed his face into a slight frown. "Hmm."

"I um, actually went to college for it."

"Oh? Is that what you teach?"

Jeremiah gasped, caught unguarded by his question. "Do you remember *everything* I said that first day we met?"

Pastor Trantham's eyes sparkled with his laughter. "I seem to have a way of remembering things about people. I may be terrible on names. Well no. I'm pretty good at that, too."

"Must be a pastoral thing."

"Maybe."

"Actually, I teach math," Jeremiah said, trying to steer the conversation back on subject.

"Not music, huh?"

"I could have. Still can if I want. I have the license for it but I chose to go a different path."

"Hmm." Trantham leaned forward, put one leg on a step that led up into the pulpit and rested the book in his hand on a knee. "Give me your name again?"

"Jeremiah Day."

"Right, right I remember. Brother Day just how skilled are you? I mean, can you play about anything?"

"Well, I guess. Pretty much. If I can't play it right away, with practice, I end up getting it."

"Mm hmm. Can you show me?"

Jeremiah's mind ran through a hundred tunes before he settled on one where he might demonstrate his knowledge of the Hammond organ, import a key change or two, and then settle into a solemn chord progression that would allow any congregation to listen, meditate on the goodness of the Lord.

"My God," Pastor Trantham whispered. "You are anointed." The Pastor turned as though he would walk away, but he stopped and turned back. His eyes were large, inquisitive. "Have you considered playing for anybody here in the area?"

The question astounded Jeremiah, who took a moment to consider an answer. "I haven't been around to get to know the churches. I've only attended here since moving to Olds."

"I don't know whether to take that as a compliment or you don't know any better than to hang around at this little church." He chuckled.

"Oh no, I enjoy the services and your Bible study. Please, take the compliment." Jeremiah turned the organ off. His moment of solitude had definitely ended. "This church has a musician though. Right?"

"A musician," Pastor Trantham hesitated, "well, let's just leave it at that."

"Okay. . ."

"Finding an anointed musician in this area – in any area is – near impossible. Don't misunderstand me. There are some great players; they do what's needed to take a church service through the motions. And thank God we even have a good musician that's not a plunker. I have pastor friends who have to struggle with mediocre music departments. I don't want that same type of problem. We're moving into a new sanctuary soon, and my wish is to move in with a truly anointed musician in charge of my music. Someone qualified to oversee the entire department. And brother, I can tell you're anointed."

"Just by that little something I did?"

Pastor Trantham waved his hand. "I'm not crazy. I know what I hear. And I sense God is ready to use you. What a gift."

"Thanks to praying parents who made me stay in church."

"Oh no. It's more than just going to church. You stayed with that talent until the Lord planted His anointing in you."

"Funny. My fiancée says exactly the same thing."

"Fiancée?" Really?"

"Her name's Arze' Chambers."

"Are-zee?" Pastor Trantham tried to pronounce.

"No-no. *Are-sha',*" Jeremiah replied, emphasizing the long a sound. "Her dad's a deacon at their church back home. The way my fiancé tells it, her father wanted a boy who would be named Ezra, after the prophet. Instead, when a girl came along, he took the name and spelled it backwards. A-R-Z-E."

"So her dad still got his prophet," Pastor Trantham said amusingly.

"That's a way of putting, I guess. Hopefully you'll meet her soon. She'll be in town in about a month or so. She has to come on a Sunday that she doesn't have to play back at home."

Pastor Trantham formed a broad smile. "Your fiancée plays as well?"

Jeremiah swallowed hard, knowing that he'd let out a something that Arze' didn't want anyone to know. "Yeah, but she's quiet about it. And when you meet her, please keep that piece under wraps."

"The secret's safe with me," Pastor Trantham said with a touch of humor in his voice. "I am serious, though. I want you to consider playing for us, even if it's on a limited basis."

"I'll definitely pray over it."

"See? That's what I mean."

Jeremiah was puzzled. "What?"

"I'll pray over it." Pastor Trantham shook his head and then smiled. "That alone lets me know that you're coming here isn't by chance."

Verse 6 ♫

*Also I heard the voice of the Lord, saying, whom shall
I send and who will go for us? Then said I, here am I; send
me. Isaiah 6:8 KJV*

About two weeks later, Jeremiah and his fiancée took
advantage of a weekend of some pleasant but often elusive
Michigan weather with swimming, horseback riding and
walking trails along Gaylord Road at the Olds Lake
Recreation Area. With over three thousand acres of marsh,
forest, lakes and fields, their weekend was proving out to be
a far cry from crowds, industrial sites and bumper-to-bumper
traffic.

Arze' Zipporah Chambers had everything it took to
keep Jeremiah's attention; flawless café au lait skin, an
athletic form, a brilliant mind, and a strong will.

Depending on the situation, he found her will to be
sometimes stimulating, sometimes insufferable. Despite her
steadfast disposition, especially on subjects that she refused
to be swayed on, he knew that he was in love and was
preparing to marry a Christian woman in every sense of the
word.

That weekend together was merely a visit for her, as
she was in the process of completing her graduate nursing
degree in her home state of Tennessee at the University of
Memphis. She was ready to be married to Jeremiah, and they
had set a tentative date in September. They made a pact: take
a more budget-friendly route for their wedding and splurge
on their honeymoon and the purchase of a new home. Arze'
had told Jeremiah that they could recite their vows before a
minister of his choosing. If that decision was truly left up to

Jeremiah, Pastor Trantham had become the front runner for that position. After several conversations on the matter, she had no issue with Pastor Trantham officiating their wedding.

As they began to walk along the shoreline, holding hands and skipping rocks against the water, Jeremiah said matter-of-factly, "You know, I've told him that I play the piano and organ."

Arze' paused and gave him a tense look. "You told who . . . what?"

"Rev. Trantham." He began looking off into the distance at nothing in particular. "I told him that I play."

"Oh," she said, as her response trailed off like the rock she tried to skip atop the lake. "I thought we agreed."

"To what, baby?" Jeremiah asked.

"To become bench members."

As long as they discussed Memphis, moving, and marriage, the day had been light and exciting. Jeremiah wasn't prepared for the subject of church music to make the afternoon unbearable. "Bench members?" He sighed out of frustration. He tried to continue their walk. "I don't remember committing to all that."

Arze' stiffened, giving him a twisted gaze that caused him to rethink moving any farther. "Of course you don't," she said. "You remember what's convenient for you. A lifetime of headaches from playing and singing in churches is what you told me you wanted to get away from."

Jeremiah bent down and removed his sandals so that he could dig his bare feet into the beach sand. "I know. In the past, I *might* have said something about headaches, you know, but-"

"You're a math teacher, babe. Remember?"

"I got it. Math teacher. That's going to be my job. But music is my ministry. No matter how hard I may try or what we *might've* agreed on, you know I can't get around it."

Arze' shook her head. "How things change when you go off to find things without me."

"It wouldn't have been any different if we'd have been riding around and searching for a church together."

There was an immediate grimace on Arze's face. It was a deceptive, disappointed look. "You're a man," she declared. "I've come to realize that you're gonna do what you want cause you don't listen. Typical male."

Jeremiah laughed. "It's not like my ability to play fell outta my mouth as soon as I met the man. C'mon now."

Arze' put a hand on her hip. "It ain't funny, Jere. It really ain't funny."

"I didn't commit to doing anything with the music department. I only told him that I played."

"I'm sure that's all you did," she said with an air of sarcasm. "You didn't commit *me* to anything, did you?"

Arze' never seemed to be confident in her ability as a musician. She always claimed that her mother was the influence behind her work as a church musician and, if she had her choice, would never have taken music lessons. Of course, her mother didn't force her to do her undergrad at Fisk – on a vocal music scholarship.

"Well . . . I kinda told him that you play-"

"What?" she shouted.

"Don't' make a big deal out of it. You have to make up your mind for yourself, Arze'. God knows I can't make you."

She snapped her head. "You got that right." She took a couple footsteps, intentionally scattering beach sand along the way. "You're positive this is the church where we're supposed to be? I mean, I've watched the DVDs you sent from their Sunday services. Pastor Trantham's preaching and Bible teaching is sound. I'm with you on that."

"What about their music?" Jeremiah asked.

Arze pursed her lips. "C'mon. Let's be honest. Their music kinda lacks - something."

Arze' had a point. Ezekiel's music was fair at best, but it did need something. It needed the push that Jeremiah felt he could provide. "I'm trying to pay attention to what God's telling me. And I know this is where we're supposed to be."

VERSE 7 ♫

*I therefore, the prisoner of the Lord, beseech you that
ye walk worthy of the vocation wherewith ye are called
Ephesians 4:1 KJV*

Jeremiah knew that the discussion of him possibly
participating in a music ministry would be a boiling point
with Arze', but he did just as he promised himself he would
do with her – discuss any matter relating to them. His
conscience was settled. He wasn't going into a strain,
keeping her from knowing his intentions, or pretending that
he wasn't playing for the church when he was planning to all
along. He didn't want anyone to have a slip of the tongue,
telling her what he was doing and maneuvering behind her
back. No, none of that would take place because she had
been given, at the least, some idea of his thoughts concerning
the matter. What he didn't tell her was that his mind had been
made up long before their conversation.

For several days following their weekend, Jeremiah
had avoided phone calls and emails from Pastor Trantham;
call me or *let me know something.* In his heart, avoidance
wasn't his intention; he felt uneasy over the responsibilities
of the position once he committed to it. He'd been in constant
prayer for the Lord to steady his apprehension.

Prior to Sunday morning service, an usher delivered a
handwritten message written by Pastor Trantham, desiring to
meet Jeremiah before the day ended.

Jeremiah realized that any further delay would make
him appear disingenuous. He gave a nod of recognition to the
usher, whispering to her that he would come to Pastor
Trantham's office after service.

When he arrived, the Pastor was in the process of removing his robe, and hanging it on the coat rack in a corner of his office. Pastor Trantham motioned for Jeremiah to have a seat directly in front of the massive wooden desk.

"Alright," Pastor Trantham said, "It's been a month, Brother Day. I have prayed about your coming on board and I have talked the possibility over with the Board of Deacons. Do you have a decision for me?"

Pastor Trantham was correct. A solid month had come and gone. Jeremiah had prayed about becoming a musician there, and he visited other area churches so that he could honestly say that Ezekiel was not the only church he'd given attention to. The Lord didn't give him the same feeling for those congregations that he received from Pastor Trantham and the membership. In fact, Ezekiel was already becoming more than just a place for potential employment. It was where he wanted to attend church. "I accept, Pastor."

Pastor Trantham clapped his hands. "Praise God," he said with a constrained excitement in his voice. "I see great things in the future music of this church."

"I hope I can live up to your expectation."

"I'm not worried about that." His dark, slow, tired eyes gazed from behind his wire-rimmed glasses in no particular direction. "Now, let's talk about the unpleasant."

Jeremiah sat back in his chair. "What's that?"

"Have you given any thought to what you might want your salary to be?"

Jeremiah relaxed, his wayward thoughts dissolved after hearing the question. "I tell you what, Pastor. You let the Lord lead you on what you think my salary should be. If, over time, you and the church see that I've helped to take your music to another level, then we can negotiate on the salary, if that is even necessary. Is that fair?"

"Oh my God! More than fair."

"Pastor, the salary from my school job will take care of me and my fiancée's needs, so having to depend on the church's money won't be my intention. And I don't believe you'll take advantage of me over something as petty as money."

"True, so true." Pastor paused for a moment. "But you just reminded me of the other thing that I needed to discuss with you. Your engagement. Did you get an opportunity to talk with your fiancée about your marriage plans?"

"Yes we did. She gave her consent for you to marry us. In September."

Pastor Trantham counted out, "July, August . . . that's really soon."

"I know, but we're not looking to have a formal ceremony. Just the vows."

"Oh?"

"We want to be married in the very near future because we're honeymooning out of the country. The Caribbean. A large chunk of money's going to that."

"That makes sense."

"Quite possibly, we'll have a formal ceremony in the distant future, at least a year from now. That'll be the formal one for our family and friends."

Pastor Trantham smiled, nodded. "An informal ceremony can be arranged. Now I conduct a series of counseling sessions for every couple before the wedding date, though. You believe we can see both of you a few times before the wedding date?"

"No problem. I'll give you the weekend dates that Arze'll be here in town. I know September is not that far away, but we're ready to be married. We've been engaged for some time now. The time is right, that's all."

"That's just great." Pastor Trantham smiled as he stood up and extended his hand to Jeremiah. "And just think. With your future wife also knowing how to play, I'll have a two-for-one deal on musicians."

Jeremiah shook his head as he thought back on his and Arze's last heated discussion of that topic. "Mmm, I don't know, Pastor. I wouldn't hold my breath if I were you."

At the following Tuesday night Bible Study, an overly-anxious Pastor Trantham announced Jeremiah David Day as the new head musician for Ezekiel Baptist.

VERSE 8 ♫

And Chenaniah, chief of the Levites, was for song: he instructed about the song, because he was skillful I Chron. 15:22 KJV

Renard reluctantly agreed to meet with Trantham after the evening's choir rehearsal leading up to the third Sunday in July. Much to his liking, meetings with Trantham were rare occasions; he despised them almost as much a Christian trying to convince him to convert. The two were never eye-to-eye on any subject, program or idea. Renard preferred to be left alone to fulfill his weekly assignment, collect his paycheck, and then be as far from Ezekiel's campus as possible.

After a half-hearted greeting to Trantham's administrative assistant, Renard walked into the main office and paused for a moment, wondering if he had come to the right office. It seemed that whoever placed the furniture, greenery and literature, had tried to give the space an update but, to Renard, their good-natured attempt was an obvious failure. In his mind, there were only so many ways to decorate a box, but that was beside the point. Renard's inability to recognize the room was a testament to the amount of time gone by since the two had met.

He concluded his brief inspection with Trantham, who was seated behind his desk, nursing a coffee cup while attempting to multi-task between two desktop computers. "Has our appointment been cancelled?"

"Absolutely not. Good to see you," Trantham replied as he remained seated but extended his hand.

Renard shook his hand while, at the same time, secretly questioned the sincerity behind the man's greeting. Renard took the only chair in the office that faced

Trantham's desk. "Something must be really important for you to demand my presence."

Trantham had resumed his tapping at one of the computer keyboards, but paused, an empty expression on his face. "You mean, you've never expected me to call you to discuss any matter?"

"To be frank, no."

"Well, Brother Singleton, I realize that I should probably meet with you more often, given the fact that up until now, you've been the one to keep our music ministry together."

"Oh! So I guess you have paid attention to what we do with the music," he said, hoping that Trantham caught his air of sarcasm.

"Of course I have. And I realize that the music department is vital in our worship services-"

Renard threw his hand into the air. "Whoa! What do you mean by *up until now*?" His jaw tightened as he took his time speaking. "You terminating me?"

Trantham shook his head. "That's not why I wanted to meet with you." He rose from the chair and walked around the desk, tracing the desktop with his fingertips. The space between them was a significant distance; non-threatening, yet conversational. "You've done a fine job with our choirs. A fine job. Commendable. But Renard, I really believe we've found the minister of music that this church needs."

"Minister of music. You mean a-"

"Someone capable to lead the music department. Oversee it on a permanent basis. Maybe on a trial basis at first. We just have to see. But he's someone we're most interested in. Someone *I'm* personally interested in."

Trantham's words took a minute or two to set in before Renard sensed his knuckles digging into his leg, just above the knee. "But-"

"I know what you're thinking," Trantham cut in, "you're probably asking yourself *why not me?*"

"An explanation would be helpful now that I know – you know – what I'm thinking," said Renard as he tried to keep the irritation out of his voice. "And on top of that, *who* are you considering for the position?"

Trantham tilted his head as if he was studying Renard. "Brother Singleton, I've known you all your life. Your family has been a part of Ezekiel at least as long as I've been here."

"Longer."

"You're right. Longer." Trantham swirled around in a swift motion, and then returned to his desk chair, sitting in a stiff, upright position. "I've considered you several times over these years. But in my mind, there is a tremendous difference between playing for a church, and being what would actually be an under-shepherd for the congregation."

Renard took a breath or two in order to keep his nerves in check. "Oh, so you're saying that the minister of music would be somewhat in position as an assistant pastor."

He nodded. "That's exactly what I'm saying."

Renard's brain raced through a fog of emotions within seconds. Disillusionment. Anger. Disappointment. "Ten years," he said. "Ten years I've given you."

"And we appreciate all you've done."

"And I'm sure that the position pays more than I'm currently receiving, huh?"

Trantham shook his head. "Yes, but money shouldn't be the central reason for any musician taking a minister's role. And, after talking with the gentleman we're considering, money doesn't seem to be his motivation for the position."

"I find that hard to believe. Money's always a person's motivation. I don't care what your guy says." Renard slumped back in the seat, stifled over what had just unfolded in the last few moments. He sighed, trying to calm himself, realizing that an ultimate goal had, at least temporarily, been placed out of his reach. "You just said a minute ago that I've done the work. I assumed that meant I should've been up for consideration."

"You do a fine job of playing. You always have. But this position involves more than just playing."

"Like what?"

A couple moments of silence entered the room. Meanwhile, Trantham's face appeared to be strained in contemplation over what he should say next. "This involves leading the people as they minister in song," he replied in a quiet voice.

"Like I don't lead."

Trantham leaned forward, and his brow creased into a frown. "Brother Singleton, I really don't want to go down this path of reasoning with you."

"Oh no, please do. I want to hear what you've got to say." Renard wanted to push the man without going over the edge, without making Trantham mention the word *termination*.

"Okay Brother Renard." Trantham sat forward in his chair. "You cannot lead where you don't go."

"Explain yourself."

"Can't be hot then cold, Renard." Trantham thumbed through his desk calendar. "You think I don't know about your weekend activities?"

"Meaning?"

"Meaning," Trantham replied, as he held out his palm and began folding his fingers down, one at a time, "you're never at a Bible study. Meaning, you never remain in the sanctuary during the sermon. Meaning – I hope you're grasping this - hip-hop bands, release parties, bar-hopping and the like."

"Who in creation told you all that?" Renard gritted in anger. "Never mind. Don't tell me. But I bet they were in the same places, enjoying whatever they saw me doing."

Trantham rolled his chair backwards, which put distance between the two of them. "My concern is what my leaders are doing, and how it appears in the congregation's eyes," he whispered.

"You're the only one with the stiff, old-fashioned beliefs. I'll bet nobody in your congregation puts on a CD of *Amazing Grace* when they're in the bedroom! They listen to the same type of music that I play on the weekends. So the congregation needs to keep their business, theirs, and leave mine alone!" Renard realized that his volume had become deafening, and he felt foolish after his last words spilled out.

For what seemed to be eternity but what was actually about ten seconds, nothing was said by either party.

Trantham sighed and then cleared his throat. "And, in the meantime, as Pastor, I have to point out the wrongs of my congregation. It doesn't matter who they are. And it's my fault. I've been aware of what you've been doing, but I was afraid of not having a church musician at all for an extended period of time. So, I ignored the things I heard and knew. I guess I have to repent for this."

"Everybody has something to repent for, Pastor, but I've got news for you. Go on and make your decision about this position for . . . for-"

"His name's Jeremiah Day."

"Jeremiah. Whatever. I'm against this move. I see no harm in what I'm doing on the weekends or anytime for that matter. It's nobody's business. Nobody can show me in the Bible about it being a sin. So I ain't stopping."

Renard left Trantham's office with a clear understanding; he would not become the minister of music. By no means, however, did he feel defeat. He was still the organist for one of the largest church music departments in Olds. Make no mistake. He could've created more havoc with the designation of music minister. A title, though, wasn't as important to him as positioning. He vowed that, through the Society, he could and would create a storm as never before. The Christian community in the city of Olds thought that they had witnessed a cloud of confusion led by the declarations of Pastor Felix Timmons. That would pale in comparison to what Renard would like to do and, if given the opportunity, would plan to do – to the pastor and congregation of Ezekiel Baptist.

VERSE 9 ♫

Fret not thyself because of him who prospereth in his way, because of the man who bringeth wicked devices to pass. Psalms 37:7b

Less than a week later, Renard went to Lelli's, a posh restaurant in the upside suburbia of Auburn Hills, arriving with minutes to spare before eight o'clock that evening. The maître de led him to the fraction of Gamma (Γ) Chapter members already assembled in the meeting room at the rear of the building.

"Lacrima, brothers," Renard said.

"Lacrima," the four men at the table responded in unison.

Renard requested that members of their local chapter of the Society of Tyrus have an informal get together. The musical assemblage was a cross-representation of various denominations: Missionary Baptist, Pentecostal, Congregational, and AME Zion. Along with Renard, they were some of the most sought after, well-paid musicians in the area.

The restaurant was an authentic Italian eatery known for their dimmed crystal ambience, family-sized individual pasta dishes and Filet Mignon cut from grain-fed cattle; cuisine, though, wasn't at the forefront of Renard's mind. "I have a serious problem, brothers."

"What's got a hold of you?" Terry McClure asked. He founded and organized the Gamma Chapter for metro Detroit, which includes the city of Olds. It was on the weekends that he was better known as TMac, a member of the grunge band Mudslinger. Terry's ever popular for engaging in Friday night to Saturday evening binges of alcohol consumption, hours upon hours of hookah, and synthesized, ear-splitting musicianship behind concrete structures that fire marshals have cited on numerous occasions for overcrowding, noise violations, and other nefarious infractions; but on Sunday mornings without fail for the last eleven years, when his chemically absorbed body made a seemingly miraculous transformation, he would be found at the piano of New Bethel Congregational Church in Flint.

Even at Ezekiel Missionary Baptist, Terry McClure the-church-musician is lauded, welcomed to the hallowed instruments on the rare occasions that New Bethel and Ezekiel worship together. Yes. Some would even argue that he's worshipped, but Renard didn't mind. Over the years, they'd become very, *very* close friends; even swapped wives during the Society's Annual October event, the Festival of Lambs. "Is Ezekiel not paying you what you deserve?" Terry asked.

"Naw. Nothing like that, doc." Renard ran his hand across his forehead, down a sideburn, and against his cheek. "Had a meeting with that boss of mine at the church. Found out that Trantham's about to hire a new musician."

Renard could judge by each brother's silent but obvious expressions that they couldn't sense his urgency. "I think, no, *I know* Trantham's considering this man as the Minister of Music."

"And not you?" Bacchus Nesbitt yelled out. He was organist at North Olds Pentecostal, a guy who seemed psychologically unstable, but could play so well that he'd leave an organ and a listening congregation begging for mercy. He'd been hailed as the go-to man for any organ track to be laid in the Detroit area, sacred or secular. His playing style was drawbars out to FULL, bass pedals at a whisper, with the manuals squalling. As for the volume of his verbal responses, the other brothers were accustomed to his

Tourette-like outbursts, showing no contempt for Bacchus' awkwardness.

Silence then stood in the midst of their table. Sounds of orders being taken and belly laughter filled the air, but the excitement seemed to fall short of the Society's immediate space.

"Wha' dya gon' do broda'? How well can de guy play?" asked Olufemi Kincaid, head musician at Friendship Baptist and the eldest son of its pastor. Renard never ceased to be amazed at how that brother could be Friendship's music director, retain active Society membership and play the keyboards for a Jamaican funk band, all under the unsuspecting nose of his Fundamentalist, old-school father.

A waitress had come around three times to get a drink order from Renard, so he took a moment and finally decided on a Hennessy and Coke. As the waitress left the table, he pondered the question still on the floor, and let out a heavy sigh. "You know what? I can't even lie. The man's a beast!"

"Jah know." Olufemi said.

"The other night I heard him combine *Jesus, Lover of My Soul* with Bach's *Jesu, Joy of Man's Desiring*. He played the chords of life!"

"He's not from around here, is he?" asked Zachary Fuller, lead musician for Opdyke Avenue AME Zion. Zach possessed an Adonis face, a confident swagger, and a keen eye for gender-neutral fashion. If he had a downfall, it would be that he was unobjectionably flirtatious toward any man that would allow him to be. Renard was positive that Zach still harbored ill feelings toward Gamma chapter for not allowing his musician-boyfriend to be inducted two years ago.

Zachary took a sip of what appeared to be a rainbow-colored, alcohol-laden drink. "I know *all* the musicians . . . umm, at least all the ones worth anything . . . around here, you know."

"No, the dude ain't from here. Heard he's from Memphis. Got that Southern churchy style with Midwest passing chords, and I'm pretty sure he told Trantham that he's a protégé of Moses Tyson." There was a chorus of low, throaty sighs from the brothers.

Among the murmuring, Zachary asked, "Why do you feel he'll be a problem?"

"I don't feel, think or wonder. I *know* this Jeremiah Day will be trouble."

"Okay . . . why?" everyone chorused.

Questions came at Renard so fast that he could hardly tell who was doing the speaking. He raised his hand to quell their noise. "This brother can read music flawlessly. Knows the Bible – goes to Bible study. Kills an organ. And this fool claims to live a godly life. At least, that's what I hear."

Olufemi shook his head. "All now. All di while for dis Ghetto bwoy run di road, claiming Gawd all, and de Christians come a 'clamoring. He's Worlian, just like most folks." He paused, picked up a steak knife and began shaking it. "You gon hafta tun up di ting."

The guys exchanged smoldering glances.

"Olufemi! You're crass," Terry said. He turned to Renard. "He does have a point, though. We'll have to indoctrinate him."

Renard sensed a slyness in Terry's voice that suggested Jeremiah Day could possibly be placed on Gamma chapter's agenda; to be dealt with. Renard squirmed at the table, a myriad of conflicting emotions and the battery of questions making him uncomfortable. "I know you're not thinking that he should be *invited* into the Society!" he demanded.

"No," Terry replied. "At least not immediately. We should feel him out. Get him to buy into how things are done around here."

The brothers paused their conversation to enjoy the appetizer plate of California rolls which the treasurer, Olufemi, assured them would be paid for with the Chapter credit card.

"I hear what you're saying, brothers," Renard said between bites. "But I don't know. This Jeremiah doesn't seem like he's easily persuadable."

Zachary pursed his lips in an expression of disbelief. "Then you have to ask yourself - are you in control of your congregation or not?"

Bacchus bellowed out, "Goes without saying bro'."

"Then getting him to see your way goes without saying," Zachary whispered.

"So ya'll are suggesting that he should be advanced into the Society?" Renard asked.

"Naw man! He'll have to start out as a murex just like the rest of us!" Bacchus yelled out to the point that it drew the attention of guests seated outside of the meeting room.

"I know what people say about keeping your enemies closer, but I don't see it. I don't want this Jeremiah as a member of Tyrus. That would make him my brother! He won't believe what we believe, and musicians that don't have a heart for this, shouldn't belong."

They had brewed over the matter long enough for everyone's entrée to be prepared. Renard toyed over his seafood Alfredo for a few minutes, and then asked for a large to-go box.

"Right now, Renard, you're speaking with your head. That's understandable," Terry said.

"Remember. We are Tyrus. Wiser than Daniel. There is no secret hidden from us. No power greater than us," Zachary interjected.

"Man, now you spoke that wisdom," Terry said. He turned back toward Renard. "Let's think about it. His membership could be to *our* advantage."

Renard, still dressed, sat on the edge of his bed in the master where Kira had opened the windows and the curtains were whipping against the walls, but the cool summer wind couldn't blow hard enough to calm his anger. He turned to the *Society's Edicts* for inspiration:

> *Those who transpire against Tyrus will like rocks fall into your path, your destiny. Never falter! Yours is the only mission that is true. Fight your enemy with your gifts, talents and resources. Follow the Ras el-Ain. This fluidic source hones rocks that cavalcade your path. Look only to Tyre – the true Rock. AΩ*

Verse 10 ♫

O my God, I trust in thee: let me not be ashamed, let
not mine enemies triumph over me. Psalm 25:2 KJV

About a week had gone by since Pastor Trantham's
recommendation that Jeremiah be added to Ezekiel's music
ministry. Pastor suggested that he give Renard a call with the
expectation that they get together, get acquainted, and
strategize on how they would divide the duties for rehearsals
and worship experiences.

While on the phone, Renard sounded reluctant to
meet, but Jeremiah remained insistent. There would be a
meeting; voluntary with the two of them or involuntary with
the Pastor present. Renard's choice.

They settled on an early Wednesday evening in the
sanctuary before Prayer Meeting.

Jeremiah went inside the sanctuary to wait for
Renard. He took a seat; second row, center-view of the
pulpit. Though his view from that angle would be brief, he
felt out of place in congregational seating. He was so used to
being on an organ. He occupied the time by looking through
a hymnal, taking a mental list of titles he might input into
upcoming Sunday services. He became thoroughly engrossed
into the book when a loud echo startled him. Renard strode
in, traces of perspiration on his forehead, and looking back
every few steps as though he had lost something. He walked
up, stopped, and then straightened the jacket of the steel gray
suit he was wearing.

"Sorry, I'm late," he said, seemingly out of breath.

Jeremiah checked his cell phone. For Renard to have
called himself late was an understatement. He rolled into the
sanctuary fifty-six minutes past the appointed time. He could
be patient. This time. After swallowing his disgust, he said,

"It's alright. I know things can come up." *Was something wrong with him calling me?*

"Honestly, I didn't expect you'd still be here," Renard said as his breathing quieted.

Jeremiah turned to face him, putting an arm up and across a seat in the front row. "Where?"

"Here. At church. I mean, since I was late."

"What? You were hoping?"

"Man, naw." Renard gave off a half-laugh. "Really though, what musician do you know that's ever on time for anything?"

Jeremiah refused to give a response. He let the silence be what it was.

"You know. Since you're here now and-."

Jeremiah interrupted, "Not going anywhere. . ."

About thirty minutes into their conversation which included subjects ranging from family to neighborhoods to great places to eat, their vocal jostling soon turned into a civil dialogue; even bordered on being cordial. Their interaction became especially refreshing when they began talking shop; engaging with someone who had more than an elementary knowledge of music. Picardy thirds. The Nashville number system. Cold calling chord progressions in any key signature. "I wish there were more around like you," Jeremiah told him.

Renard laughed. "Right, right. Funny you mentioned that." He sat back and relaxed into the chair. "We do have a group of area musicians that get together on a regular basis."

"Really?"

"We talk about things like struggles we may have in our churches, chord changes, the latest songs; things like that. You ought to become a part of the group."

"Group of musicians, huh?" Jeremiah rubbed his face, contemplating the suggestion.

"Best in Olds."

"So what's their testimony? Are they saved?" he asked.

Renard's eyebrows twisted on his face as though he was in disbelief of the question. "Really? They're *church* musicians."

Jeremiah didn't see his question about salvation as a ridiculous one. Even less was his appreciation for the humor in Renard's response, and didn't hesitate in telling him so. He spent the next few minutes giving Renard a rundown of issues he'd dealt with in his years as a church musician. "I'll have to think about your invitation. I'm careful about forming relationships with musicians until I really get to know them." He looked away for a moment, hoping that a subject change wouldn't force Renard to clam up. "So tell me more about Ezekiel's music department. You've been here long enough to know all the ins and outs, huh?"

"There's nothing much to tell. Just a bunch of choirs. Rehearsals. Afternoon services. Arguments over petty stuff. Some good singing followed by some good sermons. Just a bunch of stuff."

"You sound real excited."

Renard rolled his eyes. "Those people work me to death."

Jeremiah nodded as though he agreed, but in his mind, he summed Renard up as the lazy, careless type. "Well you might find some consolation, maybe even relief, in what I have to tell you."

Renard pursed his lips. "What do you mean by that?"

"Well, if I'm correct, Pastor Trantham plans to combine some of the groups into one main – Mass choir – for lack of a better term. That's probably what we'll call it until a more appropriate name is thought of."

Renard shifted in his seat, but within seconds, he bolted up. "Trantham told you this? When?"

"He says it's been on his mind, but he has to wait until the time is right. Maybe that time is close."

Renard turned away, leaned on the back of a chair and quieted his voice. "He's getting rid of the Chorale, too?"

Jeremiah could tell that the news made Renard uneasy, but he didn't understand why. "I don't know. You'll have to ask Pastor Trantham. He hasn't given me all the specifics."

Before Jeremiah could take a breath from his reply, Renard whipped around. He had a sharp gaze and a pointed finger. "There's a danger in making too many moves too quick."

Jeremiah returned the gaze with one of his own. "Are you talking about me making moves, or the Pastor?"

Renard's eyes widened. "I have a lot of kin here."

"Really?"

"About half the church," he replied, emphasizing each word.

My patience can run out. Jeremiah, realizing that he should remain the Christian, gave serious thought to Renard's supposed threat before asking, "Are they all in the choir?"

Verse 11 ♫

For to be carnally minded is death; but to be
spiritually minded is life and peace. Romans 8:6 KJV

Throughout the previous evening until dawn, the sky
sang a tune in discord. Severe winds threatened the
atmosphere with tornado-like clouds, patterns of thunder had
the consistency of a kettledrum ensemble, and the rain
danced in horizontal fashion. Sections of the city went for
hours without power. Radio and television stations forwarded
messages from government officials, who advised citizens to
remain stationary in their homes, jobs or businesses while the
utilities were being stabilized. Renard was somewhat fearful
that he wouldn't be able to do any recording on that day.

Fredrico texted Renard that morning, letting him
know that Sound Shocker obviously couldn't operate without
electricity. Thanks to mid-morning winds that blew the storm
in a northeastern direction, good fortune and the expertise of
Olds Power & Light, power was restored to that quadrant of
the city, and the two men were able to lay rhythm and vocal
tracks in the studio by late that afternoon.

"I got this new cut," Renard told Fredrico as he
booted up his mixing board and clicked his computer mouse
to open a new audio file for the recording.

"Oh yeah?" Fredrico asked. "What is it? Hip Hop?"

"Mm hmm."

"What's your idea?"

Renard pulled his cell phone away from the clip on
his belt. He swept his finger across the screen to open an app
designed to hold virtual notepads. "I guess you could call it a
working title, but the more I hear myself say it, the more it's
sticking to me."

"The title?"

Renard took a few more swipes at his phone screen, and centered the note he was trying to find. *"Death to a Carnal Christian."*

Fredrico stopped adjusting sliders and swiveled around to Renard, who was actually behind him, his hands frozen in mid-air. "Huh?"

"You heard me."

In the moments that followed, Fredrico was silent. Renard smiled to himself, feeling a sense of accomplishment over the shock factor he believed he'd generated. *Death to a Carnal Christian.* It was far from a mundane phrase. Pretending as though an ordinary circumstance had just occurred, Renard went on, outlining his preferences of key and time signatures, instrumentation, and groove. "I just want to get it started today. We won't get to finish it. I have a choir rehearsal to attend and some finance account files to complete for work before I go outta town this weekend."

"Alright."

"Something wrong?"

"Oh no. Let's get to work," Fredrico said as he turned his attention back to the mixing board.

"Will do." Renard still sensed the weight in the room, but he wasn't going to press an issue that Fredrico wasn't willing to bring to the forefront. *It's just money to me,* he remembered Fredrico saying.

After close to four hours of recording, Renard paused, studying the flow of each track, meticulously tweaking every synth sound, hi-hat, cymbal crash and vocals:

> *You! With yo' backbitin', fake a- - ways*
> *I might as well live for the carnal days*
> *'Til I die I'll be happy – how 'bout you?*
> *You'll be tied down and boring with yo' spiritual*
> *crew! I wanna say*

Death to the Carnal Christian
May you not live long . . !

"Fredrico, there's a sample I want to insert in the bridge that I think in which will nail the vibe on this song."

"Alright," Fredrico said, "What's the sample? Where we gonna take it from?"

"I've got a wave file. Here. Use this." Renard produced a flash drive, telling him that on it was the motif from an old Bob Dylan tune that he wanted to input at specific measures:

Even the Knights of Tyrus with their convict list;
Are waiting in line for their geranium kiss.

Two cold pizzas and an insane amount of Red Bull® kept the two of them working until the sun peeped through diminishing storm clouds and dusty studio windows, signaling a new morning. It was then that they realized every track had been laid and every harmony had been placed on the new tune. Renard removed the headphones from his ears and glanced over at Fredrico, overcome with a feeling of satisfaction for the product they had produced. "Man, I cannot believe I've only two hours to shower and get ready for work all over again." Renard let out a boisterous yawn.

"Don't do that. That's contagious," Fredrico told him. "I'll get about a half day's sleep. Call my people to get it mixed hopefully this evening. Take another day to master it." He reached across the board to make a few more adjustments on the mix. "You want me to keep this piece on the DL until you decide what to do with it?"

Renard smiled to himself. He'd given careful consideration to the timetable and scope for publishing the song days before calling Fredrico to schedule the recording session. With the tune's provocative title, lyrics and rhythm, he had schooled himself on the possible repercussions that *Death to the Carnal Christian* could create for him as a church musician. He weighed all of the problems the song could bring him against its potential popularity. Fortune. A personal legacy with his beloved Society. When he finished weighing everything against everything, his decision was made. "Naw. Pull out all the stops on this one. Digital Underground, XXL, online stations and any other connection you've got that'll play or review the cut."

"*Death to a Carnal Christian.* That's the title you wanna go with?" Fredrico asked, sounding on the verge of fearful.

"Oh yeah. That's the title I want." He smiled. "It sends a message." He stood up and headed toward the door of the studio. "Let's see where it goes."

Fredrico gave a heavy sigh. "Let's."

As Renard walked out of the studio, he sent Kira a text to let her know that he was headed home. Since all of his normal sleep time had been consumed with recording, he accelerated the gas pedal, realizing it would be a rush to get ready for work.

Kira met him at the doorway, cell phone in hand and buds in her ear. "Hey. Glad you made it home safely." She waved the phone in the air. "I got your new cut."

"I was wondering if you got it. I didn't know how many megabytes it ended up being since it was compressed at the studio. Sometimes music files are difficult to send."

Kira crossed her arms, turned around and began walking through the breezeway on into the kitchen. She spun around to face Renard, her back against the wall. "Oh no. You sent it through Dropbox®, and I downloaded it from there."

Several moments passed without either one of them exchanging a word. Renard was losing patience with people supposing to be close to him giving the silent treatment.

When Renard couldn't bear the suspense any longer, he asked Kira, "Well? What do you think of the cut?"

Kira's brow bunched in what seemed to be a state of confusion. "Death . . .?" She stared at him, a blank expression on her face.

"That's not the whole title," Renard explained.

"Oh, I know."

"Don't you want to know why I gave the tune its title?"

"You made it very clear in the song," she said. Kira pulled the buds out of her ears. "You're twisted."

Verse 12 ♫

Yea, they shall sing in the ways of the Lord: for great is the glory of the Lord. Psalm 138:5 KJV

Oh to be a witness as a church evolves one of its auxiliaries. The people's reluctance to change cannot be compared. Secondary musicians were let go. Choir officers relinquished their little power. Several longstanding singers left the choir stand for the pews, with the possibility that they would never return.

The backlash from that move would take more than a minute to calm. Maybe it never would.

The new choir, The Voices of Ezekiel, came about as a compilation of several choirs soon placed in the annals of their church history. Before the Voices, eight choirs covered a month of church services with two choirs serving each Sunday.

It was decided that eight choirs with their individual rehearsals was too much, even for a church that size.

On the evening of the Voice's first rehearsal just prior to the exact time, Jeremiah met with Reverend Micah Knight, an associate minister of the church. Pastor Trantham assigned him as a special liaison to the entire music department.

Rev. Micah Knight stood well over six feet tall with a crown of salt and pepper hair that was paired against his honey-colored skin. He was a quiet man who successfully pulled off being unassuming despite his stature. He spoke with a somewhat noticeable lisp. Jeremiah wasn't mistaken, though, in believing that a mere speech impediment would prevent him in any way from being a most powerful prayer warrior. Jeremiah would often find Rev. Knight on his knees, on his face or laying prostrate prior to church services or non-service times when the sanctuary would be completely empty. The two had spoken on many occasions, even in the short time Jeremiah had been there, on the fact that Ezekiel Baptist is poised for a spiritual transformation, but the right combination of people were needed to be in place for a change to occur. Rev. Knight wasn't aware until that evening that Jeremiah could play an instrument.

"Pastor Trantham wanted me to be here tonight mainly for support, to see that things go well. I'm wondering, not surprised, just wondering . . . how he came to choose me out of all the ministers in the church."

"I requested you," Jeremiah told him. "I've tried to pay close attention to things, especially since Pastor began mentioning that he would love to have me on staff here."

"Why? I mean, why me?"

"I want to be an asset to the ministry, Reverend Knight, not a hindrance. I do my best to hear what the Lord wants me to do when it comes to my gift and ministry. I'm not here to play around, or come to church because it's the popular thing to do on Sunday."

Rev. Knight nodded. "I hear that."

"So if we're going to be about ministry, I knew that we'd need someone who will focus specifically on the music ministry, from a prayerful aspect."

Rev. Knight led Jeremiah through double doors, and the two began pacing the length of the connector. "I see. You'll need saints to keep you covered in prayer."

"Oh yeah because people can be resistant. Mainly to change."

"That's how the devil works. Through people, chaos or fear of the unknown."

"You got that right."

"I appreciate your confidence. Just to let you know . . . our prayer band is a group of intercessors that'll begin to pray for your protection, go throughout the choir stand, anoint the chairs, instruments – everything. We will want you covered."

Jeremiah nodded his head. "I knew you were the right person for this ministry."

"I want to warn you, keep you reminded about something, though. . ." His husky voice became hushed as he looked around.

Their walking ceased. Both men stood at the door to the sanctuary. Jeremiah asked, "What's that?"

"You're going to have resistance," Rev. Knight told him.

"I know."

"No, you don't understand what I *really* mean." Rev. Knight paused for more than a brief moment. "You seem sincere in your intentions, Brother Day, and I can tell you want the music to bring in the Cloud of the Holy Ghost."

He nodded. "Absolutely."

"Then be prepared. You're going to get hit from every direction in ways you or I couldn't possibly know. The devil's on his way."

"I understand."

Rev. Knight began opening the sanctuary door. "Just stay prayed up."

"Vertical Praise? We ain't never heard of it," one of the choir members of the new Voices of Ezekiel declared.

Renard was present for rehearsal, but would be out of town on Sunday attending the National Christian Music Convention in New Orleans.

Jeremiah had only thirty minutes prep between the time he spoke with Rev. Knight and the actual rehearsal for the Voices. He had made up his mind that ninety minutes would be time enough for introductions, inform them that

Rev. Knight would be their prayer liaison, and rehearse a new song, two if time allowed, for the upcoming Sunday service. He had not factored in questions which included their misunderstanding of where and how Jeremiah wanted their praise to be directed.

"Yes. Vertical Praise. Let me explain," Jeremiah said. "Most of the songs I've heard from the choirs here at Ezekiel talk *about* Lord; His goodness, how He has blessed. I want to include more songs that talk *to* the Lord; tell Him directly of the things he has done." Jeremiah raised his arms upward. "A Vertical song as opposed to a Horizontal song."

"What do you think is going to happen with these so-called vertical songs?" Renard asked.

Jeremiah sensed and ignored his cynical tone. "All I'm going to say is that when *it* happens, you'll know it."

"Uh, you have any . . . umm . . . vertical songs for the choir to rehearse – tonight?"

Jeremiah focused on the choir members, who seemed to have a more receptive attitude. "Oh, yeah. If we rehearse one song tonight and get it ministry-ready, pray that the lyrics get into our spirits, and transfer our understanding of the song through our singing on Sunday morning, the Lord will move."

Renard chuckled. "Man, you've got high hopes, 'cause that's a tall order."

"We can only obey God's command. He'll do His thing."

*   *   *   *

For some reason, Jeremiah met with Knight for some thirty, maybe forty minutes. Renard wasn't included in the meeting. He chose to hang out in the sanctuary and greet the members of the newly formed Voices of Ezekiel. He vowed not to miss that first rehearsal with Jeremiah, even though he would be out of town on the upcoming Sunday.

Renard vowed that Trantham would regret disbanding five of the previous choirs, especially his favorite choir, the Chorale. They concentrated on singing the most popular songs from artists receiving airplay.

"What do you think this new musician will be like?" Calvin Inman, a tenor, asked him. "Have you met him?"

"Oh yeah. I met him."

"And?"

"The jury's still out," Renard said. "He'll have to fall in line with how things are done here. I've already warned him about making fast changes."

By that time, Tamla walked in and took her usual spot in the choir stand. "So," she butted in, "will I still have a chance to solo like before?"

Renard winked at her. "You know I'll put in a good word for you."

Renard watched as the new musician stumbled in, late by five or six minutes, making what didn't sound like an apology for his lateness, and then asking everyone to bow their heads for a prayer in which he led. During the choir's business session, he announced Knight as some prayer warrior for the choir. Renard was confident that the choir had never heard of some lowly associate minister being given a position like that before, thinking, *I don't think the choir will take to this.*

"I really appreciate the contributions that each of you bring to this congregation, at least what I've heard since being here," Jeremiah told the group.

Renard listened in disdain to the changes in department policy that Jeremiah proposed; not that anything had ever been in writing. Renard also wondered if the musician's enthusiastic spirit would still be present once the choir members really got a hold on him, reducing his vigor to indifference. *Just like they've done to me.* "I appreciate your compliment of the department," Renard said, hoping that his insincerity wasn't surfacing in his voice. "We'll see how things go from here."

"Another thing before I forget. I prefer that we don't predetermine the Invitational Selection," Jeremiah said.

"Why not?" Renard asked as he looked around for agreeing looks from the singers. "I mean, shouldn't we know every song we plan to sing before any Sunday?"

"We need to gear the Invitational toward the sermon, which we can only determine once Pastor Trantham actually begins preaching."

Renard grinned to himself. There was a muted hush among the choir.

"And," Jeremiah continued as though he had paid no attention to the choir's indifference, "I want our concentration of songs to emphasize Vertical Praise."

"Vertical Praise?" Calvin said. "We've never heard of that."

The musician went on to give some lame explanation about the difference between horizontal and vertical songs. He told them that he didn't care for all the songs they sang – about God. He told them to try singing – to God.

He startled Renard when he raised his hand like he was praying. "You'll see a difference in the worship experience," Jeremiah told them.

I really hope they're not buying this. Trying to impress folks with some new knowledge that a religious fool came up with. "What do you think is going to happen with these so-called vertical songs?" Renard asked.

"All I'm going to say is that when *it* happens, you'll know it."

"Any *vertical songs* for the choir – tonight?" Renard asked with a sneer.

"I think so," he answered.

He's not prepared. He won't last. "Not really ready with a song tonight, are you?"

Jeremiah appeared to shuffle some lyric sheets. "Oh no, I'm prepared. One song. And if we practice this one song with fervor, the Lord will move."

Renard did all he could to keep from laughing at the farce he called Jeremiah. "Man, you've got high hopes."

"Obey God's command and He'll do a work."

Renard had confidence that his position as a church musician was secure. He would enjoy his stay in New Orleans and come back from the convention, anxiously waiting to hear from the people of Ezekiel that Jeremiah turned out to be nothing but a one-week wonder.

Verse 13 ♫

In that day the Lord with his sore and great and strong sword shall punish leviathan the piercing serpent. Isaiah 27:1a KJV

On Saturday morning, Kira climbed into the driver's side of their Jeep Grand Cherokee, where Renard was already waiting for her, reclined on the front passenger side, his luggage tucked behind the third-row seat.

"What are you wearing?" he asked, noticing that she was bundled inside of a tan trench coat with the belt tightly cinched.

Kira closed the car door and turned to him. She pursed her lips and raised an eyebrow. "Listen honey. I'm not putting on makeup and everything, just to take you to the airport. Not this morning."

"But dang, girl. A winter coat in August. Really?"

"Don't worry about me," Kira said as she put the vehicle in gear, heading for Detroit Metro.

Ten minutes down the M1, Kira began loosening the belt on her coat. She meticulously pulled the flaps apart, revealing her once-worn Valentine's Day gift from Wilbourn Sister's Exclusives; a vibrant crimson, silk print two-piece pajama. "Let me know if the view is right." While she guided the steering wheel with her left hand, her right hand unbuttoned her top, leaving only the curvature of her breasts in sight.

Renard fidgeted in his seat, trying to referee his loins; his body, amped from her sensual exposé. "Stop, please," he begged.

"Hmm," she moaned. After outlining the cavern of her navel with a fingertip, she reached through the foot-long slit in her pajama pants, tracing the length of her leg; the whole of her body, a rich, regal coffee tone. Underneath the overcoat and the silk layer – oil kissed flesh. Her eyes gave the road her concentration, but her flawless mouth formed a Cheshire cat smile. "Bet you'll keep this in mind while you're in New Orleans, won't you?"

He was in wanting, his eyes trailing the avenue from her petite waist, along her thigh, down to her knee. Kira couldn't have had a clue how much her quick-tease fueled his undying addiction. On second thought, she must've known precisely what she was doing. Given time, he would've surrendered to her package, her offering. To his dismay, he had a plane to catch.

Although curbside check-in at Detroit Metro Airport seemed to be the busiest he'd ever known, Renard still found time to get through Concourse C, make a stop at the Delta Sky Club and enjoy an appletini before boarding.

As he strolled through the crowded concourse, Terry McClure came up behind him and whispered The Call, "Lacrima."

Renard turned around and before he could offer The Response, Terry handed him a 5 x 7 card; lavender colored, thick, quality stock, and teardrop shaped according to Society specifications. It read:

The National Officers
Of
The Society of Tyrus
Request & Require your Presence
For the XLV Conclave and Refectory
Thursday, August 8th, 2013
Place d'Armes Hotel
625 St. Ann Street, New Orleans
7:06pm

Renard took a picture of the invitation with his phone and then placed the card in his carryon bag, taking care to pack it in a secret compartment. After the two found vacant seats near his gate, Renard informed Terry about Kira's antics on the way to the airport. He placed his carryon down at his feet. "What I should've done was grab a spot in short-term parking. I would've handled her right then, right inside the car," he said amusingly.

Terry laughed several times between his *O My God's* during the story. "Whoa, player! You know to leave some of her for me! Festival of Lambs is coming up."

"Don't remind me. In about two months," he replied, as his groin briefly reignited on thoughts of the Chapter's annual October party.

Terry glanced over his shoulder as if he wanted their immediate space free of intruding ears. His look was thoughtful. "You know this year's meeting is very, very special."

"Why?" Renard asked.

"The national officers plan on divulging a scheme to disrupt churches all over the country. A kind of Pentagrammatory Attack, they call it."

Renard, strangling the handle of his bag, listened in earnest. "Five Points. The unicurse. Interesting. What's our role?"

"President Auerbach will sketch it out for the membership, piece by piece. It'll be especially interesting to us, since Gamma chapter exists near a crucial city but has never participated in one before." Terry did another quick survey of their surroundings, looking to his right, then left. "This year is our time."

Renard swallowed to calm his anxiety. A real and deliberate test of the Society was something he had longed for. "Wow. I'm glad I'll get to hear it firsthand. Can't wait."

"Tell me 'bout it." Terry glanced at his watch. "Listen, my flight's in about an hour with American, dude, so I better run on over to my gate. Ras el-Ain, my brother."

"Ras el-Ain," Renard whispered. "See you there."

Verse 14 ♫

And the people gave a shout, saying, It is the voice of a god, and not of a man. Acts 12:22

The Crescent City. The Big Easy. The vivid culture. The storied history. The mysteries detained in its known and yet to be discovered religious practices. It was one of the few cities that sparked Renard's inner core, serviced his every hunger. He couldn't wait to submerse himself in the trappings of a post-Katrina French Quarter, where fleets of trucks loaded down with restaurant supplies, liquor and beer, two-by-fours and twelve-gauge wiring, plow through urine infested streets – the same block by block inner-city grid that required a daily, early-morning power wash from the previous night's unspoken activities. One small part of a beautiful experience.

He stopped at baggage claim, secured his rental car and drove to the headquartered hotel, the Hilton New Orleans Riverside, where the National Christian Music Convention would take place. He checked his MapQuest app for the distance between the Hilton and the Place d'Armes, the hotel chosen for The Society of Tyrus' National Meeting. From A to B was slightly over one and a half miles, which was the Society's intention; to be a considerable distance from the church music convention site. He was careful in mapping out his driving route, because Society rules only allowed them a ten-minute window for entrance to the Conclave and Refectory. The invitation said 7:06pm, which was firm and adhered to without excuse.

Until that time, he had four days to enjoy the sights and sounds of New Orleans, to entertain both personal and business pursuits.

He and Terry spent one evening dining at Emeril's Delmonico. He honored Kira's request by purchasing an authentic Mardi Gras face piece from Masquerade on Saint Ann. His dad, Adrian, asked that he purchase a rare Jazz recording for his collection. "Make sure it's real wax, not that plastic digital stuff," he told him. That meant a trip to Euclid's on Chartres.

He had little concern for the Christian Music Convention workshops, where he did attend the sessions on chord progressions and vocal technique while skipping the early-morning prayer sessions and Morning Glory Worship. He found excuses for avoiding any session remotely resembling an aspect of Christian ministry. His interest on that subject was simple: Nothing pertaining to a belief in god. Nothing to help strengthen a local body of infidels.

"Hey, you attending the sessions on *Using Music to Evangelize Your Local Church?*" some preacher asked him in passing one morning.

Renard decided against a comeback remark, settling instead with a head nod in the negative.

On two days, he slept from late afternoon until early evening, waking up in time for the late night concerts where musicians and preachers with non-religious interests would be in attendance. There he played the role of recruiter, hoping that he might entice someone to consider membership into the Society. He didn't discriminate. He was well known as a church musician, making it simple to socialize with the music industry's most prominent Christian, Inspirational and Gospel artists. He was a hip-hop writer on the rise, so when the occasion presented itself – which was often - he met the onslaught of secular artists roaming the convention halls throughout the week. Secular. Spiritual. It didn't matter. He craved everyone's time, *everyone's* money. He networked, even passing out business cards which billed him: *Renard Singleton. Musician, composer, producer.*

On the evening of the Society's Conclave and Refectory, Renard summoned the hotel's valet parking attendant some forty minutes prior to the Society's chosen zero hour. He'd made it to the lobby of the Place d'Armes well before time to enter through the hallowed doors of the meeting. Members in chapters from all over the country put the Conclave and Refectory on their annual calendars, under the disguise that they were attending the Christian Music Convention only. Many of the musicians had swindled their local church into funding their Tyrus Society trips; money that had been set aside under a Music Education and Conference budget line, which were funds actually designated for the purposes of true ministry, study of the craft, or the accumulation of new choral music. Most of the Society's membership, including Renard, got away with this scheme.

"Let us call the Forty-fifth Conclave and Refectory to order please," declared Brad Auerbach, National President of the Society of Tyrus, and the lead musician for a Saint Louis Pentecostal church. "Lacrima."

"Lacrima," was chorused throughout the room.

President Auerbach continued. "The agenda has been adopted and accepted. . ."

Renard turned to his left and realized that Terry McClure had taken a seat next to him. "What's up," he whispered.

"Hey man," Terry said.

The first hour was consumed by the usual hoard of committee reports, and the special Necrology reading and observance for members who had, from September 2012 until then, *Traveled the Waters of the Ras el-Ain to Eternal Tyrus*. President Auerbach then asked that the National Doorkeepers make a special check to see that each member in attendance had in possession their Teardrop Invitation, the Codified Manual of Tyrus and the Edicts of Tyrus Society.

"Well Brothers," Auerbach declared, "it is now time to plan our annual DOA. For those of you that are Murex in the Society, you may think that DOA means *Dead on Arrival*. Well, peace be with you brothers because that's not what it means, although we do hope dead on arrival will be the end result of our church services once we're done."

There was a humorous roar throughout the room.

"Let me explain," Auerbach said, taking a moment to adjust the rostrum microphone. "Here, at the Conclave and Refectory, we plan an annual D-."

"Dicaearchy," the membership chorused.

"O-."

"Obrumpent."

"A-."

"Allotheism."

"Which is defined as-," Auerbach continued.

The membership responded, "A just government bursting forth with strange gods." The membership erupted into an applause that lasted just about a minute.

When order restored, Auerbach continued with another request. "Turn to page thirty-seven in your Book of Edicts."

That page read:

> *In your organized revolts, the totality of all your talents, gifts and resources are utilized as proof that you hold dear the ideals of the Society and that your collective power is functioning. AΩ*

After President Auerbach allowed approximately five minutes to go by while the membership familiarized themselves with the Edict, he then asked each member to go to their Codified Manuals and turn to page 20. It read:

> *At the Annual National Membership meeting, the discussion of a Dicaearchy Obrumpent Allotheism*

will take place where the membership will organize and synchronize a musical confusion of worship services around the country with specific regional chapters guiding the attack. AΩ

"Now that you have read the Society's historic references for our DOA," President Auerbach said, "let me outline how the synchronization will be carried out . . ."

Auerbach accompanied his explanation with a PowerPoint which helped the membership visualize the details of the future occurrence.

The event would be a centralized musical attack which Auerbach coined *The Pentagrammatory*, coming from five perimeter cities with Tyrus Society chapters: Chicago B (Beta), Omaha I (Iota), Dallas/Fort Worth O (Omicron), Memphis H (Eta), and Charlotte Ψ (Psi), with President Auerbach's chapter, Saint Louis Z (Zeta), being the central point for primary communication.

The collective body decided on Sunday, December 1st, 2013 as the date the DOA would commence. Each member would use a special text number – 331615, the North coordinates of the city of Tyre – to send by text message the results of their individual DOA's to their designated region.

"These churches won't know what hit 'em," Terry whispered to Renard, a gigantic grin on his face.

"Aw naw. The only thing I've got to do is figure out exactly what I'm going to hit them with," Renard said.

"We want this Pentagrammatory attack to have as synchronized a zero hour as possible. We realize that we're talking about different church service hours in various time zones, but let's make zero hour as close to 12 o'clock noon as you can," Auerbach commanded.

As the president gave instructions, Renard calculated that his DOA would need to be near the end of Ezekiel's service time. With Trantham's altar call and first Sunday Communion, he could easily launch his musical attack between 12:30 and 1:00pm Eastern. Perfect.

"Please follow the instructions for this collective DOA to the letter." President Auerbach allowed several minutes to entertain questions from the general membership. "If there are no other questions, we will adjourn this Conclave and reassemble in the hotel's Grand Ballroom for our Refectory meal. So, in the spirit of our society. . ."

The general body responded, "We owe our abilities, gifts and resources to Tyrus."

Renard and Terry remained seated until the some of the crowd dissipated from the room.

"We'll receive the rest of our general instructions from the Chicago chapter, Renard," Terry said. "But I still want our chapter to get together back home and iron out details, you know, just for us."

"I hear ya'. I'm extending the invitation now. The brothers can meet sometime at my house."

"You're on. We can share ideas on how to disrupt our church's so-called worship and at the same time, keep it from looking like we're the culprits."

"Oh my goodness. There's so many ways I can think of to prove the power of the Ras el-Ain relevant, it makes my head spin."

Terry gave him a look of wonderment. "You're in this all the way, aren't you?"

Renard took a two-second mental inventory of what this DOA could mean to him, his secular music, and his desire for influence and fame. "Oh I'm in it. More than you know."

Verse 15 ♫

And so were the churches established in the faith, and increased in number daily. Acts 16:5 KJV

Jeremiah soft-stepped into the sanctuary to power up the Hammond and then honor Rev. Knight's request to have prayer with him before greeting the choir. He made his way to the organ and flipped the RUN switch. He pressed the B-flat upper manual preset bar, adjusted the drawbars to his liking, and played a quick chromatic run – no sound. He repeated this ritual three more times before he realized; he needed to pull the START switch first.

He stood there, laughing to himself. His stomach let out a hunger growl on a full stomach. He had a bout with perspiration and it wasn't warm. It reminded him of a similar feeling before the first Voices of Ezekiel rehearsal. After correcting his goof-up, he went to the back of the sanctuary and shared his embarrassment with Rev. Knight, who was standing at the entrance, and always ready with a word of encouragement.

"Don't let a minor thing side-track you. This is a great day," he said.

"Just want things to go well, Reverend."

Rev. Knight waved his hand in midair. "I feel it," he proclaimed. "This church is being positioned for a great move of God. Pastor will bring an anointed Word." He turned to Jeremiah, a deliberate look emblazoned on his face. "Is the choir ready?"

"Vertical Praise was my message to them on rehearsal night. I've done my best to plant great songs. Your prayers have watered the music. Now, we can wait on God for the increase."

They walked down near the front of the sanctuary for prayer, selecting a front seat in proximity of the pulpit. On the row behind them, an early-bird saint, a matronly woman in her seventies or eighties, was busy arranging a silk lace napkin on her lap and adjusting the pink pillbox hat on her head. She was occupying the time with short prayers, moans, and thumbing through the pages of a large print King James Bible, but pausing long enough to acknowledge both men, offering the sweetest smile and a Sunday morning twinkle in her intense, brown eyes. "You know, son, we should enter into His gates with thanksgiving, and into His courts with praise," she declared.

Jeremiah repaid her gesture with a smile. "Be thankful unto Him, and bless His name," he whispered to her. He regarded their brief interchange as a sign. God had answered; He was in the midst. Jeremiah's first Sunday with Ezekiel Baptist would be a blessing.

The entire time that he was chatting with the woman, Rev. Knight had been sitting quietly, bobbing his head. "Let's pray for the success of the service," he said as he reached for Jeremiah's hand. Together, they closed their eyes in meditation.

Outside of the sanctuary in the vestibule, congregants wedged their way past the choir and through the iridescent, double glass doors of the sanctuary. Jeremiah did a quick count of the number of singers that were robed and ready for the Call to Worship. The conglomeration of one-hundred, thirty voices assembled in a circle as Rev. Knight led a prayer of preparation:

Lord, we're asking you for your guidance as we prepare to sing your songs. Bless the choir as they enter into the gates with Thanksgiving, proceed into Your Court with praise on their lips and worship in their hearts. Allow their songs to prepare us in receiving the preached Word as it

*comes from Pastor Trantham. Bless him to be the servant
needed for this time, even in this city. Lead us. Bless us. Keep
us. In Your son, Jesus' name. Amen.*

When the choir burst into an applause, Jeremiah
found himself feeding off the choir's spiritual energy. He
only hoped the congregation was catching the fire that the
Voices were about to bring.

The middle of service seemed to slow to a mundane
crawl, but Jeremiah pushed the musical envelope above and
beyond what might have been dismal, guided by the Holy
Spirit. He played and directed the music, holding faith that
the Lord had established an appropriate atmosphere for
worship, refusing to worry about what his finite mind
might've thought or what his naked eye might've seen. He
began striking the chords to a new song that the Voices of
Ezekiel were prepared to sing, the first of many songs they
would sing after only one rehearsal; one of Jeremiah's
personal compositions. The Voices chorused in harmony:

> ♫ *Praise the Lord*
> *Praise the Lord with all His angels*
> *And those who call Him King!*
> *From the greatest to the least,*
> *Other powers cease, when we*
> *Praise the Lord!* ♫

Through tear-filled eyes Jeremiah played, God
sanctioning him a witness in the congregation's move toward
oneness in worship. He pulled a microphone to his mouth,
one that had been incorporated into the sound system and
placed on a boom stand, one marked specifically for his use.
He ministered:

I

♫ *If we follow His command*
Take His guiding hand
He will lead us to the Promised Land... ♪

The atmosphere of the sanctuary transformed before Jeremiah's eyes, revealing to him that God had extended His ear in their direction and allowed the Cloud of the Spirit to descend upon them. Parts of the congregation fell prostrate before God. A small group of saints sprinted around the perimeter of the sanctuary. The once-sleepy, often staunch deacon's corner, who, as a body had adopted some unwritten by-law that they maintain an ultra-solemn exterior, had broken out into a cacophony of praise unequaled by any other section in the church.

Although Jeremiah couldn't see anything immortal – it wouldn't have been prudent for them to have been seen – he could feel an angelic force hovering around and above.

Pastor Trantham motioned for Jeremiah to decrescendo but continue to sing the same song. He then instructed the associate ministers to assemble around the altar and prepare to lay hands, anoint those who came forward and desired special prayer.

More sporadic shouting.

More crying out.

Still others sang in full voice.

Jeremiah raised his towel, which was a gift from one of the church members; a beige terrycloth swatch of fabric with a grand piano and the words *Minister of Music* embroidered in black, dabbed his eyes and forehead. He surveyed the Voices, where half of the singers were ministering as Pastor Trantham had instructed, the other half had ceased singing altogether, and were shouting, dancing, crying. *No! Ya'll have to keep singing!* He bowed his head and ashamedly self-corrected his thinking. Praise was supposed to be the result when their song was sincere.

Pastor Trantham made his way out of the pulpit with a microphone in hand. "I don't know what I'm supposed to do," he declared. "I thought that if I walked over here to the podium, God would reveal to me what's supposed to take place next. Maybe He'd tell me that it's preaching time. Right now though, we're bringing the slogan that's written at the bottom of our bulletin full circle: "*Subject to change according to The Spirit.*" He reached for his Bible, which sat open on the podium. He read from II Chronicles 5:13, 14:

> *The house was filled with a cloud, even the house of the Lord, so that the priests could not stand by reason of the cloud, for the glory of the Lord had filled the house of God.*

Pastor Trantham closed the Bible and placed it under his arm. "I'm to get out of the way and allow the Spirit do His thing." He walked up the short stairway into the pulpit, went to his chair, and sat.

The chorus of the song was sung twice more.

Pastor Trantham, an anxious look on his face, again leaped up from his seat and walked down the stairs from the pulpit to the floor. In that same instant, a trio; Jeremiah, Tamla and an alto named Sherrie Brill, sang the next strain of the song:

♫ *We feel the power of His presence*
We know the vict'ry in His name...

Then Voices sang a medley of various songs that ministered for another twenty to thirty minutes.

Pastor Trantham spoke out, offering an invitation; *opening the doors of the church.* Sixteen new converts accepted Christ and dozens of others came forward in rededication.

Had anyone ever known a time when Ezekiel Baptist Church lost its sense of composure? Jeremiah wouldn't have had a clue but, on that Sunday, he witnessed a celebration of the spiritual kind.

Several minutes later, Pastor Trantham returned to the pulpit and again began speaking to the congregation. "If you're still waiting for the service to reach a peak today, then you've already missed it. I was prepared to start a series of lessons on *True Worship* today, but this Sunday, God did the teaching," he shouted with conviction.

He gestured for the deacons and ushers to come forward. "Folks, you may not believe what I'm about to say. We're going to take the offering; praise the Lord. If we're not careful, the people will forget to give! Amen!?"

"Amen!" the congregation chorused.

"Then we're going to have the benediction." Pastor Trantham hunched his shoulders, leaning into the rostrum. "After this move of the Spirit, what can I say, what am I gonna add?" There was a hush among the congregation, a low murmur of agreement that could be heard throughout the sanctuary. "The Lord preached the sermon that *He* wanted preached. So, after the offering, let's prepare to leave the sanctuary with a praise on our lips, and joy in each heart."

"Worship today was something, wasn't it, Brother Day?" asked Rev. Knight as he and Pastor Trantham stepped down from the pulpit, both ministers appeared to be in spiritual afterglow.

"Vertical songs, Reverend," Jeremiah replied. He walked out of the choir stand with a satisfied feeling, believing that a work had been performed in that appointed time and place; that a small part of metro Olds had seen barren ground broken, and then restored. "Vertical songs bring vertical worship."

Verse 16 ♫

Because the carnal mind is enmity against God: for it is not subject to the law of God, neither indeed can be. Romans 8:7 KJV

Renard found himself involved in red-eyed flight layovers that lasted from 10:00pm Saturday evening until early Sunday morning. Under most circumstances, he would have caught a nap under the rumble of jet engines, but, for some reason, sleep didn't find him, and precious hours were spent in a restless state. If he dreamed a dream during his travels, he did it with opened eyes.

When he arrived in Detroit around 5:00am, legs intensely numb from cramped seating and body slightly inebriated from on-board cocktails, Kira rescued both him and his luggage from curbside. They made the twenty-five minute drive up the M1 to their home in Olds.

"Did you remember my-"

"Yes, I did," he interrupted, predicting her reference to the blessed mask she so desired.

"Did you get anything for your dad?"

"Girl, yeah. I got him an album. Actually two." Renard tried to coerce, even con his restlessness into sleep by reflecting on the kinship he felt with the freewheeling atmosphere of New Orleans. He'd swore others had to have been similarly affected, and wondered how anyone could escape its diabolic clutches once they'd visited that city.

He reclined in the vehicle, recalling the camaraderie of the Society brotherhood as they exchanged ideas, swapped chord progressions, and inducted new members during the Conclave and Refectory. He nurtured the thought that he had been given permission - one could even say he had received *explicit orders* - from the National Chapter of the Society, to carry out a programmed DOA. Inwardly, he smiled a wicked smile. *Yes.* That could be the mental formula for a restful sleep.

"Are you playing for church this morning?" Kira asked, matter-of-factly.

Her question caused Renard to quicken, forging his mind into an unsolicited whirlwind of thought. It *was* Sunday morning. He'd made no music preparations for the service, which had been on his to-do list, even while he was out of town. Nothing came to mind. Not a Morning hymn or choir selections. Nothing. It took him a minute to gather real composure before he finally said, "I gotta be there today. There's no getting around it."

"Naw Baby. Actually you don't," Kira said with clear, crisp confidence.

Renard was already alarmed over the last-minute preparations he knew he'd have to make, and he waited for a sign from Kira that she was joking, but she did nothing to pick up the pace. Her eyes held no panic. Her face never twisted in a smile. Her foot never accelerated the gas pedal. He knew that showering, shaving, general I-need-to-get-ready preparations were ahead of him, and time was wasting. "Why don't I have to go?" he asked.

Kira shot him a brief glance and then returned her attention to the road. "You don't remember? The new guy will be there. Pastor said his name last Sunday, but I forgot it."

"Huh?"

"The new gentleman . . . umm-"

"Jeremiah? Day?" He tried to take the surprise out of his voice.

"Yeah, that's his name. Won't he be there?"

Renard shrugged. He just wasn't sure.

"C'mon, make this a day off for yourself. For the two of us, honey." She slid her hand across and down to his seat and gripped his inner thigh, massaging everything within reach.

Renard's mind traveled back about seven days or so, when on the way to the airport, he left some business unfinished, but reality stepped in the way. He took hold of Kira's hand, giving it a squeeze. "Aw naw." He hadn't given Jeremiah another thought; not during his trip, not since the last rehearsal. And he hadn't thought to ask. He actually *did not* believe that the new musician would've survived past the previous Sunday. "I definitely cannot take a day off."

Kira's eyes opened up and her mouth parted. "Why not?" She wrenched her hand from his grasp and began waving it in the air. "Never mind. You know your job. I'll be at Bedside Baptist. Resting. You know I don't sleep well when you're out of town," Kira told him in an angry purr.

"Well I'm here in town now, babe, so you stay home and rest," he said, trying to sound settling. Renard was gratified that Kira didn't try to press him into staying home, even though her spoken request was his desire; but he *had* to play that morning. Now that he was back in town and the Society had given him a renewed vigor, that morning wouldn't be just about playing the organ and getting a check. Now he was on a mission. If he were to find the right opportunity during that morning's 10 o'clock service, he would play a hymn or song out of character with their worship. If he could seize a moment, his efforts would disrupt anyone or everyone within earshot of the music. What better way to test the Dicaearchy Obrumpent Allotheism formula and prove the power of the Society of Tyrus? What better time than the present?

The thought of what he might accomplish on that Sunday would make going to church and operating without rest . . . well, worthwhile.

Verse 17 ♫

Let his days be few, and let another take his office.
Psalms 109:8 KJV

Renard dropped his luggage in the foyer, showered, changed into a suit and tie, jumped into the car and hurried down the road to Ezekiel. As he arrived onto the campus and parked, Deacon Elginor Steele, a bristly-haired man in his late-sixties who evidently cultivated an undying affinity for thick, disproportioned, glen plaid three-piece suits a couple sizes too large, crowded Renard at his vehicle, with just enough room for the driver's side door to crack open. "Welcome back, Brother Singleton. Listen. Whatever else you have to do, you need to see Pastor before service begins," he said smugly, sticking out his pudgy hand.

In a single motion, Renard shook and withdrew his hand. "Okay. I will." He preferred not to be bothered with Steele on that morning, a man he regarded as opportunist, heralding associations with others in-the-know, not realizing that those same associates have only the appearance of solid financial stature, but were truthfully less than a paycheck from poverty.

To be honest, greeting congregants wasn't Renard's forte. Whenever possible, he sought out entrances and exits that avoided as many people as possible. He didn't care for them, unless they became servants to his purposes. He had categorized the entire bunch: there were those using the church as a pickup spot for the opposite – rephrase – the sexes. Several cliques full of aints with nose-trouble who found nothing constructive, taking the time to chitchat with fellow churchgoers on matters they had no business attending to. Bible-quoting aints attending morning services while contemplating which nightclubs they would hit that same evening. It was their behavior that helped Renard form the opinion that Christians are worthless, convoluted message-bearers.

He thought even less of speaking with Trantham before service but, because of the request slash demand, Renard barreled down the administrative hall to the pastor's office.

Renard rapped on Trantham's office door and peered inside because it was already open. One of the associate preachers motioned for him to enter. Renard examined the room, where the head usher, deacon board chairman, and several of the associates were scattered about. Renard positioned himself near Trantham, and though he was offered a seat, opted to stand. He didn't have to guess the meaning behind the scornful expressions of that crowd. One thing he was confident of: they couldn't have disliked him more than his hatred for them.

"Brother Singleton! Good to see you back!" Trantham almost passed as sounding genuine.

"Hey. Steele said you summoned me."

As if on cue, every individual cleared the office, each one pretending in some way that Renard had not been a topic of discussion prior to his arrival. With the office vacated except for the two, Trantham asked, "Should I be concerned about you and Brother Day's working relationship?"

"So I can assume that he's still here."

"I don't see why you thought he wouldn't be." Trantham picked up a pen and scribbled something on a notepad. "Yes. Last Sunday was blessed. That's the only word I can come up with to adequately describe the services. And from what I've heard from several singers and the other musicians, the choir rehearsal this week was just as productive."

"There must've been a problem with my rehearsals." Renard hoped that Trantham understood his statement to be more of a question.

"At this juncture, I'm not trying to compare the two of you. Bottom line is, Brother Day is now the lead musician for our church, and it's important that he gets every opportunity to lead our music down a path without any obstructions."

"Umm hmm."

"I've been lax on how our choirs sounded. That's now history. I'm ready to see our music taken to another level in worship. I have to know that everyone beginning from this point is on board. That includes you. Especially you."

"I'm on board. I still don't see why the attention's on me. Like I'd hurt the ministry."

"You've been here the longest," Trantham said. "You probably feel some kinda way about this move."

"You mean like being the experienced guy on a job who looks around and sees some young buck getting hired? Then, the old guy has to train the young one on *his* job. So forth and so on the story goes."

"Look, Brother Renard, It's not up for discussion about who's been set in place for any ministry at this church. Not as long as I'm pastor."

"Whatever you say." *You're doing some big talk Trantham. I don't know why I keep having to say this is my family's church and you can't run me out.* "I'll do my job. I intend to be here. Forever," Renard stated.

Trantham stabbed the desktop with the nub of the pen in his hand. "But it's *my* ministry. My vision."

As if Renard didn't already feel a sense of desertion from choir members he'd known for so long, his favorite soloist approached him wearing a black and blue color-blocked zip-up dress that proved her every symmetric curve;

Tamla stood just outside the robing room. "Oh my God, Renard! You should've been here last week."

"Really?"

"Yeah. Service was awesome. And *Praise the Lord*, the new song we sang? I don't have the words."

"I'm sure you don't," he replied.

Renard abruptly ended that conversation by walking away, trouncing down to the end of the administration hall, where Jeremiah met him just as he passed the robing room.

"Here's the list of songs for worship this morning, Brother Renard," he said. "We will start using this song service document from Sunday to Sunday so that each musician will have a general idea of the songs that will be sung."

Renard looked the list over. "This is pretty much concrete?"

"For the most part. It depends on any turn the worship service may take. Then we'll make adjustments."

Adjustments? "I'm not sure how to prepare for that." Renard knew he'd just lied. Impromptu performance was a specialty of his.

Jeremiah, showing no concern what he'd been told, said, "It's something I want us to get used to. We may practice one thing, but the Holy Spirit may lead us in another direction; we have to be prepared to follow."

Renard took another look at the potential songs for service. "There's no Invitational song listed."

"I know."

"Why?" Renard hadn't planned to sit in the sanctuary during the sermon. For him, any piece-a song would've sufficed, thinking that Jeremiah was putting too much effort into what should have been a simple task.

"Really? You have to ask?"

"Uh-yeah."

"The Invitational song needs to line up with Pastor Trantham's sermon. And since we have no idea where the Lord is going to take him, we have to leave that portion of the service open."

"Of course. According to the spirit," Renard said.

Jeremiah waved his finger in the air. "See? You're getting it already."

Did Jeremiah think he was a fool? He sensed the sarcastic tone. It didn't matter to him how much authority the new music minister tried to employ. Renard's mission to destroy Ezekiel's faith was not going to be hindered. Not by Jeremiah, not by his father, Adrian, not by Trantham. Not even by the Society if they got in his way. No one.

C'mon, c'mon. Renard began to play a series of disruptive chord progressions during a point in the service that Trantham called, "An opportunity of praise." He sent the Leslie speakers blaring, forcing the drummer, Phillip, to follow his rhythm. He purposefully kept the meter of his playing off-balance. He ignored signals coming from the musicians and Jeremiah, who was to the left and rear of the choir stand joined in praise, stopped, zoning in on Renard with a straightforward stare.

These folk don't have a clue. From Renard's vantage point, the congregation's worshipful state lessened to inexplicable despair in a matter of minutes. He figured there would be no familiarity with the song he had incorporated, but it didn't matter. The Edicts of Tyrus Society had taught him that lyrics don't have to be the impetus that drove people into submission. The congregants became afflicted as he moved his chord progressions from a joyful major to hauntingly minor. The people were muddled as the music moved them from exhilarant to vexed, disorderly.

Then the atmosphere became a horrendous fermata, the same type of long embarrassing silence that audiences reward a performer for an aria gone wrong.

Trantham turned in his pulpit chair and gazed at Jeremiah, inquisitively. In turn, the new musician responded with a facial expression that Renard interpreted as, "I'm just as baffled as you, rev." The remainder of service never recovered from the damaged he had caused.

Renard, beaming with pride over his accomplishment, was confident that the only ones with any possibility of knowing what he had done were the musicians, particularly Jeremiah, whose glare seemed to last on end. *He might as well get over it. It's done.*

After service, Jeremiah captured him as he proceeded down the connector, yelling so loud that overtones rang out in Renard's ear, the combination of the new musician's warm breath and screeching voice came off like a clanging bell. "You think I don't know you changed the mode of the music?"

Renard, determined to play ignorant, began to move on down the hall and asked, "I changed the mode?"

Jeremiah moved as well, cornered him, forcing him to lean against the wall. He spouted off a monologue of acidic words, battering him verbally. "Please don't play me. You know what you did."

A couple deacons were at the other end of the hall, peered at the two arguing, and then went in the opposite direction. "Musicians interject patterns in the music all the time when praise breaks out," Renard rationalized. "What do you think *War Cry* is?"

Jeremiah shook his head and a finger from his free hand violently. "Stop trying to justify what you did. You can't compare Bishop Moales' *Praise Break* with what you did this morning. You and I both know the difference."

Renard refused to have his confidence shaken. "There was no difference. You sound sensitive," he said with an intentional jest.

"Sensitive?" Jeremiah turned away, and then snapped back into the squabble. "You right. I've been charged to be sensitive to the music going out, and what our congregation receives. A child, really, a *fool* could hear what you played this morning and tell that wasn't right for church."

"Mister Day, I'm trying to understand your way of doing things and all the changes you propose to make, but judging my chord changes? We haven't known each other long enough for you to know how I do on the organ."

"Man, please. Any real Christian can figure it out. They might not be able to express it in music terms, but they're not stupid. People know when something doesn't sound right to them. Jeremiah slapped the hymnal in his hand, shut. "It better not happen again."

Verse 18 ♫

Whoso findeth a wife findeth a good thing.
Proverbs 18:22 KJV

Arze' came up from Memphis the following week for their third and final pre-marital session with Pastor Trantham before their September 20th wedding date. Jeremiah refused to tarnish her visit with the particulars of last Sunday's service or his ridiculous argument with Renard. Moreover, he didn't want her to remind him of her thoughts against taking a church music position in the first place. For sanity's sake, he would keep her outside the realm of knowing.

They had a short wait with Pastor Trantham's admin before Pastor escorted them into what he called his "transitional office."

Once inside, Arze' commented on the Philodendron vine that had snaked its way along the office wall, the miniature water feature that sat in one corner, and the floor-to-ceiling bookshelf holding various Bible commentaries and concordances occupying an adjacent corner. A serene backdrop of Ben Tankard's Gospel Jazz provided an ambient blanket for every other decorative element in the room. Pastor Trantham expressed his pride in the furnishings as the couple surveyed the surroundings. "My office in the new sanctuary won't be as cramped a space. I don't need or care for the abundance that the building committee has planned for me, but it's what they want to do so I won't argue them down on the matter. It'll be comfortable, but not important to my church work."

"I'm sure you deserve it," Jeremiah said. He was being sincere. Since working with the Pastor, he'd been a witness of his compassion and devotion to the congregation.

Pastor Trantham arranged the chairs in his office so that Jeremiah and Arze' faced each other. "I need you as one as you ponder your decision to marry," he said amusingly, motioning for Arze' to take her seat.

Jeremiah didn't find the assignment to look into the bright, pecan eyes of his fiancée difficult. His love for Arze' and the desire to have her as his mate had grown, the accelerando to his open heart. He gazed over at Arze', who returned the expression with her own. The half-hour appointment turned into a two hour session, with Pastor asking how long they've dated, what the parents thought about their future plans and in what manner do they go about settling or compromising their personal convictions for the good of the marital bond. "Study His Word together. Never go to bed angry. This is some of the advice I can give you for a loving and lasting, God-fearing relationship," were his words to the couple.

Jeremiah and Arze' confirmed their preference for a simple office ceremony, an elaborate honeymoon afterward, and sometime in the following year, go to their hometown and host a reception for family and friends. "Would there be a problem in having Rev. Knight as a witness to our marriage?" Jeremiah asked, wanting his ministry intercessor involved in what he regarded as an ultimate stepping-stone in life.

Pastor Trantham saw no issue in it, and consented for the vows to be exchanged in his office.

"Now I hate to be pastoral, but where do you plan to make your church membership as a couple?" he asked. "Actually, I don't apologize for the question. I want to know."

He glanced toward Arze' for confirmation. "We're going to be right here, Pastor," Jeremiah told him.

"Good, good." Pastor Trantham turned, eyeing Arze' without a blink, and then extended his hand. "Now dear, I hear you have a gift or two that'd be a blessing to our church. Now tell me I'm correct."

The scowl that she gave Jeremiah had him hoping praying, that he wasn't about to be embarrassed or worse, maimed or killed right there in the Pastor's presence.

"I know that my fiancée told you that I play and sing. I do – while I'm still living in Memphis. When we get married, though, I plan on being in some ministry; promise, but I very seriously doubt that it'll be music, which is also what he should've told you."

Pastor Trantham bowed his head, his eyes, moving, seeming to find an object to settle on. "We'll make a place for you, dear," he said with insistence, "wherever you desire."

Arze' nodded. "Thanks Pastor. But it's no to the music department."

Honestly, Jeremiah couldn't help but be in agreement with her decision. Considering the music department and its events of late, he didn't think it wise that she joined him in that ministry. Not right then.

Verse 19 ♫

The path of the just is as the shining light that shineth more and more unto the perfect day. Proverbs 4:18 KJV

Olds Central High School, a sprawling campus situated on the city's east side, had been in the middle of its own little war. Being the oldest accredited high school in the state of Michigan didn't seem to matter to the local school board, which voted in favor of its closure a year ago due to tremendous budget shortfalls and anemic student decline. Closing would have placed the pre-cast concrete architectural wonder into the hands of vandals, looters, and souvenir seekers. But something could be said for Central's powerful alumni association, whose membership had boastfully included everyone from the three Russell brothers of NBA fame, to the infamous assisted-suicide physician, the late Dr. Jack Kevorkian; rallying and petitioning against the government's desires. Olds Central High went down as one case where Indians - the school's mascot – survived an attack.

In Jeremiah's not-too-distant future, he would be witness to thirteen hundred half-grown freshmen, sophomores, juniors and seniors invading the school grounds, so he set aside wedding plans, church issues and anything of a personal nature, to concentrate on his nine-to-five.

He spent the following day at school doing the things that teachers do in preparing for a new year: attending staff meetings, cleaning rooms, copying worksheets . . . etc.

During their opening staff meeting, over ninety faculty members introduced themselves as part of the principal's ice-breaker; each person giving their name, the subject they teach and something interesting that others may not know.

The gentleman sitting next to Jeremiah introduced himself as Leopold Richter, an athletically built man anyone would've been hailed as a prince of Counter-Culture upon first impression; a greasy blonde, fashion-absent male who had emerged right out of the sixties youth movement; a nomad thoroughly educated in psychedelic music and well-versed in altered states of consciousness. He made it known to that group of educators that he preferred to be called Leo, and no, he wasn't intentionally named after the German painter or the famous soccer player. After finishing his introduction, he turned to Jeremiah, and in a whisper he asked, "You're the new musician at Ezekiel Baptist, aren't you?"

"How did you know?" Jeremiah gave his musical talent as an interesting fact for the ice-breaker, but he didn't specify the musical genre and where or if he did any live performing.

"Oh, word gets around. There's not that many musicians in the area and even fewer that anyone would want to listen to. Churches scramble and throw big dollars in the way of the most popular musicians, trying to scoop them up."

"You know, I've heard that on more than a couple occasions since moving here. What a way to hire a musician. It's really pitiful."

"Yeah, but think about it. What musician worth big dollars would stay in this city? Most of the churches around here are having a difficult time paying a *preacher*. I mean, he or she would have to really be dedicated, especially since you can go to Detroit where there's a better opportunity."

"I don't see where they can do that much better. At least, I don't guess," Jeremiah said, knowing that the Motor City couldn't boast an economic windfall. Fewer jobs meant more people attending church – to pray, not to pay.

"Yeah," Leo replied, "I don't think I would travel fifty miles roundtrip just to play for little more than gas money."

Jeremiah paused for a second to listen to the principal's rant on lesson plans or some other uninteresting topic, and then he turned back to Leo. "Oh. Do you play?"

Leo rolled his eyes back of his head and spread the fingers on his hands as though he needed them to think. "Lessons from six to eleven years old. Started getting serious about my music around twelve. I've been paid for playing ever since I was thirteen. Got a piano performance degree from Michigan State. I'd say yes, I play. But I teach Public Speaking and Drama here at school."

"That's probably as peculiar as having a music degree but teaching Algebra and Calculus. You play church music?"

"Is there any other kind?" Leo asked. "I mean, I only play Christian music. I've been out in the world with women, dope, alcohol, and worldly music. God helped me get a release from that stuff before it killed me. I'm not interested in going back into that lifestyle."

"So you've played secular music?"

"Lord yes. I've played everything from light rock to heavy metal. I've done it. Now that I've accepted Christ and committed to the Lord, I play to please Him."

"Me too. I think that if I'd even tried to play something else other than church music when I was younger, my old-line Baptist preacher daddy would've killed me. Now I'm too afraid of tempting God into doing something to me if I were to corrupt the gift He's allowed me to have."

"Your talk is totally different from the usual conversations that come from out of Ezekiel."

"What does that mean?"

"I'm sorry. I didn't mean folks in your congregation. I don't know them. I'm referring to your organist. Re'Re'

Singleton never speaks with any Godly conviction; I wonder if he's saved. So it's refreshing to hear another musician confess a belief in Jesus Christ."

"Re'Re'?"

"I grew up and went all the way to high school graduation with the man. That's what we call him. What? I guess you call him Renard."

"Yeah. Well basically, Brother Singleton."

"I hear you. At any rate, I shouldn't have judged what I thought you'd be like based on how he acts. Honestly though, from what I know about Renard I don't see how the both of you get along."

Jeremiah's mind went back to last Sunday, and then he wondered how much if anything had Leo heard about the tug-of-war that took place in Ezekiel's choir stand. He was just making Leo's acquaintance, so he felt better keeping church business close to the heart. "We've had a couple growing pains, so to speak, but we do okay."

"Really?" Leo said.

"In fact, Renard asked me about becoming a part of the association of church musicians that meet occasionally to discuss issues we face in ministry. You know what I'm talking about?"

"Oh yeah."

"You a member?"

"Well, let's see. How do I put this?" Leo said after giving a wordy, round-about, senseless explanation.

Jeremiah sat back in his chair, ruffled over Leo's answer. "Something wrong?"

"Let's just say at one time I was seriously being considered for the Society, but . . . my church wasn't large enough to suit them."

"What does that have to do with being in a group designed to assist church musicians? Church size. Really?"

"I play for a relatively small Episcopalian congregation. Your church is pushing what, some three thousand or so?"

"I guess. And I have to remind myself that a new sanctuary is being built to accommodate the ever- growing congregation. Why?"

"For the Society of Tyrus, church size is everything. And let's stop calling it a group because that's not what it is."

"Then what is it?"

Leo's eyes met his like a laser. "You have time after school to get together and discuss this . . . away from here?"

Jeremiah knew between finalizing plans for life with Arze', church work and the preparation for the opening of the school year, he had more than his share to do. But he was curious to hear what this Leopold Richter had to say. "I've got nothing but time."

"Great then. Let's grab a bite to eat later. But I'll tell you this. If Renard is trying to get you to be a part of what he's involved in . . ." Leo's voice trailed off as he looked around, "I can't just call it a group. It's a whole lot more than that.

"Yeah?"

"It's a cult."

Verse 20 ♫

. . . For the battle is not yours, but God's.
II Chronicles 20:15 KJV

When Jeremiah phoned Leo and told him that he had a craving for a hamburger, Leo laughed boisterously and then asked, "How hungry are you?"

Little did he know that his colleague was leading him down Michigan Avenue to eat what he assured was the "Original Slider." He seriously doubted that Leo's recall of culinary history was correct. To Jeremiah's dismay, he ended up eating his words.

So between bites of squared-off, greasy, onion laden, but surprisingly delectable White Castle burgers, they sat as Leo began unfolding an abbreviated account of the Society of Tyrus, how the local chapter came to be, and instances where former members had, more than likely, experienced some wrath of God because of their devotion to the art of demonic musical deception. "That cannot be for real," Jeremiah said in amazement.

"I was first considered for membership in the Tyrus Society a couple years after I had converted to Christianity. I stopped playing guitar for Mystic Brew, this groove metal band based out of Port Huron. They're only regionally popular but still together, from what I hear."

"A metal band." Jeremiah had already judged by Leo's appearance and demeanor that he could've fit in a band of that genre, so he wasn't surprised by Leo's revelation. "In your heart, Jesus and metal didn't mix, huh?"

Leo nodded; his expression was submissive, almost apologetic. "No way. In my heart, the Lord was convicting me. Something just . . . during that time, nothing in my life turned out right."

"What a testimony. Now God uses you for His work."

"And I praise Him every day! I became the music minister for Centennial Methodist Church in Waterford Township. They were pushing close to four thousand souls. I was even instrumental in the conception of a Contemporary Worship Service as an alternative to their traditional service. With a music degree, a secular music resume, and employment with a mega-congregation, the Society showed a definite interest in my becoming a member, and I was willing to begin the initiation process. But before I could become a full-fledged Society member, I left Centennial. I decided that that church just wasn't for me."

"Why'd you leave? The money?"

"No. Oh the money at Centennial was good. Very good. But the teaching and the messages didn't feed me, you know, for what I needed at that time in my life. I moved my membership and started playing where I am now, which is a fine church with about three hundred wonderful believers.

"You have to go where you know the Lord is calling you. That's a huge shift in congregation size."

"Huge shift. But no regrets. Once the Society found out that I was no longer at big Centennial and I refused to play any more rock music, they immediately halted initiation."

Jeremiah nearly choked off a huge swallow of Coke. "Wow. I can't believe that."

"It was an amiable parting, believe me. So Renard has asked you about joining, huh?"

Those one-bite burgers were in his system and beginning to digest, fighting for air space. Jeremiah held the next sandwich between his hands, studying whether he had the strength and room to devour it. "He's casually mentioned membership me. To tell the truth, I hadn't given it another thought."

Leo's brow furrowed. "Oh?"

"The way he talked it up, he made it out to be more of a club than anything else."

"Let me tell you, brother, it's no club. The history of the Tyrus Society proper goes all the way back to the mid-eighteenth century. And some parts of their rituals can be traced back to Biblical times."

"You're kidding."

"I wish. The Society of Tyrus is nothing to play around with. They're as dangerous as the KKK. Maybe even more so. They try to follow their books and rules to the letter. They believe they have a demon on their side, working on their behalf. And truthfully, I believe they do, too."

Jeremiah stifled his laugh.

"I know, I know," Leo said. "It sounds preposterous, doesn't it?"

"Uh, yeah."

"I don't know everything it is to know about them because I never crossed over, but I know enough to know if they ever tap into the power they believe they have, they could turn each one of their church's music programs upside down. Please understand... Renard is in the middle of that stuff. And now you, in the same church with him?"

"I'm not going to let him run me."

"If you don't stay prayed up, you may not have a choice. Doc, I'm telling you. That group studies ways to keep what we might call normal church drama going, just like any other music department, all the while they're spreading layers of satanic activity. And the bad part about it is that they do it right under the noses of their congregations."

"It just sounds amazing. Almost impossible to believe."

"Well believe it, brother. Before you know it, the Society will have dug their heels into your church, so that only God Himself can clear them out."

Jeremiah spent a few moments reflecting on what Leo told him. He had never dealt with anything or anyone that attacked him beyond mere childish bullying, which was often mindless adolescent behavior. If Leo was factual and his own assumptions were correct, his faith, his existence, was being challenged. If his deductions were in the right, Renard and his comrades were more than casual stirrers of confusion among singers and musicians; they were strategic practitioners of demonic activity, using the churches they played in as headquarters for their operation. But there was one thing he was certain of: he would never have a genuine interest in Renard's society. "You know, I recall something I heard a while ago."

"What?" Leo asked.

"It was on the radio, and I hadn't asked anyone about what I heard, because I didn't know how to explain it. The whole message was unclear at the time."

"When?"

"It was a Gospel station. This dj talked about a pastor and congregation being put out of their church-."

"Say no more, bro," Leo interrupted, shaking his head. "I know." He chomped on a fresh burger, following it with a slurp of his drink.

Jeremiah stared at Leo and began whipping his free hand in a circular motion, hoping to press him on. "Don't leave me hanging, man! Tell me what you know."

"What you heard on the radio was the work of the Society of Tyrus."

"C'mon man! Really?"

"I'm trying to tell you, brother, this is no joke. Pastor Felix-."

"That's who I heard," Jeremiah interrupted.

"I know. That pastor's a former musician for a world-wide ministerial organization before he accepted his call into the preaching ministry. Had a thriving ministry, with people flocking by the droves to The Open Door."

"That's the name of their church?"

"That *was* the name of their church here in the area."

"It doesn't exist anymore?"

"Dissolved." Leo snapped his fingers. "Just like that."

"Wow," was all Jeremiah could say.

"Pastor Timmons and his minister of music began studying the history of the Society, and before you know it, Timmon's musician started incorporating weird-like music progressions in their services."

"Chord progressions?" Jeremiah asked.

Leo nodded. "Progressions that conjures spirits. And not the Holy one."

"Unbelievable."

"Okay. Keep thinking that," Leo shot back. "I'm guessing that before those two really realized what was happening, they began experiencing the power in the music's hidden messages. Over time, the musician got high-minded, and the pastor began denouncing Christianity as the only religion in which people could be saved. And they were both . . . members of this thing you wanna call a club."

"So that's why the guy on the radio that day kept using the word heretic when he referred to that pastor."

"Yeah. And rightly so. When I was in the initial portion of the Society's intake process, I did learn that Timmons and his musician had become what Tyrus calls 'teeth which had sprout into warriors for the cause.'"

"Well, do you have any idea what has happened with the two of them since their fall?"

"The pastor has moved to some city farther west with some congregation that was foolish enough, willing to take him in."

"And the, umm, musician?"

"The musician left Olds a hero in the eyes of the Society. Disappeared."

"A hero?"

"You know. He was like a bee that's stung a human. After he accomplished his mission, he died. In a sense of speaking."

Jeremiah began to think back to his brief history with Renard, the encounters they've already had, every move and habit he'd witnessed so far. He gave careful consideration to his situation, coming into the realization of what may lie in front of him. "But wouldn't it be difficult for Renard to do anything like that at my church?"

Leo shrugged his shoulders.

"I mean, think about it. Pastor Trantham has designated me as the head musician. I'm running the department. Renard can't do anything about that."

"Brother, let me be clear. Whatever might be going on is not about you. When I look back on the part of my life that included the Tyrus Society, I almost pledged my allegiance into an organization that proposes to fight a war in a realm no human can see."

"Don't they realize they're fighting on the wrong side?"

"You know when the Bible speaks of principalities and *high places*?" Leo asked.

"Of course. Ephesians six, twelve."

"You got it. You may not be in the fight with them - yet. But your day is coming."

Later that evening, the walls of Jeremiah's sparsely furnished apartment were his sole companion. With Arze' still in Memphis, he sat on his couch in silence, listening to himself. Given all that Leo told him and his experiences with Renard so far, he considered his moments alone as a prime opportunity to speak with God and for God to speak to him. *Dear Lord . . .*

As he prayed, his teaching position, his upcoming marriage and all that entailed his move to Olds came before him with confidence juxtaposed against realization; he very well may be in a fight against Renard and his choir members, mortal foes and Satan, the immortal enemy. This made him restless, forcing his prayer to intensify, causing his eyes to well with tears.

Verse 21 ♫

The field is the world; the good seed are the children
of the Kingdom; but the tares are the children of the wicked
one. Matthew 13:38 KJV

Just as he promised Terry during the Tyrus Society's
National Conclave and Refectory, Renard hosted an informal
gathering of the Gamma chapter at his and Kira's home on
Walton Boulevard in Rochester Hills, an outskirt east of
Olds.

On that evening, Kira served her signature punch of
ginger beer, cinnamon sticks and pineapple juice; endless
salsa chips topped with a ground beef, Rotel and Velveeta
dip, taking moments now and then to listen in on the men's
idle banter. "Alright brothers, let's drink up, Renard
demanded, lifting up a Highball glass that he had filled with a
healthy portion of Dewar's and topped off with ginger beer
leftover from his wife's punch. "Bar's open. The punch is
great, but if you're like me, I need something with a little
lead in it." As if on cue, the brothers went to the kitchen
counter and helped themselves to the bottles of Seagram's,
Crown Royal, Johnnie Walker and other libations. While the
brothers congregated there, he pulled Kira aside and sweetly
requested of her if, once the brothers started into serious
discussions, she would excuse herself from the room. She
gracefully consented, telling him that she knew the essence
of the get-together was for Society business.

After everyone had a plate of snacks and a drink in
hand, they retreated to the family room.

"Dude, that new cut of yours is something crazy!"
Bacchus screamed. His impulsive action caused a part of his

drink to fly into the air, but he retrieved the drops, which was entertaining to the group.

"Where'd you hear it?" Renard wanted to know. He had been so busy with his job at Freestar Financial and preparations for the Society DOA that he hadn't been in contact with Fredrico at Sound Shocker since the day they completed and agreed to begin some promotion and marketing for *Death of a Carnal Christian.* Once he was sure that Bacchus was referring to this latest release, Renard knew that, in his absence, Fredrico had taken some tremendous initiative on getting the song in rotation.

"WJLB 98 played it on *Cool Flight Indy Night.* DJ Big Blast asked people to call in, Tweet, Instagram or instant message the station's Facebook page with a yea or nay on the cut. You got a great response," Bacchus explained.

"Alright, alright." Renard didn't want to appear too ecstatic about the news, but he knew that as soon as he had opportunity, he and Fredrico would ramp up the promo on that cut, and possibly start writing another song ASAP. "Now I've got to figure out how my music can make me some cash, not just make me popular."

"Pretty soon, you won't be able to distinguish between your church music and your Hip Hop riffs. Whatcha gonna do then?" Terry asked with a sly smirk on his face.

Renard, sensing the facetious nature of the comment, pondered the thought for a moment. "Give me more credit than that. With a hit song, I can't be stopped. Church folk don't really care what you do on the weekends. As long as the music is right on Sunday, they're willing to turn their heads."

"Dat's what you *Dink*?" asked Olufemi.

Renard sifted an understanding out of his Ghanaian accent before responding, "I don't *think* the Ezekiel members are that stupid. I *know* they are."

"Okay everybody, let's uh, come together," demanded Terry, trying to sound presidential.

Renard knew the brothers should postpone the lauding of his latest musical accomplishment, and that Terry needed to get them brothers on task because if they weren't careful, they'd spend half the evening talking about everything except actual Society business.

"You've had more than enough time to think of ideas for your individual DOA's. Let's hear what you have and make some decisions on ones we believe will be the most effective," Terry advised.

"We know what chord progressions will work for us when we do this. The people get stirred when we stack minor sevenths, open up the eight, four, two foot drawbars on the organ, and then crank up the volume during a ministerial exhortation. Right?" Renard asked, not wanting to wait for a response. "Well let's alter the chord progressions a bit." He hesitated in the moment, realizing that his rapid fire speech could be perceived as overzealous. Thing was, he *had* launched a successful faux-DOA, so he figured his suggestions carried at least a little weight.

"You're on a roll. Don't stop now," demanded Zachary, who bolted through the entrance of the room, sounding winded. "Sorry I'm late fellas. He pointed to Renard. "Gone on brother, because I need some ideas."

Renard nodded. "Like I was saying, we can alter our progressions, or instead of a smooth key change of a half or whole step, make it a step and a half. Difficult key- change transitions like that throw choirs off, making the music sound off-balance to the congregation."

Terry, Zachary, Olufemi, and Bacchus – that mix of Baptist, AME Zion, Pentecostal and Bapti-costal musicians – agreed that Renard's idea sounded like an ingenious one.

"We can't go through our service using that method," said both Mercer and Merle Dobbins in harmonious chorus. They were fiery redhead twin brothers and musicians from Cokesbury United Methodist in downtown Olds. They were among the first brothers to arrive at the gathering, commandeering a corner of the room for themselves the moment Kira welcomed them in. "Our music is pretty resolute, and it leaves us little chance for the improv you guys get to do. Playing outside of the script just doesn't work for us. We're not comfortable doing it." Mercer stated.

Bacchus sprang up from his chair, startling a couple of the brothers. "The majority of your services are hymns!"

Both Mercer and Merle appeared jolted from Bacchus' proclamation, but they nodded in agreement.

"Keep your chorus intact, but alter verses two and three or two through four, bounce from major to minor modes; it will have the congregation off-balance for sure," Bacchus shouted in what seemed to be at the top of his voice.

"And for those of us who do it at their churches," Renard paused, looking to everyone except the twins, "you will refuse to give an instrumental acclamation to your preachers when they're in the drive."

"Huh?" said Zachary.

"Don't bump the preacher in his squall, fool!" Terry said. "Don't pay attention to their sermons, and don't give a musical response to anything they do, no matter how much they signal for your help."

"That's cold," Zachary said.

"That's how it's meant to be," Renard told him.

"Listen fellas," Terry said, "be sure to practice whatever chord progressions you're going to use by December first, so that each one of your plans goes off without a hitch."

"If any of you need chord progression ideas, I don't mind practicing with you or writing out a set of effective progressions," Renard said with a grin that he hoped was obviously menacing to his brothers. He couldn't have asked for a better date to pull off his scheme. A December 1st DOA would be the Sunday after Thanksgiving which, from his remembrance, was occurring later than the DOAs of previous years. It would also be a Communion Sunday, giving him an additional forty minutes to pull off his plan as compared to other Sundays in the month; prime opportunity to disrupt one of the Baptist denomination's wretched ordinances. "I'm not waiting until December first to do what I plan to do. You all can do whatever you want," he announced.

"What does that mean?" Terry asked.

"Oh, I don't mean that I'm not participating in the DOA in December. I mean that I'm going to do a kind of practice run." Renard cocked his head to one side and began nodding, hoping that the brotherhood would see his air of confidence. "It'll be on some Sunday in the near future."

"What?" Zachary drawled out.

"Now that's what I'm talking 'bout! Defiance!" Bacchus shouted.

Renard resolved to remain calm, keep his tone inviting. "I don't mean it to be defiant, not against the brotherhood. It's that I've done something similar at Ezekiel recently, on a smaller scale. The actual DOA is a national thing, but frankly, disrupting worship services should be on our agendas all the time anyway."

The Dobbins brothers interrupted each other asking why Renard would want to do such a thing. Renard regarded their disagreement with him as mere noise.

"What will you do concerning your other musician?" Olufemi asked.

Renard knew that Jeremiah was planning to be out of town for both the rehearsal and the Sunday in which he would wage his personal little battle, making for a perfect opportunity. His self-assurance was incomprehensible to the brothers. He pointed a finger in Olufemi's direction. "That my friend is not a problem," he said.

"It won't work. You can't do that," Terry stated with a sharp dryness in his voice.

Renard was surprised at the mixed bag of emotions and responses from the rest of the brotherhood, but he wondered why his friend felt a dissenting voice of reason was something that he needed. "Which is it, Terry? It won't work or I can't do that?"

"Both. You can't get all independent on us. That's why we make decisions as a brotherhood," Terry said. He was seated until Renard made his declaration. He stood up and began to pace the length of the room. "You were there, Renard. Our Dicaearchy Obrumpent Allotheism exercises are approved by the general membership and only through our national meetings. We don't fly off as lone birds in the name of The Society."

"I guess he's right, Renard," Zachary said apologetically. "It probably does go against Society Edicts."

"Maybe even the Ras el-Ain itself," Mercer Dobbins chimed in.

"Since one of the through-lines of The Society is the musical display of our power, I would've imagined that how often we demonstrate our power wouldn't be a problem, *especially* to the general membership," Renard argued.

"Believe it or not, Renard, it would be. Man, c'mon. Let's stick with the program," Terry shot back.

"I am with the program. I support The Society one hundred percent. I'm supportive and I'm financial. And, I have secular releases that prove my versatility."

Terry's pacing stiffened. "Now I see where you're going with this," he said. "Okay. So now you're the virtuoso, the ultimate Society member." A few of the brothers chuckled at his comment. "Bro', don't start believing your own hype just because we said you may have a hit record on your hands."

"That ain't got nothing to do with my plans for this Sunday. You can believe I'm on some personal vendetta or that I believe my own press if you want. I'm no hype-master. I'm just going to do a little test run on what the Society says is our right as members. I don't have to make up what or when I can do something that aids our cause. Our Edicts tells us we have power and authority. And I intend to use mine." In the moments that Renard made his declaration, the way he would implement his plan became clear.

Verse 22 ♫

*My son, hear the instruction of thy father, and forsake
not the law of thy mother. Proverbs 1:8 KJV*

The brotherhood had dispersed and Kira had retired
for the evening. Renard rushed up to his office to look for a
particular piece of music. At the same time, he decided to
phone Adrian Singleton, his father, to tell him of his plan and
the commotion his fellow brothers made concerning them.
He also decided that hearing his father's opinion about the
whole incident couldn't harm.

"Sometimes artists can claim that they're doing
something simply for art's sake. Disrupting churches
though?" He cussed loudly. That seems a bit over the top. I
don't see the art in it," Adrian said.

"Well, everything can't be for art's sake," Renard
replied. A neatly shelved stack of books received a frantic
shuffling as Renard held the cordless phone to his ear.
"Countless times, artists use a platform to make a statement."

"To an artist, it's the only way. But you can't
compare refusing to perform because of Jim Crow or, or you
know - artistic censorship . . . look, I've just had the good
sense to steer clear of any church if I can't be a help to
them."

"Dad, forget you." Renard tried reading through his
father's rhetoric to determine what he meant. "I was as
honest with the brothers as I could possibly be. There
would've been a problem for sure, had I kept my intentions
to myself and had refused to warn them."

"You've told me what you said to your brothers,"
Adrian said. "But are you being true with your intentions?
This isn't some hole-in-the-wall or despicable music venue
that you're planning to do harm to. It's a *church.*"

Renard attempted to retain a group of music books from falling off a rack, but failed, also causing the phone to slip from his ear. He snatched the phone up off the floor.

"What the devil are you doing, son?" Adrian asked.

"Nothing. Go ahead. I'm listening to you." Renard tried to keep from sounding breathless.

"Who knows? Church might be good for you. I mean, other than you just collecting a paycheck."

"You're one to talk. I don't seem to recall you as a regular churchgoer. We didn't when I was a kid. You don't go now. At all."

"But I've never used my musicianship to disrupt a church like I hear you're about to do! And for crissake, Renard, don't play me stupid. I know for a fact that this is what your group, lodge, whatever you call it, has *always* done."

"Yeah. Okay." By then, Renard had turned his attention to another bookshelf filled with various songbooks by prominent artists. He adjusted the phone against his ear. "Like you know what the Society does. You ever been pulled for membership?"

Adrian, seeming to ignore the question, repeatedly asked him what some noise was or why Renard sounded distant on the phone. Renard never divulged that he was trying to locate an item while talking to him. That went on until Adrian said, "I guess people have to feel drawn to be a regular churchgoer. Trustees. Church musicians. Even preachers – they'll know that feeling when it comes. I know one thing, Christian or not. We're all supposed to do right by other people. You should at least give in and follow that philosophy. Or get beat up by it."

"I'd have been willing to change or even drop my game plan if the brothers had made sense with their explanation that I'm doing something wrong."

"But . . . son-"

"What?"

"I'm not going to say that what you're doing is wrong, but you could suffer-"

"*Me?*" I'm doing fine, thank you very much. I may have a hit tune down the road, real soon," he declared. "Have you been paying attention lately?"

"Yes. I have. *Death to a Carnal Christian.* Your indie cut is gaining popularity. You're doing things that I have never done," Adrian said in what sounded to be a belligerent tone.

The man was right. Renard's music had taken turns that Adrian's never had. He still felt, though, that he hadn't reached the pinnacle of expertise that his father possessed. He wanted to *surpass* that. Throughout his childhood, Renard marveled at Adrian's ability to whip out classical rudiments and scales in the hall of their Detroit apartment from a broken down ten dollar piano they once labeled the Eight Hundred Pound Monster. As Renard matured and developed an affinity for various genres of music, it was nothing to hear his father emulating an Art Tatum embellishment, a Herbie Hancock chord sequence, or even a Twinkie Clark riff on a Hammond B-3 Adrian purchased before Renard was born and eventually passed on to him as a college graduation gift. "I hear what you're saying, dad. I really do. But my life is mine."

"I've got to tell you that your life in the short-term may look rosy, but long-term . . . I just don't know."

Renard slumped into his office chair, feeling somewhat exhausted. "Man please. Spit it out."

"Just because I don't attend church, doesn't mean I'm against what it stands for."

"Well I *am* against what it stands for, and I feel honored in showing my defiance to it."

Adrian mumbled something indiscernible.

Renard chose not to respond to his grumblings. "The great thing about musicianship decisions and overall decision-making as an adult is that you *can* make independent decisions – because you are an adult."

"And the thing about being a father or mother is that all decent parents try to steer their children free of making decisions they know will harm them – even when their children brag about how grown they are."

"I'm trying to see how you know without a doubt that doing this will harm me."

"There are some things about destiny, things that come to the heart, even things parents do and speak into existence that harm their children. Maybe not immediately, but in the long run – it shows up. Please. Trust me. I know what I'm talking about."

Renard grew weary of Adrian's banter. He tossed a stack of papers across the room where they landed against the wall, sprayed over the floor. "Whatever. Daddy listen, I've got to go. There's something I gotta do."

"Okay, okay. But listen. I don't just know things because I'm a father," Adrian said. "Trust me. I know what you're in and what you believe because it's my responsibility to know you. I can't speak for anyone else. Other folk's children ain't my concern. I'm *your* father."

Verse 23 ♫

He that is soon angry dealeth foolishly, and a man of wicked devices is hated. Proverbs 14:17 KJV

What A Friend. Blessed Assurance. O For A Thousand Tongues. So many hymns. Anthems. Spirituals. So many songs that helped establish the foundation of the Church Universal.

Renard wasn't interested in just any familiar song or hymn. Besides. The familiar or orthodox just wouldn't work. Not for his scheme. He needed a song. No. He needed a hymn. A *morning* hymn, because, if he was going to attack the very psyche, yank at the so-called spiritual heartstrings of that congregation, he would need to do it before they got too far along in the service. So, the song should be the one that took place in the beginning of the – worship. *And now let us stand as we prepare for our Call to Worship and our Morning Hymn . . .*

He would apologize later for rushing his father off the phone. Their conversation hindered what he really wanted, what he felt he needed, to do. Adrian, after all, wasn't saying anything that Renard wanted to hear. Why continue listening?

Renard spent the next two hours searching for a song; one somewhat obscure to many churches, and relatively extinct to Ezekiel, outside of a few crotchety old aints who weren't members of the music auxiliary anyway.

As he tossed one hymnal after another on his office floor, his anger increasingly swelled. There were so many particulars about the song that he needed. It couldn't be just any song.

It had to be in the key of E-flat, but easily worked in C-minor. *My Faith Looks Up To Thee?* Nah. Not obscure enough. And his faith didn't look. . .

He quieted the noise he was making, afraid of awakening Kira. Book after book, paper after paper, desk drawer after desk drawer. Contents were crumpled, thrown into corners, impetuously shredded. When he thought his efforts to find the perfect song would be futile, there it was, sitting in front of him. His heart began to race.

He found the perfect song. It was though the waters of Tyrus had sent the message themselves. It was E-flat, C minor. Obscure? Ezekiel hadn't seen this song in years. Decades. Maybe never. And he knew just what to do with its lyrics and notes.

He booted up his computer and opened up Finale® while simultaneously setting up his keyboard. Realizing the amplifier would take his wife out of her sleep, he went to the closet, pulled out a set of headphones, and plugged them into the electronic setup.

He picked up the pages of the hymn, looked them over, studying the song's melodic algorithm; pondering its degrees of discord and scaling. After rehearsing the song a few times, managing the few difficult parts until they were perfected, Renard set his computer program to MIDI implementation, and began to record the song in real-time. It took three or four takes and a bit of heavy quantization to get the rhythm correct, but he completed the process. He then exported the file as a JPEG in order for it to PRINT. The score was perfect.

Then, he extracted the Electric VOX part from a recent recording and set it to PRINT. So far, his efforts were working in sync.

He sighed; part exhaustion, and part, coming in the realization that his next step in the process would, likely, be the most difficult.

Slowly, he superimposed one score over another, and examined the result.

An augmentation there. A diminished chord change or so. A subtle fluctuation of the tempo marking. Then, he would have what he wanted.

Renard marveled in personal genius. All he needed was to teach the hymn to the Voices of Ezekiel, and to send a PowerPoint file of the lyrics to the audio-visual ministry so that the congregation would be able to view them on the screen.

And then, it would happen. Renard would set in motion the scheme to confuse the mortal, please the immortal. His personal Dicaearchy Obrumpent Allotheism experiment was out of the theory, passed through the development, and awaiting the implementation stage. He would be the only knowledgeable witness as to how Ezekiel Baptist's congregation became de-spirited, rendered into a state of confusion from a morning inspirational hymn, once the choir finished singing *Give of Your Best to the Master* as he played the chord progressions of *Death To A Carnal Christian.*

Verse 24 ♫

And no marvel; for Satan himself is transformed into an angel of light. II Corinthians 11:14 KJV

About three weeks later, Jeremiah informed Renard that he'd be out of town and away from church because of his honeymoon, giving him the specific dates that the responsibilities of third-Sunday rehearsals and service would be in his hands.

Renard beamed over the thought of an opportunity to inflict his own non-sanctioned, Tyrus Society DOA test run. This was his opportunity; the perfect time to incorporate the morning hymn of his selecting, using alternative chord progressions and musical fillers in the service without any interference from the new guy. His plan could not have fallen into place any better amidst discouragement from the brotherhood and his father's outright rejection. They would all eat their words. Every. Single. One of them.

On the evening of the Voices of Ezekiel rehearsal, Renard entered the church through the breezeway, and could hear voices milling around in the administration hall. He figured it was probably choir members who had come to the church early, and they were just hanging out until time for rehearsal.

Renard went into the sanctuary, pausing to steady his nervousness. He did a brief reconnaissance to ensure he was the only one in the room. He walked into the pulpit, very aware that no one was permitted to tread that hallowed spot without Trantham's express permission. He picked up the pulpit Bible and opened it to the Book of Revelation. From his pants pocket, he produced an intricate piece of felt; lavender, tear-shaped, 3' x 5" in dimension, a beamed set of eighth notes is centered on the swatch, accented in hues of goldenrod. Inscribed in embroidery at the base of the piece were the geometric coordinates: longitude 33° 16' 15", latitude 35° 11' 46", the global positioning of the ancient city of Tyre; numbers which all Society of Tyrus' members have committed to heart. Emblazoned at the crown of the entire piece was the local chapter's Greek sign, Γ, Gamma.

There are mysterious powers formulated by none but immortals; irreversible powers existing within the scientific conglomerations of numerals, alphabets, and symbols. When and where you may be able to exercise indiscretion, place these symbols of your belief in your midst. Implore the power of the Society to germinate where you plant these symbols. Lacrima AΩ

In between pages of the Last Book of John the Revelator, he placed an arcane device, the official insignia of the Society of Tyrus. "Now, Ras el-Ain, do your work," Renard whispered.

The choir members filed into the stand for rehearsal; heads covered in rags, steel-toed boots covered in mud, attitudes covered in – who knows what? Renard kept himself occupied by separating lyric sheets he had printed.

President Georgia, a withdrawn, wearied look in her dark, shadowed eyes evidently from handling middle-scholars all day long; strutted up to the point his personal space was being invaded. "We usually have prayer before rehearsal," she felt inclined to inform him.

Anyone else having the upper hand or the last say-so would not take place that evening. "We can pray after rehearsal. We need to get right into the music. Then your prayer can honor the success of the rehearsal. Afterward," he replied.

"If you say so." Georgia hugged her hymnal, adjusted her glasses center of her face and gave Renard a motionless stare.

"Let's get started with rehearsal," he said while returning an annoying glance at Georgia. "Look. I want everyone to turn your hymnals to page four, seventy-one."

He watched in amusement as the choir began exchanging puzzled looks as they flipped through the songbook in search of the correct page. He'd been at Ezekiel long enough to know that the choirs didn't recognize their hymns by title or first line, they knew them by page number. He could've told them the title of the song outright, but that would've taken away from the overall mystique and his right to be entertained; something he did not wish to be deprived of.

Renard played an unusually rousing introduction to the hymn in hopes that the choir would loosen their overall appearance, but it was evident that their attention was on their ignorance of the song. He recognized the tension, a cauldron of expressions stirring hotter, boiling; he could tell that each singer wished someone else would speak out on behalf of the group.

As it turned out, the predictable president Georgia raised her timid hand. "Uh, brother musician?"

Renard was determined not to freely offer an explanation to anything they weren't daring enough to ask about. "Yes?"

"This song, umm. When was the last time we've sung it?" Georgia asked.

Renard's heart churned in hilarity. He found it extremely difficult not to outwardly scoff at their stupidity. "I don't know. Do you have any ideas?"

For a moment, Georgia chattered nervously with a singer sitting next to her. "Well, no," she said, "Uh, I don't think I know the hymn. I don't think anyone here knows it."

Renard couldn't resist the temptation to escalate her idiocy. Maybe if he rode her enough, she would be compelled to resign from her position, maybe the choir altogether. "You should have this song in your repertoire, although it's been a while. You don't remember it?" Renard asked.

The murmuring among the choir increased to a level of pure confusion. Calvin Inman spoke out and said, "Look here. I've been in various choirs here at Ezekiel for the last fifteen or so years. In all my days here, I've never sung this hymn. The words don't come across as even vaguely familiar to me."

Renard clapped his hands together. "Well, this is a good time to get familiar with it again. You know? Since you've forgotten it," he declared, fully aware that Calvin was correct. They've never sang the song. His little game, though, was fun while it lasted.

Give of Your Best to the Master. Give of the strength of your youth. . .

The choir labored through the song with missing notes, botched phrasing, and sketchy enunciation. To Renard, the result was spectacular. He could readily tell that they hated the hymn, and were using every opportunity to show it during rehearsal, but they were too proud a group to damage that or any other song when it counted. Morning service. As long as they performed the hymn without an emotional attachment, he could fulfill his purpose.

After they had rehearsed each verse and the chorus to some satisfaction, Georgia then asked, "When are we singing this hymn?"

"It'll be the first song. The Morning Inspirational Hymn," Renard said.

"The first song?" William Rand asked. It was rare for Billy to speak up. He was a quiet, in the shadows type of choir member. He held his tune, but never tried out for solos. It's been rumored, though, that he was spiritual as long as things were to his liking, but if he felt like there would be contention over a matter, he would let you know that he was in disagreement. Word was that he'd shot someone in his early years. Never repented for it. "You're going to use this as an *inspirational* piece? Really?"

"I don't see anything wrong with it," Renard replied.

"It sounds strange. It has no life. It doesn't make you look forward to the rest of the church service."

"That's your opinion," Renard said.

"It just plain sounds funny," Calvin said. "Let's just be honest."

"Brother Day wouldn't choose a song like that," Georgia said. Everyone else sat, supposedly stupefied at her honesty.

Renard sat at the instrument in pure, undiluted rage. "What?"

"I said, Bro-"

"Oh, I heard what you said." Renard began tapping a pen on the organ cabinet. When he realized the rhythmic beating could be irritating to the choir members, he increased its volume. "Look, I see what you're trying to do. It won't work, folks. You had a good service this past Sunday. I've heard this from everyone I've run into. But there's one thing I know. You're only as good as your last performance, and your next one is coming up. So, holding out on me won't do anything but make you look bad. If I were you, and I'm glad I'm not, I'd pick up the pace."

Renard hushed, feeling like he'd said all he needed to say, until he swore he'd heard someone speak some profanity under their breath. With a pile of sheet music in his hands, he walked along the front row and stood center of the entire group, eye to eye. "Look. I don't get paid to babysit you. And you know what? Jeremiah Day ain't here tonight, and he won't be here Sunday. So you might as well do as I'm telling you, because I'm running the show this week."

Verse 25 ♫

*Thou believest that there is one God; thou doest well:
the devils also believe and tremble. James 2:19 KJV*

Renard arrived at church early that morning, which
was an uncommon practice that he wouldn't care to make a
habit. *But today is special*, he thought. Since he had the time,
he decided to sit leisurely at the Hammond and observe the
aints as they filed into the sanctuary.

A few people came over and greeted him, each one
either trying to kiss him on the cheek, hug him or shake his
hand; all of which he found detestable. Most displayed telling
expressions on their faces, undoubtedly because they'd never
seen him waiting for the service as opposed to the service
waiting for him. The topics of the people's banter ranged
from pleasant to critical; the critics making it known that
they'd heard his secular tune, which did nothing but confirm
his belief that they listened to and watched more than just
religious stations, surfed more than just religious websites.
Some felt comfortable enough to broadcast their personal
problems and declare an unshakable faith that their god
would solve them, which Renard found hilarious. Their plan
of action was to spend time on their knees praying, end with
the usual "Amen", and then proceed to solve the issue
themselves instead of waiting on the one they prayed to. No
wonder they were constantly asking their messiah, "Help my
unbelief."

Renard didn't fault any of the people. He didn't
believe in a messiah either. At least, not theirs.

About thirty minutes later, he went to the robing room
where several of the singers had blockaded the entrance. He
gave them an apocalyptic look, and then they cleared the

way. He came within earshot of a small group of them, not letting on that he'd heard someone say, "It's an abomination if you ask me." Their guilty eyes and whispering voices helped him surmise that *Death to a Carnal Christian* was the topic of discussion.

He forced himself to say, "Good Morning everybody," without trying to speak to anyone in particular. It didn't matter to him whether he received a response. The air was filled with controversy. Controversy among church folk made great press. Great press sold downloads. Downloads made him money.

Georgia Fisher approached him in her usual portrait: her hair, finger-waved with not a strand out of place. A Bible, hymnal and a notebook full of music lyrics were nestled under her arm. "What's on schedule for this morning, Brother Singleton?"

Renard didn't have the patience for Georgia acting under her presidential authority. "You already know the morning hymn, right?"

She pursed her lips. "Mmm. Yes. I do."

"Just know that we'll likely use what we've rehearsed, but if there are changes to our music, it'll be because the spirit led us in a different direction. Okay?"

It was amazing to see how Baptist, Methodist, or Church of God in Christ aints would squirm if the word spirit was used in conversation. Spirit. Spirit – *spirit*. It was church folk's kryptonite, and it worked on Georgia for sure. She turned and walked away without giving the faintest response.

During the Instrumental Prelude, Trantham emerged from a side doorway up into the pulpit, followed by a small entourage of associates. After using hand gestures to assign each minister a seat, Trantham walked up to the rostrum. "Good morning!" he said in a boisterous voice.

"Good morning!" the congregation echoed.

Trantham went on to make what seemed to be an endless roster of announcements with each one more flagrant than the one before. "I've saved the best announcement for last," he declared with raised hands. "The construction company has informed our building committee that they need ten more weeks to put the finishing touches on our brand new sanctuary. Thank God! Amen!"

He paused as the audience riddled the air with applause.

"So, he continued, "I've spoken with the deacons, trustees and the building committee. Plans are to move into the new edifice and dedicate it on December first." He rapped his fist on the rostrum. "Get ready, saints! We're moving!"

Amens, hand claps and shouting went on for the next two or three minutes.

"December first, December first . . . December first!" Trantham kept repeating. He motioned to Renard with a ready sign, a cue to begin the introduction. "Now Ezekiel, let's prepare for the Morning Worship and sing the morning hymn with vitality. The Lord is in His Holy temple. Let all the Earth be silent before Him." He picked up the Sunday bulletin, which earlier had been placed on the rostrum by one of the ushers. He flipped to the first page. "This morning's hymn is number four, seventy-one, *Give of Your Best to the Master* . . ." His voice trailed off.

From the first to the last verse with the chorus between, Renard performed what he had meticulously rehearsed, remaining insensitive to the numerous mistakes the choir, ministers and the laity had made during the song. Blending *Give of Your Best* and *Death to A Carnal Christian* proved to be an artistic and apocalyptic success.

By the end of the hymn, the choir's volume had lowered to an embarrassingly low hush. Adolescents had begun mimicking vulgar dance moves they'd evidently seen on a hip-hop or video channel. A trio of deacons, sitting on the front pew located to the right of the pulpit, were engaged in chatter that seemed to be steeped with tension.

From Renard's view, the entire congregation's countenance had been dislodged, putting the body of people in a virtual desert, a subset of purgatory.

Even the choir's four remaining selections couldn't lift the congregation above the haze that had fallen upon them.

Trantham seemed to be in the worst condition of all. He had gulped down a small bottle of water, and wiped his beading forehead with a handkerchief. He sat slumped, in a mental fog, appearing to have misplaced his composure. One of the associate ministers reached over and touched Trantham's arm to get his attention.

As Trantham got up to deliver his sermon, Renard slid off the Hammond, walked over to one side of the choir stand and sat within clear sight of the pulpit. He brewed in contentment, marveling at the physical outcome the Edicts of Tyrus Society had predicted.

A trail of villainous thoughts entered his mind as Trantham opened the pulpit bible on the rostrum. Some have called them hexes, voodoo, curses or afflictions. If the pastor had known an arcane device had been placed in the book, he probably wouldn't have read from it.

Trantham used 1st Chronicles, 22nd chapter as his text, the story of when David gave Solomon the charge to build a house in the name of their god.

To Renard, the scripture seemed predictable; Trantham having announced the upcoming completion of Ezekiel's new sanctuary. The pace of his reading was noticeably unsteady, his sentences and punctuation had a cautious flow. He read the last verse of the scripture, closed the bible and paused for a moment. There was a disturbed look sweeping over his face.

"You know," he said, "it feels like something else needs to be done before I get into my sermon, but I don't know what." He reached for a handkerchief, wiped the beads of perspiration on his forehead. "If I were a singer, I'd render a song, but I'm afraid that would make things worse," he said, forcing a smile in his vain attempt to lighten the sullen mood overtaking the atmosphere.

Trantham strained through his sermon. Renard was being entertained as he sat the entire time, refusing to accent the pastor's phrases with chords from the Hammond.

After the Invitation, Altar Call and Benediction, everyone filed out of the sanctuary as though they were a host of humans wading through quicksand. A solemn funeral recessional where Worship was the guest of honor, and Renard had laid her to rest. He could not have had a more satisfying feeling.

Renard tried to collect his check from the church treasurer, make it out of the church and to his car without having to confront a single soul but, somehow, shuffling his way through the throng of congregants in the parking lot was Deacon Steele.

"Brother Singleton," he announced while throwing his forefinger in the wind.

Renard huffed. "Yes?"

Steele placed his hand on the hood of Renard's car and leaned in. His expression was taut, his eyes were glassy, and sweat was running down his forehead. "Didn't service seem out of sorts and peculiar to you?" he managed to ask between heavy breaths.

Renard surveyed the disgraceful old man and smiled to himself. He had to respect Steele, him being the only one with audacity enough to inquire about that day's events and desiring an honest answer. Renard contemplated the deacon's question, deciding that someone else would have to give him the honesty he desired. He slammed his car door shut, let down his window. "We had music, we had preaching. To me, everything went as expected. You take it easy, okay?" He put his car in gear and sped off, leaving Steele standing on the pavement with a dumbfounded look on his face.

Still glowing from his accomplishment during Sunday's service, Renard checked his company email account that evening, **rsingleton@freestarfinancial.com**, hoping to have a head start on his Monday morning responsibilities. He briefed one correspondence and set it aside as priority: *Prequalified Home Mortgage Applicants Week of 09/16/2013.* He looked over the next dozen emails, making a decision to prioritize or delete each one, and then, his entire body halted, as though someone had interrupted him mid-sentence. He returned his attention to the email that listed the prequalified applicants, carefully noting the names included in the message. *Fred & Marcy Allen.* No. he punched his finger on the computer screen, forgetting that he needed his mouse to scroll down the list. No last names with B. Five last names with C. Then, his finger came to an abrupt stop. "I'll be darned." The gods of Tyrus couldn't have been any better to him on that day. In his profession, he had learned that the greatest way to maneuver human psyche was through a person's finances, and 57 Central Avenue was in his hands. *Jeremiah & Arze' Day*, $150,000.00.

Verse 26 ♫

...Wherefore their anger was greatly kindled against Judah, and they returned home in great anger. II Chronicles 25:10 KJV

Jeremiah and Arze' left the skies and waters of the Eastern Caribbean behind, knowing that he'd never let the wonderful memory of his time with his wife diminish.

It was their honeymoon, but it didn't matter how beautiful the adventure or vacation – Jeremiah's course of reality had a way of catching up, rising above the fantasy, and maneuvering to the forefront of his life once he and his bride returned to the States.

At Olds Central High, his students were still in the first quarter of learning, struggling to comprehend the concepts of Algebra II and Introduction to Calculus. The real reality, however, was in full blossom at Ezekiel Baptist, where the dilemma of dealing with Renard Singleton awaited. One day real soon, Jeremiah would thank Leo for being spot-on with his prediction that Ezekiel's tenured musician had to be watched.

While Arze' spent one Monday in mid-October at St. Joseph's Mercy Hospital trying to secure one of the two open positions in Critical Care Nursing, Jeremiah occupied his morning hours increasing the capacity of young minds. After school, he drove to Ezekiel where he met briefly with Pastor Trantham, who did his best to retell the callous details of Sunday's service. "Don't ask me what went wrong," he said. "For the life of me, I don't understand it. I wish I had a better reason for Sunday, other than telling people that a wayward spirit entered the sanctuary."

"And you think the music had something to do with it, Pastor?"

"To tell the truth, I thought that if anything could lift the weight that fell on the service, the music would. Instead, the choir seemed to weigh the atmosphere down even more."

"Something was wrong with how the choir sounded?"

"Well, no. I don't think there was. It was . . . I can't put my finger on it."

"You think I can get a DVD of the service, Pastor?" Jeremiah asked. "If I can view the service, I might get a better understanding of what took place."

Pastor Trantham's admin walked into the office with a small stack of documents. She pointed to a spot on a paper at the top of the stack. Pastor Trantham glanced at it, signed it, pulled it off the pile and handed it back to her. She walked out. "Sure," he said. "Get whatever you need. Go by Audio-Visual."

Jeremiah walked out of the Pastor's office and down the hall, where the Audio-Visual Ministry had set up temporary offices until the new sanctuary was completed, and they would move into their state-of-the-art facility. He didn't want to take up precious viewing time by driving home, so he pulled up a chair inside of the viewing room, loaded Sunday's video, and began watching.

With each rewind, Jeremiah became more disturbed. He watched particular parts of the service over again. He took notes. He toiled between waiting for another day to speak with Renard, or tackling the issue head-on, that day. When he gathered enough calm, he took out his cell, dialed Renard's number.

Within two hours, the two were at the church, in the sanctuary, face to face.

"What?" Renard asked. "Is there something wrong with *Give Of Your Best To the Master?*"

"I'm not dealing with the hymn just yet. I first want to talk about you injecting those useless, horizontal, seven-eleven songs," said Jeremiah.

"What?"

"Exactly. *What.* Makes me wonder whether you've paid any attention to anything I've said or done since I've been here. I specifically said during the time of Praise and Worship that I wanted songs that sing *to* God, not ones that speak *about* Him."

"The songs you use don't make a noticeable difference, man. Really?"

"Like I said . . . you haven't paid attention." Jeremiah began toying with the on/off switch on the Hammond.

"I've been paying attention, but listen . . ." Renard went on to give an explanation why some choir members might have a problem with Jeremiah, which in his rambling, turned out not to be a bona fide explanation.

"I can take that two ways, Renard. I want the choir to like me. I do. But if they choose not to, that's okay. As long as I get my respect."

"Humph."

Jeremiah ignored Renard's grunt. "But from now on, if I ever have to be out of town, I'll just prepare a list of songs that you're to rehearse and use for that Sunday service, with directions not to deviate from what I give you. My God. I thought I could trust you to carry out service in a way that the people would be blessed. Foolish me," Jeremiah said.

"You're making more out of it than it really is."

"Am I?"

"Absolutely. There's nothing wrong with the hymn or the choir songs I chose."

"About that hymn. The chord changes were out of line with the song itself."

"No. It wasn't," Renard said, referring to the hymn's progression from Ionian to Dorian in the third line of each verse.

"That song was out of place on so many levels, it makes me mad to even think about it. First of all, I've never used that song . . . ever. It's such a seldom used hymn, because of the strange progression. Then, you used it during a time in service when the atmosphere needs to be upbeat. Jubilant. And then - correct me if I'm wrong - you added some strange . . . series of chords. If I didn't know any better, I'd believe that you were *trying* to throw the people off. What was the problem?"

There was an eternal silence in the room. Jeremiah stared him down, deciding not to press Renard for an answer. Not at that time, anyway.

Verse 27 ♫

Then he said unto him, Come home with me, and eat bread. I Kings 13:15 KJV

"The windup . . . and the toss," said the television announcer.

"There it goes!" yelled Jeremiah.

"Aw naw, he swung on an outside pitch!" Leo hollered between bites of a sandwich.

"Steerike!" the umpire yelled through the screen.

In that same week on Saturday afternoon, Jeremiah and Arze' invited both Leo Richter and his wife Sarah - a svelte, refined, natural golden-blonde, athletic type with an easy-going personality - over for a day of relaxation and to discuss a possible strategy for searching out a permanent residence.

It was October 19th, and the Tigers were matched up against the Boston Red Sox in the American League Championship. Jeremiah had become emerged in the Tiger's baseball culture since moving to Olds. He had been a Brave's fan while living in Memphis, Tennessee not having a pro baseball team. Now that he was in the North, he felt comfortable in moving his alliances. Jeremiah was sprawled out on the couch in true baseball lover's fashion. Men feasting on Cracker Jacks. Italian sandwiches. Sipping on Vernors, a Detroit original soft drink, while watching the game on a flat screen with high definition sound. A sports lover's fantasy. Jeremiah relished every minute. "Leo, you want another Kielbasa?" he asked through the wad of gum in his mouth.

Leo had reclined in a chair, rubbing his half-exposed belly. "Yeah, why not?"

Jeremiah turned toward the kitchen. "Hey baby, can you fix up another sausage? Mustard and onion?"

"Okay, although your hands ain't in church", Arze' shouted.

Leo leaned over to Jeremiah. "I don't mean to put your wife to work," he whispered.

"Arze' doesn't mind. She'll probably end up having your wife to make the sandwich. You ain't considered company anymore, you know." Jeremiah reached for his glass. "And fixing us something to eat is Arze's way of being nosy, keeping track of us."

Leo laughed. "That's how she'll keep up with *you*."

By then, it was the seventh inning stretch, giving the two men time to discuss whether or not the Tigers would make it that year to the World Series, given their mediocre win-loss record.

"Man, I wish I was up in Boston watching this game live," Jeremiah said. "I know it's got to be cold up there. Just chilly enough to make great game weather. I'd be in love."

"We should do that next season," Leo replied as he popped open a Vernors. "You know, Jere, I'm an outdoor lover. Always doing some kind of camping, hiking. Anything in cold weather."

"You? Me, too. Those are things I did every year in Tennessee. Not Arze' though. She's uh, how do I say this . . . prissy."

"We must've married twins!" Leo joked. Sarah doesn't do camping. In that arena, she's my polar opposite."

"I feel ya."

"You can always go with me on this trip I usually take in January. It's a wilderness area in the UP that has great fishing, hunting. Everything outdoorsy."

"Now that sounds like a trip. I'd go in a heartbeat."

"Let me warn you," Leo said. "You'll have to take a couple unpaid personal days to go."

Jeremiah did have to remind himself that school would be back in session, and Leo's proposed trip was after the Christmas break. He didn't want to make a bad impression since it was his first year in the Old's school system. He took seconds to give the trip serious consideration. "No worries. Count me in."

"You know," Leo said, "I fancy myself a pretty good hunter, too. Got a new gun for this season. A Browning twelve gauge. Gold plated trigger. The rabbits and grouse better be very afraid this year."

"You? A hunter? Man, you couldn't hit . . . I could take a weak little four-ten single shot and kill more game than you."

"Sounds like a challenge to me. Leo replied. "I'm-"

"Ball on the outside," was the game announcer's voice.

Jeremiah and Leo witnessed the Tigers play to a disappointing 5 – 2 loss. After the game, the two couples traveled to Fifty-seven Central Avenue, a vacant house sitting on the western edge of a twenty block radius in East Olds; that slice of the entire city currently on the city council's radar for urban renewal, where the previous citizens had aesthetically neglected their neighborhood.

Jeremiah pulled up to the curb, placed the car in park. "I know we've talked about houses." He pointed toward the house. "This is the property Arze' and I have talked about." He angled his body so that he could see the others in the car. "And listen. Before you judge, picture its potential."

East Olds immediate history was a landscape of diminutive, shotgun houses occupying the majority of the land, with a few updated homes dotting the remainder of the vicinity. A local barbershop, backyard mechanics, crack dealers, cut-rate prostitutes and a truck farmer had been the central collectors of that locality's revenue, where its perimeter had been protected by a teenaged gang. A new mayor, police chief and groups of citizens that wanted to see their neighborhood shown in a better light, saw to the eradication of illicit and illegal activity.

In that part of town, a closed down lumber mill still remained. An open field faced the Central Avenue houses; a field which had been a railroad and trucking stockyard. Children used the area as a place to break up bottles and stomp on cans for entertainment.

The two couples were in front of a house that, with the exception of its slightly over-grown lawn, was surprisingly neat. It appeared to be part of a block of homes forming a boundary separating renters from home owners.

"It's a diamond," Jeremiah said with genuine enthusiasm. He took a glance at Arze'. She responded with a pleasant smile.

"Oh yeah, and it's definitely in the rough," Leo added.

"So you all are seriously considering *this* house?" Sarah asked. Her question seemed to be directed more toward Arze'.

"You don't understand," Jeremiah interjected, "We've researched this piece of property. At one time it was a duplex. We can turn it back into a single family dwelling by continuing to live in our apartment until one side of the house is ready and live there while we work on the other side."

Leo nodded in agreement. "Oh. That makes sense."

Jeremiah threw his arm forward as if introducing someone. "And then what will we do baby?"

"Sell it!" Arze chimed in.

"Okay that sounds good," Sarah said with tremendous doubt in her voice. "But what's it going for?"

Jeremiah leaned in and whispered, "Twenty thousand dollars."

"You're kidding!" Leo said. "Then in that case, go with God. At that price you should be arrested, 'cause you stole it."

Arze' looked up at the roofline, and then tried to look in through one of the windows. "We could put another forty, fifty thousand dollars in this house and make it what we want. We'd still be well under appraised value."

"Well, it sounds like ya'll have really thought it out," Sarah told them.

"I know." Jeremiah began testing bannisters and bouncing on the tongue-and-groove planked porch leading to a colossal front door that had been painted with endless coats of eggshell colored exterior latex. "Appraisals have it at about eighty grand. And that's before fixing it up. We're already prequalified, so the process should go off like clockwork."

Verse 28 ♫

How could I do such a wicked thing and sin against God? Genesis 39:9b

It was evident. It would have been useless to have tried to convince Renard otherwise.

Jeremiah had become a weed; an unwanted plant intruding on Ezekiel, growing out of control and able to escape eradication. For the choirs, he'd become a positive influence. To Renard it was a foolish supposition. And Trantham had crowned Jeremiah as the confidant for all things music related. That was too much trust, too much growth, too little time.

To Renard, Jeremiah was a phantom; a pariah that had methodically closed in on those that knew no better. He was a destroyer of Renard's ambitions and the strangler of his pursuits.

And he needed to be watched.

Over the past several days, Renard had reminded himself of Terry's words: *Give yourself time to really think how this new guy's membership could be to our advantage.* Maybe Terry was right. With the actual Dicaearchy Obrumpent Allotheism about six weeks away but fast approaching, he wanted to remove as many hindrances as he could that were within his power to manipulate. True, he was armed with the knowledge and the authority of Tyrus Society. True, he had the knowledge of Jeremiah's qualifications as a homebuyer, and that his mortgage paperwork would likely require *his* stamp of approval before the Days made it to the closing table. *But that's not enough,* he thought. So, keeping the ultimate goal in mind, maybe showing Jeremiah some favor wasn't such a bad idea.

Renard made a call to Terry and discussed the idea of inviting Jeremiah to the Festival of Lambs.

"Now you're thinking," Terry told him.

It was after morning service, exactly a week after Renard pulled off his successful stunt and just days after their argument, that he asked to briefly speak with the music minister. To satisfy Renard's feeling that walls had ears, they met outside of the church building; "C'mon and join us, Jeremiah. It's a time when some of the musicians in the area get together to . . . celebrate," he said as he gave a brief, but detailed invitation to Jeremiah.

Jeremiah took a step back from Renard. "Celebrate what?"

"Umm, thankful that another year has almost ended."

Jeremiah frowned. "Most people would wait 'til the end of the year for that kind of celebration. Actual God-fearing people call it *Watch Night*," he said.

Renard sensed that his point or persuasion wasn't having an effect. "C'mon man, really? This is your time to know some of the other musicians. Wouldn't it be great to talk shop and relax with comrades outside of the job site? We share a common bond, not to mention our spouses and what they have to go through." He mindfully felt regretful that he sounded almost angry, desperate.

Jeremiah's eyes widened. "Hmm, yeah. It is difficult being a musician or the spouse of one. Especially those true to the calling."

"Uh, ok. I hadn't thought of it exactly like that," Renard replied in a softer, more assuring tone.

"I mean, you've got a point. I don't know that many people outside of Ezekiel church members."

"And your wife, of course. Don't forget she needs to get to know people here. Who better to know than other musician's significant others?"

"Arze' is a peculiar girl. She's not the cordial type when she meets you the first time."

"She'll enjoy the company of our group."

"Possibly." In that moment, Jeremiah cleared his throat. "But, come to think of it . . . why would I join in partying with you, Renard? We can hardly get along here at church."

Renard, surprised at the comment and question, sighed, struggling to conjure an answer. "J-just testing your intentions, man, c'mon." He reached up and gave Jeremiah a gentle slap on the shoulder. He found it a struggle in keeping his goals forefront and his real thoughts in the background. "Look. It's nothing personal. Here you come on the scene rather suddenly. You're from out of town. Nobody really knows you. Not everyone would have good intentions for Ezekiel. No harm done." Renard reached out his hand.

Jeremiah responded with a hand shake. "No harm done."

A bit of Renard's anxiety relaxed. "She will, trust me. And besides, what woman doesn't want to dress up and look cute?" he asked as he mindfully formed Arze's silhouette. Nude.

"Dress up?"

Renard hesitated before giving any further explanation. He felt the need to spoon-feed Jeremiah on all the particulars of the Festival. "Uh, yeah. It's a black tie, masked, formal type of thing. At a very posh hotel. It's an annual thing."

"When is this get-together?"

"Thursday, October thirty-first, eight pm," Renard replied.

Jeremiah shook his head. "Thirty-first? Masked? Sounds like a Halloween party."

"It is, in a way. But we call it Festival of the Lambs."

"Hate to disappoint you. The party sounds tempting. But we don't do Halloween."

"But it's not, really," Renard said as he began to feel another bout of anxiety.

"You're partying on the thirty-first of October?" Jeremiah pulled his cell phone off his belt clip and peered at the screen. "That's choir rehearsal night anyway."

Renard swallowed. "It is a rehearsal night, isn't it? Then you can count me absent on that evening."

"Your group couldn't have considered the event, maybe, on November first instead?" Jeremiah asked. "It would be a Friday and you wouldn't have to miss rehearsal. You could forget the idea of some hideous, demonic face masks. Christians partying on *All-Saints Day*. That's novel."

"Get serious, Jeremiah. It's just an innocent party. Nothing more."

Jeremiah started backing up, walking away. "Oh I am. You can scratch me off the list. Take Arze' off, too."

Verse 29 ♫

For we ourselves also were sometimes foolish, disobedient, deceived, serving divers lusts and pleasures. Titus 3:3

Renard took a glance at his watch, realizing that the Festival of Lambs was yet two hours away. He and Kira were in their suite at the Atheneum Suites® Hotel, preparing for the evening. Fully dressed in a black tux, he occupied himself by having a seat in front of the wardrobe mirror and taking glances at his wife, who was barely covered in mauve La Perla lingerie. When Kira retreated to the bathroom with her dress in hand, he looked around the room suspiciously. Satisfied that Kira wouldn't return from out of the bathroom, he pulled out his book of Society Edicts and read:

> *Pertinent thought in Tyrus Society is that, as part of the universe, we are gender specific beings, capable of nihilism of the sexual kind, with traditional thought being unfounded and archaic. As a member, become conditioned to the fact that creation of every kind is sexual in nature, for sexuality is and will always be – natural. Eros is to be cultivated, worshipped, and consensual among companions within the membership. AΩ*

Renard closed the book and smiled. He was intent on relishing the dictates of the edict and enjoying himself to the fullest that evening.

On the annual evening when children traditionally pounce on houses door to door in neighborhoods for candy and other treats, the Rhapsody Room of the hotel had been transposed into an adult playroom, an atmosphere of elegance; classically decorated in black and white tapestry, accents of lavender toile, and elements of the Cadmus sitting atop six foot Corinthian pedestals with an arrangement of Asters at each base. Silver trays had been strategically placed around the room, filled with party trinkets of all varieties: Macadamias, Dagoba® Chocolate, Trojan, Durex, Lifestyles.

The DJ received his instructions. Play to the audience's choosing, no matter the genre of music. The atmosphere lacked bodies, though.

Then the zero hour came.

Bodies began to file into the room. Each person donned masks, which added another level of decadence to the vibe. Over thirty Society members attended from out of town; members from Chicago (B) Beta, Cleveland (Δ) Delta, and the Milwaukee (E) Epsilon chapters. Each member of the Society brought a significant female companion.

Renard surveyed the attendees. The men were arrayed in tuxes of various styles. He could recognize that there had been considerable attention given to their appearance, but it was the women. Oh, the women.

There was such a fine arrangement of African-Americans to Pacific Islanders to Caucasians that, if Renard didn't know any better, he would've thought the females had been leased specifically for that evening. He was aware, though, that every female in attendance was either married to or spoken for by a brother of the Society. Each had on a dress or gown that exposed their navel and almost every other seductive crevice for which Renard had a peculiar affection. He was especially drawn to the female navel. He regarded it as the center from which all hungers exists.

The Festival of Lambs was ready to commence.

When Terry and Val McClure arrived a full and fashionable hour late, Renard made his way to them and the men embraced. "Lacrima, my brother."

"Lacrima."

"You look wonderful, Val," Renard told her.

"Thank you, Renard."

Renard eyed Val, and stood speechless. The fuchsia neckline on her gown plunged south, exposing her vanilla kissed flesh.

Val let go of Terry's arm, casually moved closer to Renard, and whispered, "You interested?"

His ear tinged with the coolness of her breath, he drew in a nostril full of her scent. His senses battled for the next experience of her. Renard found himself caught in a state of surprise as Val continued to privately state how she wanted him to be the one to pleasure her. *I know I want her this evening.*

Renard knew that Kira would also accept someone's invitation that evening, and he wasn't bothered by that. Most of the members of the Society would end up in each other's hotel suite before daybreak because of a Society understanding; free exchange of partners was a part of the festivities. He would do Terry's wife, shower, go play an hour of craps at the Greektown Casino, and then he and Kira – if she wasn't already worn out from the evening – would play the nightcap.

Verse 30 ♫

For in the days of David and Asaph of old were chief of the singers, and songs of praise and thanksgiving unto God. Nehemiah 12:46 KJV

Rev. Knight asked Jeremiah to join him in a personal fast to seek direction from God for the music ministry. "Let's fast for a week."

He told Rev. Knight, "Yeah, okay. Do we begin on November 1st?" Jeremiah wanted perfected music; songs that would summoned a cloud of the Spirit, stir a move of the Holy Ghost, bring about a collective power unlike any their music department had seen before.

For the most part, Jeremiah managed to get through a month of Sunday services drama free. The rehearsals, however, were another story. They were war.

It was Tuesday, November 26th, two days before Thanksgiving, and the Voices of Ezekiel had their last opportunity to polish the selections for Church Dedication and opening of the new sanctuary, a mere five days away. The weather that evening was boisterous and in uncommon form - God speaking a unique language that only the prophets understood. Jeremiah's inner man felt a glint of fear but not to be afraid; an awe of the skies as God moved nature in tumultuous concert. God's thunder was a monologue, and Jeremiah interpreted The Almighty's natural activity as a commission to clean up the choir and set them on a right path. A purging. A commitment to abolish much of what he thought he had already rid the choir of: profane activity among choir members, arguing over solo parts, and a litany of other deeds carried out by evil, dispirited singers. He saw that night's rehearsal as a start toward the choir's redirection in Godly purpose.

Jeremiah stepped into the choir stand and switched on the Hammond. After a collective prayer and vocal warm-ups, he motioned for one of the directresses to come forward and individually sing an alto part on *Cover Me*; a piece they'd been working on for two weeks.

"So will the rest of the section get a chance to go over the phrase, too?" Tamla asked.

"Oh yeah, absolutely," Jeremiah replied. "This song *will* be included in this Sunday's service."

Tamla rolled her eyes, smacked her lips. "Well we didn't know." A few of the choir members whispered "Amen" in support.

"What does that mean?" Jeremiah asked to no one in particular. No one in particular answered back. *Really? I wish they'd stop playing me stupid.* The defiance by the choir to any of his input and ideas had noticeably increased. The shift of attitude seemed to have sprouted during the weeks following his honeymoon absence, but he made a conscious decision to not address it with anyone until he was positive that it wasn't his imagination playing games.

Jeremiah pressed the C-natural manual presets and shoved the bass pedal drawbars to 0 on the Hammond, not wanting to accidentally make a wayward sound because, whether they realized it or not, he was getting ready to chastise them. "I don't know where this is coming from, but listen. We're preparing for one of the most important times in the history of this church."

Jeremiah watched as the singers gazed at each other with a *do-you-know-what-he's-talking-about?* expression. "Sometimes Christians lose sense of their real purpose. Take my word for it; losing focus happens often and easily in choirs. But I'm determined. This Sunday will be a time for us to move out of the way, bless God with our music, and allow Him to bless the building effort. I'm not going to willingly allow the devil to hinder us. Now I'm serious. If any of you plan to take on the mind of Satan against the rest of the group on Sunday morning, I got no problem in asking you to excuse yourself." Jeremiah paused, giving each singer time to make his or her decision.

While Jeremiah spoke, Renard had somehow retreated from the choir stand, and began lurking around the unlit perimeter of the sanctuary like a scampering cat in a back alley.

"You wanna join us, Bro. Singleton?" Jeremiah asked, not wanting to yell but assuredly wanting to be heard.

"Just checking something," was all Renard would offer.

A million thoughts ran through Jeremiah's mind as Renard seemed to reluctantly make his way into the choir stand and onto the piano. What had he done to deserve that? Nothing had gotten any better. In fact, it was worse. He was thankful that he turned down the Halloween party invite; he never felt right about it anyway. At that moment, he felt even less for the person who had offered.

Although he refused to let the choir see it, he felt embattled, but not defeated. His way was right. He would not be deterred. He whispered a brief prayer for patience. "Alright ladies and gents," he said, let's roll on and get finished."

Pastor Trantham walked through the sanctuary during the final minutes of choir rehearsal, waving and greeting the choir. He approached Jeremiah, leaning in close. "Let's talk briefly after rehearsal. Just a few details for Sunday. At my office. We won't be long, I promise."

When Jeremiah got to the office, he found Pastor Trantham carrying on as though he had contracted an adult's version of Attention Deficit Disorder: shuffling papers, loading boxes, checking emails from both his phone and a tablet. "Oh. Brother Day. C'mon in." He had a stream of music related requests for Dedication Sunday. His desires weren't unusual, but it was out of the pastor's character to lay out such a list of particulars. Everything he asked for was doable. Then, from what seemed to be from out of nowhere, he asked, "Do you have any concerns you'd like to share with me, Bro. Day?"

Jeremiah paused for a moment. It was his pastor, a man who had shown a genuine concern for him, his family, and the church. "Yessir." He skipped any pretense and dove right into his concern. "Is there a church policy that says something about members interfering with the duties that I carry out?"

"What? Have you run into a problem?"

"Well, I think Brother Singleton is trying to discredit me. Like he wants the music ministry to fail."

Pastor Trantham gestured for Jeremiah to take a seat. "Okay, let's get something straight right now. Renard's not a member. So church membership policy doesn't apply to him."

"Oh."

"He is what he is. *An employee.* Someone who can be fired."

"But he's constantly throwing up in my face that he has relatives here."

"Doesn't give him membership rights. As far as I know, he's never expressed a desire to become a member of Ezekiel."

"I'm not saying that I want him fired, Pastor, but while I pray for him, I'm going to set some things in place so that his efforts aren't as easy for him to sidetrack what we do. Hopefully he'll see that whatever he's trying to do, it won't work."

"However you want to proceed. This church is seeing a transformation like they've never seen before. I know the people don't really realize what's happening, not just here, but in their lives."

"Praise God." Jeremiah heard the accolades in Pastor Trantham's voice, but he refused to take any credit for what he knew God was doing.

"And this new building that's about to be finished and dedicated? Naw. We're not going to let the music department settle back into any of their old habits and mundane ways."

"That's my hope. Renard's a good musician. A great musician. I just get the feeling that he wanted to be the minister of music, or the lead musician like he once was."

"I assure you, Brother Day . . . that charade should never happen again. Not while I'm the pastor."

"Pastor I want to be really clear. I wasn't coming to you to see how I might get rid of him."

"Our music department's been at a low point for years. It's been this way for a lot of churches in this area. Urban blight, attitude, multiple issues."

Jeremiah shook his head in agreement. "You should visit the schools. You can see it in the children, firsthand."

"Well, my friend, we needed and have found someone that's true and is leading the choirs into true ministry. You."

"Okay. I'll take that. But it's God in me. And I want to do it right."

Pastor Trantham reached up to a bookshelf above his computer, and pulled down a particular Bible reference book. "You've been teaching our choirs that singing for the mere sake of performance isn't Godly, and now our church hears music that convicts, restores and blesses."

"I'm only trying to get the congregation ready for the preached Word."

"Oh, you do. The bad part about it is that Renard's never had a desire to do it, no matter how many chances he gets."

Jeremiah smacked his lips. "So you *do* know what he's doing. I wondered."

"Most people don't think I'm watching, but I am."

"So you know that he means the choir no good?"

Pastor Trantham nodded. "There's no time for being an outside show – parading ourselves as holy when we're no holier than the rest of the world. Oh yes. I know what he's doing."

"Good," Jeremiah said with a sigh.

"It's my job to let the wheat and tares grow together. Let's allow the Lord do the separating. We tread a fine line as Christians. True, we're not to act like the sinner, or are we to make them feel like they don't belong at all. We are here to save them. If we don't even try to lead them to salvation, then the only difference between the church and Satan is that our gathering place isn't called a juke joint."

Verse 31 ♫

O full of all subtlety and all mischief, thou child of the devil, thou enemy of all righteousness, wilt thou not cease to pervert the right ways of the Lord? Acts 13:10 KJV

On Friday evening, Renard began counting down from thirty-six hours before the Society's DOA; the same amount of time before Ezekiel's church dedication. He found that time to play lazy, opting to enjoy the freedom with Terry since Kira claimed she wasn't feeling well, unable to hold anything down. In a way, he wanted to claim the evening as a time of celebration. With his wife resting, he and Terry could drink, talk, and cut up.

"Got something to show you. Just keep it to yourself," he said to Terry as he handed him a document that he had printed from off his computer.

"Fifteen grand?" Terry posed the question after looking over the one-pager, sighing loudly.

"Yeah. Ain't that something?" Renard replied. It was a royalty statement from MusicSweep, an online company that collected and distributed funds for independent music artists. "Posted into my bank today. *Death To A Carnal Christian* is on fire." It wasn't a mistake. Sixteen thousand downloads minus company commission wasn't a bad take for his independently produced, original tune. "Money, notoriety. That's the name of the game."

"And that ain't all that tune is bringing."

"What dya mean?" Renard asked.

"Well, it seems as though that tune of yours has caught on to the underground crowd. Mudslinger did a gig in Dayton last week-."

"I remember." Terry had texted him after the Dayton gig, bragging about the insane number of Red Bulls he'd downed to stay alert for his drive home.

"As it turns out, the imprint you created for the cut was hanging on the wall of the venue. I guess someone color printed it from off the Internet," Terry said.

"Get serious."

"I'm telling you. It's true. I'm shocked you didn't know about it."

"No way I could've."

"One of the band members pointed the poster out to me and I shouted my excitement. Much too loudly."

"So what?"

"Soo . . . a gang of women overheard me, and asked if I knew you." Terry hunched his shoulders. "Why lie?"

"OMG."

"I told them that of course I knew you. And I got their phone numbers." He reached into his wallet and unfolded a small piece of paper, handed it to Renard. "I mean, promise me that if a bunch of women recognize my picture on a wall that you'll make their acquaintance on my behalf."

Renard glanced at the paper, laughed. "Yeah, yeah."

Terry raised his hands like a referee's touchdown signal. "I mean, ain't it always good to have a piece in reserve?"

"I guess you make sense. A little."

"I'll admit it," Terry said, "I'll always be a player, always be a schemer. My church is so dumb to what's going on. Simply amazing."

"Oh yeah, it's interesting to hear the drama. See, that's the reason I can't get with church. Why should I let myself be judged by other folks that pretend like they're holy? You can't tell me nothing! I see the same people clubbing on Saturday, shouting on Sunday." Renard went to the bar, poured himself a glass of Zinfandel. "Have some more?"

"No thanks. This glass is giving me a pretty good buzz by itself."

"Suit yourself." Renard took a sip and a seat. "I know without those people, I wouldn't have that job. But now, I'm looking to do greater for the Society. Now, it's not about the job. I know it's my mission. I know my power. I have the uncanny ability to get things into people's spirit."

"And you think your mission can be carried out while you're still at Ezekiel?"

"You better believe it. Nothing can stop me."

"Brother, you got confidence 'cause I don't see how you'll be able to complete anything there with the minister of music you claim to have. I'll bet you wish for the days of Dr. Murphy again, don't you?"

"Oh my god, those were the days." Renard was reminded of Farris Murphy, Ezekiel's pipe smoking music professor that was more of a vocalist than pianist. He existed at the church for decades until senility set in, and he was remanded to a nursing home. On a weekly basis, Renard would devise schemes that worked Dr. Murphy's nerves. "I couldn't stand that man. As the years went by, I tolerated him more. On one day only, I got to like the man. That was the day that wife of his died." He cursed, calling Lillian Murphy out of her name."

Terry asked, "But what about now?"

"What do you mean?"

"Dr. Murphy ain't there. You seem to forget that you've got a Jeremiah Day trying to block your path."

"Please! I don't even think *he* realizes we've got him in a battle. He just does what he does."

"I don't know. The dude don't sound like he's ordinary. I think he knows things and can see into people. You say that he can speak without getting riled up. He may not know we've got him in the crosshairs, but he may not be totally dumb to what's really up."

"Trust me. He's got no clue."

"Uh-huh. You got guts because I wouldn't mess with him."

"Maybe that's the reason the Ras el-Ain has me at Ezekiel, and not you."

"Hey. You must see the victory in this. I just hope you don't find out that Jeremiah already knows the outcome."

Renard knew a hidden meaning was in the comment, but he resolved not to let it bother him.

From the Edicts of Tyrus Society, he read:

Your craft is your gift. Study, rehearse, and practice it with diligence and fortitude. Your weapon is to be honed to a fine point so that you as a soldier may be confident in its ability to strike. Defeat your enemy who lives in defiance of what he believes, understands. The notes, verses and choruses are an intricate roadmap to success, the Society, and life. AΩ

On into the ungodly hours of the night, Renard did what the Ras al-Ain directed. He rehearsed. Every chord, every rudiment. Every strike of the ebony and ivory. Every progression was committed to memory, committed to making every melody fight with a more complex counter- melody; positioning a fugue to poison real life, real people. He knew that the DOA was a universal attack, and that it would take every member's intricate input; he didn't want to be the weak cog in such a well-previsioned machine. If anyone were to be successful in the venture it would be him. And then, Ezekiel would witness a fall unlike any other church.

Verse 32 ♫

...And your sons and daughters shall prophesy, your old men shall dream dreams, your young men shall see visions. Joel 2:28 KJV

Olds High School's head custodian, Michaelangelo, chased Jeremiah on foot out of his classroom and out the door of the school to the south parking lot. He looked over his shoulder, estimating his distance to be about fifty feet ahead of what he hoped was just an apparition. Despite aching legs and shortened breath, he got to his car, unlocked it and started the ignition. Jeremiah looked out over the hood of his vehicle. From what appeared to be an eye-level storm cloud, the custodian leaped out toward him, landing on his car hood. Jeremiah's fear heightened when the flames from the janitor's widened pupils scorched his face, even through the windshield. Michaelangelo ripped the auto's wipers out of their sockets. Jeremiah put the car in gear. He sped off. Michaelangelo slid off the car, slamming onto the concrete.

Jeremiah. Safe. For the moment. He looked at his watch. Ten seconds passed.

Within the eleventh second, he peered into the rear view mirror. In amazement, he beheld Michaelangelo who had sprouted five foot legs and beginning to catch up to his vehicle. His brain ached, bruised from banging his head inside the car after making a series of right and left turns, trying to deceive his adversary; trying to veer him down an elusive path.

His efforts were to no avail. Michaelangelo remained hauntingly within arm's reach.

Jeremiah decided that his best option for losing him was to speed down Wide Track Boulevard. He took a left off Whittemore St., stomping the accelerator. Michaelangelo was on his bumper. Jeremiah raced past St. Vincent DePaul's parking lot, clipping a stop sign, losing a headlamp along the way. He made it onto Wide-Track Drive.

A string of eighteen-wheelers were parked along the side of the road, which was an unknown obstruction for Jeremiah. Heart racing, he wheeled past one, two, three trucks. The fourth truck, a monster grain hauler, had pulled out in front of Jeremiah. In that same moment, he drifted off to sleep with less than a second in time before colliding with the truck. He lacked the strength to even brace for the impact. Then, the inevitable happened.

He thought.

Jeremiah quickened, looked forward. Darkness. He glanced into the rear view mirror. Michaelangelo was gingerly lowering the grain truck onto the ground. As the truck's tires connected with the road, the angel's wings retracted into his shirt; a Kelly green janitor's uniform with the insignia of Olds Central High adorned on the breast pocket.

"Jere, Jere! Wake up honey!" Arze' had rolled over onto Jeremiah's shoulder, shaking his hand, kissing his ear. "What was that about?"

Jeremiah smacked his lips and began to blink, allowing tears to salve his stinging eyes. He lifted his face out of a pillow, cold and damp from perspiration. "Huh?" He managed to clear the haze from his eyes. He reached over to the night stand, switched on the lamp. "Ooh, baby."

Arze' adjusted two other pillows, carefully propping them against the headboard. "You were making crazy noises. And breathing funny. That must've been some kind of dream, huh?"

He sighed, giving himself moments to gather his thoughts and composure. He sat up and curled forward with the strength available, trying to bury his head into his abdomen. He allowed the sting from stretching to take its toll.

Arze' had hurried out to the kitchen and returned with a glass of tap water. "Here." She palmed the crown of his head, and then caressed his back and neck. "You're clammy."

Jeremiah uncurled his body, took the glass, and sipped a few drops of water, using the liquid to clear his voice. "I know babe."

"You awakened me. That dream lasted a while. I started to leave you alone, but I got worried. I thought you were going to turn and fall out of the bed," she said.

"That dream took a lot outta me. I'm glad it was just a dream."

"You remember what it was about?"

"I remember. And I understand it, too." He proceeded to give the details of the dream.

"You really understand it?"

"Clear as daytime." He explained that the car chase was actually a trial that he would face. The school janitor represented God's protection. The truck that stood in his way was a road block set up by Satan. His falling asleep at the wheel symbolized his faith that God would keep protection nearby, allowing him to rest assured that hedges will be lifted, moved out of his way. "Something is about to happen. I just know it. It's getting to the point where I'm afraid to think otherwise."

"You believe, something's about to happen but you don't know exactly *what*, do you?"

"No. I think . . . it may have to do with my ministry. I'm not sure, though."

"When?"

"I have no idea. I'm sure the message for me is that I've got to remain faithful."

"Don't be afraid, honey, but I think you can be fearful."

What's the difference?"

"Afraid could make you want to run away from whatever you're destined to face. God doesn't want you to do that. He wants your respect. That's fear; respect in a Godly way."

Jeremiah laid there, amazed at her insight. "My God, I love you girl."

Arze' smiled, turning over in the opposite direction. "Try to get some sleep, honey. The church has a big day in just a few hours."

"Yeah. Dedication Day. Don't remind me. Somehow I don't think I'll be able to sleep after that dream, but I'll try. In just a little bit."

Jeremiah crawled out of bed, left the master and went into the bathroom. He switched on the light and the vent fan, believing that the noise would shield his talk with God. He sat on the edge of the tub, and buried his face into his hands. He lifted his face and began to sing:

Bring back the days of yeah and nay, when we could plainly see the way. When it was up to us to choose, whether to win or lose. . .

Despite his efforts, he couldn't retain his tears. He began to pray:

Dear Lord, I know you're trying to tell me something. I just don't know exactly what. If it's your will, give me just a little more understanding. If I'm about face something, let me know what I'm up against. I want you to know that whatever you were trying to tell me in that dream . . . please, increase my faith in you. I want to be pleasing to you. Protect me and all that is mine. Let me call, whatever trial this may be, Victorious. Amen.

Verse 33 ♫

*My heart is inditing (OE) a good matter: I speak of
the things which I have made touching the King: my tongue
is the pen of a ready writer. Psalms 45:1 KJV*

Finally. The day that had been in the making had
become the day.

The weather that day had started off with a lake effect
chill, but it rapidly warmed up with the bright sun, resulting
in a pleasant Sunday. The perfect day for a dedication.

A speaker system had been set up on the walkway
leading to Ezekiel's entrance, to the new church sanctuary.
Chimes rang, mystically heralding the congregation along the
walkway. An opening prayer was offered by Deacon Steele.
Pastor Trantham emerged from the entrance door in a gold
colored pulpit robe' that Jeremiah was sure had never been
worn before.   "The Lord is most assuredly in His Holy
Temple," he declared. "Let all the Earth be silent before
Him." A gold, silk ribbon running across the entrance of the
new sanctuary and connected to two Roman pillars on the
outside had been cut. Pastor Trantham beckoned toward the
entrance and then the congregation, as if on cue, processed
through the doors and into the new building.

The exterior of the edifice was North Carolina red
brick – no veneer, but the straw and clay quality. Inside, the
vestibule held a wide array of live exotic plants, with a floor
of Italian marble and accented with inlaid tinted concrete.
Ezekiel's official church seal was centered in the molding on
the vestibule floor.

Pastor Trantham requested that Jeremiah and Rev.
Knight come to his office to be included in a special prayer
for the morning service. Care had been taken to decorate
Pastor Trantham's suite for the occasion. On an oval table in

the center of his office was a cut floral arrangement of coleus and hyacinth with accents of leather leaf, courtesy of the pastor's aid committee. The new furniture, a complete office suite in walnut, had been polished like a cobbler's spit shine. Jeremiah observed in wonder as Pastor Trantham glanced up at a wall clock and then began frantically searching his desk. "Can't seem to find my Living Bible. I've got some notes in there that I want to refer to this morning," Pastor said.

Inside of the sanctuary, mammoth exposed beams of mahogany accented the ceiling, with towering brass chandeliers giving lumens to the interior walls. Along the perimeter were broad windows of stained glass, each one visually depicting a glamorous Biblical story.

Additional musicians had been secured for the occasion: Asaph Paschal from Flint, Solomon Gerhardt from Romulus, Moses McKinney from Kalamazoo finished out the combo. A crème de la crème of Michigan's Gospel musicians. With that additional melody, harmony and rhythm, the choir could hardly get through the morning hymn.

And then, the service took an unwarranted turn. He glanced over at Renard, whose eyes seemed to be two bonfires residing in a mind, a woodpile burning in contempt. The chords coming from the organ were conflicting with Jeremiah's piano playing. It didn't take a clairvoyant to sense the friction in the sanctuary. The discord and imbalance was audibly recognizable, musician or not.

And then, something dramatic happened. Jeremiah felt chords in his fingers that he'd never practiced. His sub-conscience brought back to him a precept that had been drilled into him. *Don't just play the instrument, prophesy at it.*

At that point, he couldn't even hear his own playing. He'd memorized the written notes, but his fingers wouldn't follow the script. Maybe it was the result of the choir's collective contemplation of Minister Knight's Morning Prayer. Whatever the reason, Jeremiah felt compelled to begin singing a personal composition that they'd rehearsed on Thursday:

> ♪ *Cover Me*
> *Cover Me;*
> *With your Holy Spirit, Lord*
> *Cover Me* ♫

A few more bars kept the song flowing. The choir reprised more times than Jeremiah could recall. It became evident that the Cloud of the Lord had rested on Ezekiel in those moments, on that day.

> ♫ *Let me feel your righteous pow'r*
> *Encircle me, Lord this hour;*
> *Let me feel your Latter Rain*
> *Cover me, my Lord, again.* ♪

Pastor Trantham rose from his pulpit chair and stood at the rostrum, silent.

Shouts rang from every direction of the sanctuary.

The pulpit ordered another reprise of the same song.

> ♪ *With your Peace, Lord, cover me*
> *With your Grace, Lord, cover me*
> *With your Love, Lord, cover me*
> *Cover me, Lord, Cover me.* ♫

Pastor Trantham opened his iPad and swiped the screen until he found what he wanted. "Can you feel Him church?"

From the congregation came shouts of, "Amen!"

"I pray you recognize Him, 'cause He's here!" Pastor Trantham shouted among the applause. "On this day of dedication, The Holy Ghost has made His way in, and has found a congregation of worshippers. He's going to be here for a while!"

The congregation chorused, "Amen!" Women shouted, fainted and danced. Ushers and nurses attended to the saint's needs. Youths clapped, children giggled. The deacon board was awake. The Voices had taken over where Jeremiah and others had left off. During those moments, the music department of Ezekiel melodically elaborated on and in the reality of the Lord.

After the church took several minutes to calm their emotional state, Pastor Trantham revealed his text and subject for the sermon. "The Lord has led me to Romans chapter eight, the twenty-eighth through the thirty-first verses. Please turn your Bibles to this letter from Paul. If you've found this scripture, say Amen."

"Amen," was heard throughout the sanctuary.

Pastor Trantham switched on a transmitter clipped to his belt. He began speaking into his lavaliere microphone. "The scripture reads as follows: *And we know that all things work together for good to them that love God, and are the called according to His purpose.*" He read the remaining verses with an obvious inflection on certain words. "And verse thirty-one reads: *what shall we say then to these things? If God be for us, who can be against us?* My friends, on this Dedication Day, I'm going to use these verses I've just read to speak to you from the topic, *The Making of a Christian.* Look at your neighbor and tell them, 'You Are in the Making.'"

The saints looked in front and behind, to the left and right, proclaiming, "You are in the making!"

Pastor Trantham's message began to flow from his mouth as he gave a Biblical history on through to a contemporary relevance of the scripture. "God has predestined this very day. He knew how this edifice would be erected, and who would be the under shepherd when it was finished. We are built the same way."

"Speak, Reverend," said a deacon.

"He knows us, predestined us-."

"Preach, preacher," said one of the guest ministers, sitting in the pulpit.

"We are heirs with Him, and joint heirs with the Son, Jesus, the Christ. What a God!" he shouted.

In those next moments, the excitement in the air amplified as Pastor Trantham and Jeremiah David Day worked with the fluency of conjoined twins: a pastor preaching with the enthusiasm of an evangelist, a musician accenting the spoken Word with screaming tri-tone chords from the Hammond.

"So now, church, here we are on this day, a day of dedication. We must dedicate ourselves, not to a new work, but to our work anew. Are you willing to say, *Send me, Lord I'll go?* Because if you are, the Lord is willing to use you. Say yes!"

"Yes" everyone shouted.

"Say yes!" he repeated.

"Yes!"

The congregation acted in approval of Pastor Trantham's words with a reprisal of charismatic exploits. With that, he did a one-eighty and returned to his seat. The church was through – in a Holy Ghost sense of speaking.

After service, Renard cornered Jeremiah in the back hallway near the choir's robing room. "What was that about?"

Jeremiah wasn't sure whether to ignore, answer, or try tossing him out of the way. "What? The saints aren't dumb. They're aware that something was going on by the way service played out."

Renard shook his hand in the direction of the sanctuary. "Th-that! This morning. What was that? Were you calling yourself speaking, like, some kind of truth to power?"

Jeremiah laughed to himself over Renard's obvious anger. "I'm speaking to the sin. That's what I have to do whenever a person obviously tries to disrupt a worship service, acting on their own. So I can't hate you. You're my brother. But I can hate the sin. What do you call what I'm doing?"

After several attempts to get Renard to answer his question, Jeremiah gave up, taking a moment to gather his thoughts. "Maybe you're right. I was speaking truth to *a* power." Had Renard shown himself to be more receptive, he would've told him that the morning service was epic, and no devil in hell could've stopped the flow of The Spirit. Jeremiah's voice – the choir's voice – became the pen of a ready writer.

Verse 34 ♫

*And I will rebuke the devourer for your sakes, and he
shall not destroy the fruits of your ground... Malachi 3:11a
KJV*

The argument with Jeremiah exhausted Renard, who
went back into the sanctuary and sat on the piano bench,
dumbfounded and embarrassed.

He looked around and over his shoulder for prying
eyes, pulled out his cell phone. Forty texts from Olds,
Detroit, all over Michigan, and the far reaches of the United
States:

*Eta chapter: Pastor couldn't preach! Memphis is
troubled!*
Beta: Chicago's in trouble! Pentagrammatory rocks!
Prez Auerbach: Zeta: Tweet #mychurchissungtoahalt!
DOA works! All Hail Society of Tyrus! Iota chapter

Renard read those texts, and then stopped reading as
frustration over his failed DOA effort mounted in his mind.

Members of Ezekiel's congregation passed by him on
the way out of the sanctuary, where many tried to speak,
making comments about the new building. He was swift to
let them know that he didn't feel their enthusiasm. Others
called themselves offering what sounded like consoling
words, and he returned their favor with a comment that he
wasn't at all interested in having anyone studying him. He
knew the aints were disingenuous.

Frantic, he called Terry, wanting to meet at the
McDonald's on North Telegraph. He wasn't interested in the
food, it was just a place where he could unload.

Once they were together, Terry chimed right in, bragging on the successful ploy he had waged against New Bethel Congregational. "That pastor was helpless. Absolutely no power. The man couldn't even preach, he was so confused."

"Really," was Renard's only reply.

"I guess it was a combination of things. I put an arcane device in his Bible, and the music I played. You're right, Re'Re'. The DOA works."

"Umm. Happy for you." Renard was sickened at the thought of his failure. "Thanks for rubbing it in my face."

"That's really not what I'm trying to do. You should be happy for me. Moreover, be happy for our chapter."

"Yeah, yeah. I am. I wasn't so successful."

"Well, okay-."

"But you know what? *Nobody's* getting in my way the next time! I'll plan and implement my own full-scale DOA, and it will work."

Terry wielded a doubtful look on his face. "What makes you think your next plan will work? This one, according to you, didn't do so well."

"Oh you think today will stop me? Think again!"

"Leave it alone, Renard! Things happen. You weren't the only one in Tyrus whose plan wasn't as successful as they planned. Guys all over the country have reported in with mediocre results. Shoot! Some of the guys in our *own* chapter said their plans didn't run perfectly!"

"Who? Name one!"

Terry sat, staring blankly.

"I thought so. Don't lie to make me feel good, brother!"

"I didn't think I needed to. Really."

"Today? Over at Ezekiel?" Renard shot his arm out in no absolute direction. "Today was just a hiccup. I've already tried Tyrus, and I know it works. Remember? It wasn't that long ago. You know . . . when all the brothers tried to fight me on it, calling me a renegade. Well bro', you ain't seen nothing yet!"

"Your wife said you might need to see someone. A professional. I sometimes think that you're breaking up."

"*My Kira?* When did you talk to her?"

"C'mon, man, ain't nothing to it. Ain't no woman gonna sit around forever, saying nothing. She had to express her feelings to someone. You refuse to listen to any reasoning. Since most people wouldn't understand Tyrus, who better to speak to about a brother than a brother?"

"I'm not breaking up. You think I'm crazy? All ya'll are crazy!"

"Here we go again," said Terry.

Renard cared less about his friend's sarcasm. "Naw, naw. You think you understand me-."

"I do understand what you're thinking, because you've said so before. *A higher degree in Tyrus*, you've said."

"Like I thought. You *don't* understand me. Me? A higher degree in Tyrus is impressive, but that's just settling. I'm aiming for greater than that. I'm shooting for *immortality*."

Verse 35 ♫

*He said unto them, An enemy hath done this. The
servants said unto him, Wilt thou then that we go and gather
them up? Matthew 13:28 KJV*

Jeremiah wanted to cut off his cell phone and take
those last remaining hours Sunday afternoon relaxing with
Arze' before his weekly work routine resumed, but in the
early evening Pastor Trantham called.

He commended him again on the blessed music
rendered in the morning service, but Jeremiah knew that the
topic of conversation would evolve toward the
embarrassment Renard had caused. "It's not nightfall yet, but
what happened today seems to be on the tongue of the entire
city of Olds. Some of the pastors in the area call what they've
heard disturbing." Pastor Trantham paused, breathing into the
receiver. "I know today wasn't some unique incident."

"What do you mean?" Jeremiah asked.

"Frankly, they were troubled over some incidents that
happened during their church services as well. Too bad-."

"What?"

"None of the pastors had an explanation for it," Pastor
Trantham replied, his voice fading away.

The earliest Jeremiah could meet with Pastor
Trantham was Tuesday afternoon. He was offered a seat
adjacent to Pastor's desk. In came Sis. Leah Wade, the
pastor's administrative assistant, into the office with her iPad
in tow. On her way to the chair next to Jeremiah, she grabbed
a handful of individual chocolates from a candy dish centered
on the oval conference table. She positioned her electronic
device to a readable level. "Pastor, this is somewhat

confidential. You want me to read this information in his presence?" she asked.

"Absolutely," Pastor Trantham replied. "Brother Day needs to hear this."

"Yes sir. Let's see," she said, focusing on her iPad screen. "Since Sunday, you've received over fifty calls, mainly from members who felt the need to express their thoughts about Renard's future. What they really want, is to know whether he will continue to play at our church."

Pastor Trantham began wringing his hands. "You see, Brother Day-."

"And," she interrupted, "I don't think the calls are about to stop."

"Thank you, Sis. Wade." Pastor Trantham paused as she excused herself from his office. "Brother Jeremiah, I feel like my members. I'm divided on what to accept as truth and whether I should do something about him."

"We are talking about Renard?"

Pastor Trantham sighed. "Yes."

"The employee . . . Renard?"

"Yes. Yes."

"You really don't feel like you have to do some kind of damage control, do you?" Jeremiah asked.

"Listen Brother Day, what you did with your music was in order with God's plan. You can't return your own evil for evil. Right will always come our way if we continue to follow God's direction."

"You're right, Pastor. It's just sometimes you want to get even in a major way."

"To tell you the truth, there's probably so much sin embedded in that department because Renard's been with them so long. And really, I can't be sure that the majority of the choir members desire to do right themselves. Some of them probably wanted to help him in that mess."

Jeremiah smiled. "You think?"

"I mean, everything came out as blessed when you think about the total worship experience. Don't be mistaken. I'm human too. If I had a vindictive spirit, I would want to retaliate as well."

"I hear you."

"Nothing surprises me. In this quest of really looking to God and paying attention to His desire in us, Satan's going to be busy, more than ever before."

"I guess you're right, Pastor. Now I've got to watch the visible demon, and keep my eye on any imps in hiding."

Pastor Trantham, who had been glancing in a book, paused. "I know that neglecting to dish out a remedy can make a problem bigger. But I'm not neglecting. I'm allowing Renard every opportunity for repentance."

Verse 36 ♫

And he did that which was evil in the sight of the Lord his God, and humbled not himself before Jeremiah the prophet speaking from the mouth of the Lord. II Chronicles 36:12 KJV

The urgency in Fredrico's voice made Renard feel as though he wasn't getting to Sound Shocker fast enough to hear what his recording engineer and friend had to say.

When Renard walked into the door, he found Fredrico smiling as he rushed to close out a conversation he was having on the phone. He swiveled around in the high-backed chair. "You ready to make an extra twenty-five grand?"

"I don't know that I'd call any money extra, but yeah, twenty-five large sounds like a great deal."

"Here's what's up." Fredrico went on to explain how Wretched Killer, a Canadian gangsta-rapper, wanted to commission Renard to write a tune for him. "This guy has long money, and he wanted to use some new talent instead of old heads for his next project. Artists on corporate labels would be too busy hugging their Grammys to write something with any true inspiration. He figured some independents would be the best bet to provide him with tunes that have grit."

"How'd he hear about me?"

"*Death to A Carnal Christian.* I'm telling you, man. That tune's on autopilot. Do I have to remind you that we live in a powerful age?" Fredrico spread his arms out wide. "It's called the World Wide Web. Emphasis on world-wide."

"So, what? Does he want to buy me out on *Death*? Put that on his next album?"

"No. But he wants you to write in that same vein."

"Okay. I guess I'll have to pull out my idea book."

"Listen bro'. This rapper's got specifics."

"Oh?"

"Listen to this." Fredrico sat back, cool, casual, into his seat. "*He* wants you to write lyrics and a tune about and against organized religion."

"Wow! He could've chosen an abundance of producers to write something like that." Renard stroked his chin, likening his jaw to his ego. "So glad he chose me."

"Man, just think about it. In less than nine months or so, your artistry has catapulted."

Renard sat back in a contemplative state. "Things have happened pretty fast, haven't they?"

"Yeah. I can see it. With this kind of notoriety, you won't have to continue dancing between hip-hop and church."

"What!? Is that what you've been hoping?" His egotistic buzz had come to a halt.

"Well, it hasn't been on the forefront of my mind, but you gotta admit . . ."

"You don't friggin' get it, do you?"

"Get what?"

"This is part of my duty, my responsibility in the Society of Tyrus. Our bylaws say that we must play an active part in a church or worship center." He paused, remembering who he was talking to. "No disrespect, but you're not a member. I've already said too much."

"Man. I really don't believe you. Where you comin' from?"

"Not where am I coming from. The question should be, *What am I achieving?*"

"Okay, I'll bite. What are you achieving?"

"Power. Infallibility. Unstop-ability. Indestructability. Immortality." Renard went on a rant, spouting close to a dozen more terms. "I got all night."

"You can't force your will on the universe."

"The hell I can't. I'm in a great position to do considerable damage," he disputed, keeping in mind that he held cards to at least one of his enemy's immediate dreams. As long as he felt that he could parlay his positions and his talents into the ruin of human understanding, he was on his way to achieve everything he wanted.

"Okay Renard. I guess I can tell Wretched that you're on board, yes?"

"Absolutely. I'll write him a hit. Or die trying." Money from downloads. Money for producing songs. Playing master puppeteer to an artistic foe. Confused worshippers. He had work to do, but he took the time to briefly savor that moment. He could even see a prosperous Christ, no – Xmas – season ahead.

Verse 37 ♫

May the God of hope fill you with all joy and peace in believing, so that by the power of the Holy Spirit you may abound in hope. Romans 15:13 KJV

Leo, whose natural height already had him head over heels to Jeremiah, was on the ladder as the designee for hanging Christmas ornaments at the top of the Day's tree. "I don't mean any harm, Jere, but your wife's got us working like slaves."

"Really? I don't mean any harm either, but what does a roguish White boy like you know about slavery? What do you know about work, period?" Jeremiah asked comically.

"We work on the same job, Bubba!" Arze' and Susan were standing at the base of the tree, directing Leo on the placement of the tree topper, a brown-hued female angel. "Now I guess, with all this work, you all will come to our house and help us with our Christmas decorations. What you say, Susan?"

Susan was busy viewing the tree topper through a frame which she had formed with her fingers. "They don't have to do that. We don't mind coming over here at all. We enjoy the fellowship!"

Leo let out a friendly grunt, grinning through the beard which surrounded his face. "She's just talking! You all will come over, won't you?" he asked, although it was unclear whether he wanted Jeremiah or Arze' to answer.

Arze' backed a ways from the tree, still keeping it in view, giving the decorations a final check. "Of course we will. And Jere will gladly assist just like you have, Leo."

"I guess I will, especially since Leo's taking me on this trip. Free." The excursion they'd planned was less than a month away, and Jeremiah was looking forward to discovering the Upper Peninsula for himself. "Thanksgiving's gone. Christmas break is just around the corner. A great guy-trip for us in January. Moving into a new home soon. This is too much excitement in a short period of time."

"We do have a lot going on," Leo agreed. "When are you set to close? Pretty soon?"

"Haven't received an exact word, but we expect to close sometime in January. Pre-qualifying is the way to go, and we just had the home inspection done. We've got a lot to accomplish, but everything's flowing smoothly."

"Good. Glad to hear it," Leo said.

"And we do look forward to helping you move," Susan chimed in. She grinned at Leo, who grinned at Jeremiah.

Arze' motioned for anyone to get closer and give her a hand. "We need boxes, because there's items we can start packing and preparing now. I know we have to keep living in the meantime, so we can't pack everything. Then, once we get the final word from the mortgage company, we can pack bedding, extra toiletries, cookware."

"Speaking of cooking . . . what's around here to eat?" Leo asked. He dropped a handful of decorative lights into a box and started looking around.

The two couples decided to abandon the decorations for a short while and go get some lunch, but Jeremiah wanted to check emails from his computer.

The majority of his emails were deleted without his opening to fully view them, but he paid particular attention to one dated the day before, which was sent by Freestar Financial:

Dear Jeremiah and Arze' Day:

We have started the process of assembling your loan packaging and closing documents for the property address of 57 Central Avenue, Olds Michigan, 48056.

We have noticed that there are several items either misplaced, incomplete, or have not been initiated for completion. In addition, there are discrepancies in the information contained on your inspection report. We will need to clear this abundance of items before we can proceed with a set closing date and, if the items are not addressed, we will have to deny the completion of this purchase. Please contact us in person or through your realtor at your earliest convenience.

Sincerely, Freestar Financial (313)664-9291.

Lord. What's going on? The news would keep Jeremiah from having a pleasant lunch but he chose to keep the news to himself right then, at least until he and Arze' could talk privately that evening.

Verse 38 ♫

For the Lord knoweth the way of the righteous, but the way of the ungodly shall perish. Psalms 1:6 KJV

Even twenty-four hours seemed too long to hold the news that Renard had to share. It didn't matter the genre or the artist, he knew that music production among professionals was a fickle business within itself, and mistrust was elevated when working with gangsta rappers; screwing around, sharing their deals and agreements with the wrong person could possibly get you killed. At the least, you'd never get work of any decent caliber again. He was aware that the specifics of his newfound luck could not be shared with just anyone. His bloodline, however, was a music pro, one who wasn't fazed by contract talks and negotiated deals. The news would be safe with his father.

Adrian came over to his house after he had been in a long, exhausting recording session on that day. After seeing his weary condition, had some regret in asking him over, but he wanted to give him the news in person. It would've been impossible to hold the news another day.

"But it's *gangsta rap!*" Adrian scolded after Renard shared the details. "My God, son, don't you feel any shame?"

"Oh my goodness, can I ever please you? I call myself giving you good news!" Renard picked up a miniature statue of *The Thinking Man* from off his desk, threw it across the room. The statue, being wood, didn't shatter, but left a visible dent in the wall. "I really don't believe you, man! So let me try this again. I've been commissioned to write some music. For major money. I'd think you'd be happy for me."

"My concern isn't about the money."

"What is it, then? Something may happen to me? Maybe I'll suffer the same fate as Biggie or Tupac?"

"Not exactly. It's more personal than-."

"Oh I get it," Renard interrupted. "It may be that the artists in this genre will make me one of their elite."

"You'll pigeonhole yourself into this genre and nobody'll take you seriously in another style of music. You'll be branded. But that's just part of my worry. You see-."

Renard tilted his head and cupped his ear in jest. "I'm trying to hear the bad part of what you're saying. I ain't heard anything terrible yet."

"But-."

"If I did twenty-five, thirty grand a month for the next decade, along with some endorsements and other royalties? Humph, sounds good to me." Renard took a few seconds to sum up Adrian's dissention. "You speak like a crazy man. I ain't feelin' you."

Tension thickened as father and son stared each other into submission. Renard made the decision that he'd said all he needed to say about the matter, and he would be the victor in their silent contest.

"C'mon son," Adrian said, breaking the standoff and pleading with sincere desperation in his voice. "There's something I've got to tell you-."

"Hold on." Renard caught the home phone on its last ring before the answering machine took over. "Hello?"

It was Terry. His voice sounded distant, peculiar. "Hey bro. Have you h-heard or s-seen the evening n-news?"

"Naw man. What's up?"

"Just go to your computer. I'll shoot you a link."

"Why don't you just tell me-."

"Just read what I send you." Terry abruptly hung up.

"Son?" Adrian said.

Renard was disarrayed over the last few minutes and how a series of events had unfolded, forgetting that he and his father's conversation was left unfinished. Since Terry's message seemed to be the most urgent, whatever Adrian had to say would have to wait.

With his computer on and booted up, he clicked on the link that Terry sent, skimming the headline, focusing on three recognizable names. "Oh no. . ."

FRANKFORT, KY (WAVE) – *Emergency officials recovered the bodies of five victims from separate accidents Sunday morning.*

Nelson County officials were called to investigate two vehicles trapped in flood waters of the Rolling Fork River along Walter Hall Road and Dee Head Road, near New Hope, Kentucky.

According to Nelson County EMS, the vehicles drove into the water with five people inside. Two passengers were able to survive the flood waters, but three people were unable to get out. The bodies of those three were recovered and turned over to the Nelson County Coroner for examination and identification.

EMS transported the two passengers who escaped to Flaget Memorial Hospital. Their condition is unknown.

Positive identification of the fatally wounded revealed twin brothers; Mercer and Merle Dobbins of Olds, Michigan; and Brionna Dobbins, wife of Mercer, also of Olds.

Funeral arrangements are incomplete at this time with Cobb's Funeral Home, Orchard Lake Drive, in charge.

Verse 39 ♫

When I consider the heavens, the work of thy fingers,
the moon and the stars, which thou hast ordained.

Psalms 8:3   Trust . . . in the living God, who giveth
us richly all things to enjoy. I Timothy 6:17 KJV

"Oh. My. God. Leo, I wouldn't have missed this for
the world." Jeremiah was fixed on the elegance, the natural
symmetry of the Upper Peninsula's hills and mountainous
regions against a wintry sky, with roaring streams in the
foreground. God truly was a magnificent Creator.

"Aw, man. You ain't seen nothing yet."

Jeremiah thought that their vacation week would
never arrive. The anticipation had overwhelmed him. Now,
he was there; it was their second day of a six-day trip, and the
excitement had far from subsided.

"I miss my wife, I miss my wife. I really do miss my
wife, Leo. But this – it's absolutely overwhelming." Jeremiah
sucked in a lung full of fresh, frosted air, raised his arms and
looked toward Heaven, observed the burnt orange sun as it
rose above the mountainous horizon. His eyes started welling
with tears. "No school with whining teenagers and algebraic
equations. No church with a devilish-."

"Hush man. This ain't the time, and definitely not the
place. This is the getaway, make the best of the opportunity.
Just take it all in and appreciate it," Leo advised.

Sault Ste. Marie was a true spectacle, everything Leo
promised and then some. They visited the Soo Locks, the
Point Iroquois Light Station, and Whitefish Bay – all of the
usual tourist spots – but it was when their excursion took

them to Tahquamenon Falls that they felt the greatest freedom and closeness to God himself.

"You do realize that we're off the beaten path, don't you?" Leo asked.

Jeremiah's heart palpitated. Aware that they couldn't possibly take in all the massive acreage of untamed wilderness, he felt settled in capturing some of his fascination on film with Arze's Christmas gift, a high-end digital SLR camera. "Oh yeah. You like it, I love it," he replied. He walked over to the river and bent down, cupped his hands like a bucket, scooped up the ice cold liquid and drank. "Man. Wonderful. Try some?"

"Oh no. That water'll freeze my teeth out. I don't see how you drink it that cold."

"Cooler the better."

"Let's do some fishing. I know they'll be biting."

"And tomorrow, we'll see who has the better hunting skills," Jeremiah kidded.

It was day five when on that evening, Jeremiah and Leo were warming by a fire inside of the Canadian cottage they had rented for the week. They busied themselves by cleaning and oiling their rifles after a dinner meal of lake trout and smallmouth bass that they caught earlier that afternoon.

Between conversations that ranged from church to school to marriage to money to life – and scheduling for when they would do that vacation again – Jeremiah kept having to run outside or to the bathroom. "Maybe something I ate," he would say to Leo. But he seemed to get steadily worse."

"Anything coming up?" Leo asked.

"No," Jeremiah replied between coughs. "Just dry heaves."

"You'll no doubt feel better after you vomit."

"God. I hate that feeling. The only time I remember ever doing it was in college, the one party that taught me a lesson about liquor. *Don't do it*," Jeremiah said.

Leo let out a belly laugh. "I'm glad you learned your lesson in one party. It took a bunch of kegs for me to learn. Even now, I slip up, I have to admit. I remember the time when . . ." His voice trailed off as Jeremiah felt another urge to go to the bathroom.

Kneeling over the toilet bowl while wetting a cold face towel was the last thing Jeremiah . . .

Verse 40 ♫

And as it is appointed unto men once to die, but after this, the judgment. Hebrews 9:27 KJV

On a dismal Friday afternoon, January 3rd, Renard was parked on a pew of the Cokesbury United Methodist church with Kira at his side, disheartened over the way his 2014 year had begun. It didn't matter that he had successfully set traps to delay Jeremiah's home purchase. It didn't matter that his music career had taken monumental leaps into positive territory.

What did matter was that two Society of Tyrus brothers, two Gamma chapter brothers had crossed over the eternal waters of the Ras el-Ain. It was sudden. And tragic.

A reporter from the Olds Free Press had picked up the story from a national wire service, taking the time to fill in the missing details from phone interviews with Kentucky patrolmen and visits to the Dobbins' family home.

Merle, Mercer and Brionna left on their trip Friday, December 20th, for a Christmas vacation that would take them into the mountains of West Virginia, Tennessee and Kentucky. The majority of their travel took them southbound on I-75, but in snow-capped mountains, travelers had to be cautious.

According to the Patrolman report, a transport truck clipped the back end of their automobile, causing the vehicle to skid sideways into the side of a tunnel.

The auto's front windshield dislodged. Mercer was decapitated. Merle and Brionna died on impact. They were found in the water, but contrary to news reports, drowning wasn't the cause of their deaths.

The Dobbins family decided to eulogize all three at the same time in a closed-casket service. And Renard regrettably had to witness to the entire event.

A slow death gave opportunity for affairs to be made right, if such was needed. When a person died slowly, family and friends had a progressive way to say goodbye to the one departing, and visa - versa. Cancer, AIDS, Huntingdon's or an abundance of other debilitating diseases heightened a person's chances for redemption.

Speedy, accidental deaths were morbid. Morbid was the way Renard's brothers died. They left without the benefit of saying, "Good Bye."

And morbid was the grief shown on the day of the service.

With a sanctuary filled to capacity, the minister in charge sat in the center pulpit chair, legs crossed, beads of sweat rolling on his dark chocolate forehead like fresh dew on pitched black asphalt. His movements were taut. Renard continued to observe the man as he fumbled with his tie, crumpled his shirt lapel, and pinched the tassels of his shoes.

The music, Hawkins's *I Won't Be Satisfied*, provided the only pick-me-up as the other parts of the service fluctuated from a draining silence to loud bursts of screaming and incomprehensible rants by family members claiming that the deceased time on Earth was too short, or that they wanted to go where Mercer, Merle and Brionna have already gone. *Right*. It had to be the emotion talking.

And then came the eulogy.

The minister, father, pastor, rector – whatever he was – rendered more of a recitation than a sermon. Renard cared less what the man said, but thought that he could've given more of a message of hope to the living; someone might have gone on their way with a renewed faith. Not Renard. But someone.

He was grateful that his Society brothers were granted permission to administer their own rites as other family and friends left the gravesite. The brothers: Renard, Terry, Olufemi, Bacchus, Zachary, and five new musicians that had begun their three month intake process as Murexes locked arms while holding their Codified Manuals of Tyrus in their hand. They read:

> *We now take time to separate the spirit of man from his body. In the spirit of Ras el-Ain, we commit these our brothers to the heights of the being for which no one in our realm may reach. Send him thirty-three degrees, sixteen minutes, 15 seconds north; thirty-five degrees, eleven minutes, forty-six seconds east. Body returns to Earth, spirit live in us. LACRIMA AΩ*

As they reached the end of their funeral rites, Renard thought he heard his name being called out but, believing it was just his imagination, gave it no regard and began saluting the brotherhood with consoling words and their secret handshake; the four fingers of only the right hands interlocked, thumbs hovering over the forefinger of their comrade.

"Re!" He heard again, but this time louder, crisper and distinct.

Renard turned in the direction of the scream. He observed his wife slowly falling onto the freshly mowed lawn of the gravesite, but whose fall was slightly broken by two women standing near her. "Kira!"

Verse 41 ♫

And call you on the name of your gods, and I will call
on the name of the Lord. I Kings 18:24a

The triage nurse at Olds General was able to contact Kira's OB-GYN, Dr. I. Nassar Haddad, who walked into the exam room with a chart in his hand. He didn't have the apprehensive look that Renard expected. On the contrary.

"What you experienced," the doctor started with, "was more than likely light-headedness from standing in the cold weather for a period of time. But because of what happened to you, we were able to quickly assume and diagnose your gestational diabetes."

Both Kira and Renard looked at each other, sighing deeply and in sync. Renard didn't quite understand what he was hearing, so he couldn't feel relieved just yet.

"Nine times out of ten, the diabetes will go away as we often see . . . in about nine months." The doctor smiled, shaking his hand in a twisting motion at the wrist, like he was opening a jar. "Other tests can help us get closer to an actual date. This will give us a timeline on how long you will have to deal with this form of diabetes."

"Date?" Kira asked.

"Why of course," Dr. Haddad replied, "your date of conception."

Kira's eyes widened. "Oh my God."

Renard's heart skipped. He swallowed, foolishly believing that clearing his throat would resume his pulse to a normal rhythm. He knew. His wife was in the one physical condition that he could be happy about.

All Kira needed was a few days for planning and guests to RSVP, and then she took a page from her mother's recipe book to prepare a complete Southern soul food meal for a dual celebration with mixed emotions; a home going. *And a soon-arriving.*

"A toast," Renard offered as he raised a glass full of Hennessy, "to our fallen brothers, and to their families."

The adults responded with, "Cheers."

"I'm not into prayer and such, but can we have a moment of silence in Tyrus for our deceased brothers and Brionna?" Terry asked.

"Let us do wit," Olufemi chimed in.

On a silent cue, the brothers began to gather in a circle, held hands, and stood silently. A few seconds rolled by, and then they shouted in chorus, "Lacrima."

The chapter brothers, their wives and children participated in and enjoyed a buffet feast of meatloaf topped with a tomato basil sauce, broccoli and cheese, glazed yams, mustard greens seasoned with ham hocks, corn bread. Renard peeked under the glass saver and saw his favorite dessert: carrot cake with crème cheese frosting. He smacked his lips as he dove into the dishes, filling his plate.

"Have you decided on names for the baby?" Bacchus' wife asked.

Kira, who was busy overseeing the table to make sure that the dishes remained filled and that children didn't butt in and reach for an item without adult supervision, replied, "Everything's happened so fast! We hadn't talked or thought about it."

She was right. They really hadn't talked about it. Renard glanced over at Kira. Her loving expression and sparkling eyes seemed to turn dark, devious; *I'm gonna get ahead of you in this baby-naming process, boy.* And she would do just that as soon as she had an opportunity. On the other hand, she would know how he's thinking. He was enjoying the company of his brothers and their families, but at that moment, he wanted to rush them out of the house so he could get started on what he thought his boy - or girl – should be named. He was about to have an heir:

> *You have another power in Tyrus, given only to you only by paternity. Biological power rests in your seed. Through your genetics, you duplicate yourself. One, two, fivefold. Nurture those who carry your name, teach them the culture, the morays, the concepts of Tyrus Society, but be advised; the secrets of Tyrus are only revealed through membership and induction. Guard the secrets until they pledge loyalty to Tyrus. When they have done so, your genetic sons and your daughters also become your brothers and sisters. Lacrima AΩ*

When the last family cleared from the Singleton household and the last dish was set away for cleaning or the refrigerator, Renard performed every quickening movement short of sprinting to his office. He sat down at his computer, embarrassed at himself for the ridiculous blessing that his machine was just in sleep mode instead of having to wait for a time-consuming reboot.

Google. Baby names.

Boys. Junior? Malik. Nick, Nicholas; whatever. Girls. Reva. Dania. Too many names. *Maybe I'll have more luck with babynames.com.* The website confused him even more. He came to a realization that he was going about the process all wrong. Since he was already on his computer and going nowhere fast with that task, he decided it would be fun and relaxing to goof around, do some idle surfing. He wanted to see what the cyber world was saying about *Adrian Singleton, Musician, Olds, MI.*

Great. *Death to a Carnal Christian* was #1 in the search engine results. *Let the people download,* he thought. Sure enough, Arizona.edu did have him listed as an alum; he expected nothing less that since it was his alma mater. His association with Ezekiel Baptist Church showed up, which enraged him slightly. He clicked NEXT under the search pages. "What's this?" he asked himself aloud.

State of Michigan

July 27th, 1984

Adrian Singleton & Tracy Wilkes

Name Change Declaration Hearing

Statutes MCL 711.7, MCL 711.2, MCL 711.3

He bookmarked the site, and then began another search, trying to pinpoint any information that could clear up what he'd just seen. He tried his relative's Facebook pages. He had no luck there, so he went to his father's Wikipedia page and found nothing, except that he was the only offspring of his parents and that his given name was the only name he'd ever known. Nothing else. It was though someone had named his parents in a prank court case. Was it a hoax? Was this about him? Was there a sibling that he didn't know about? With his mother deceased, there was only one person that could immediately answer his questions; the only other person whose name was on the site.

His fingers trembled and his palms clammed up. Five times he tried to reach Adrian within a matter of minutes, only to realize that he had dialed the number incorrectly. He didn't know what to expect to hear from his father, if anything at all.

Baby names. Renard tried not to sound desperate, but he wanted to skip any cordiality, no matter how jovial Adrian's voice sounded on the phone. "Hey dad?"

"Yeah?"

"I need you to talk to me. *Now.* And please don't lie to me."

"What's the problem?"

"Why can't I find my name?"

Verse 42 ♫

When Jesus heard that, he said, This sickness is not unto death, but for the glory of God, that the Son of God might be glorified thereby. St. John 11:4 KJV

When Jeremiah regained full consciousness, he found himself, somehow, in Marquette General Hospital. He ran his hands across the hospital bed linens. With his head nestled in the comfort of the pillow, his eyes took inventory of the room; sterile, white ceilings accented with mauve walls in a glossy finish. A Cal Stat hand sanitizing dispenser was embedded above the room's phone. The needle for an intravenous drip had been inserted and taped to his left arm.

He looked over to another corner of the room, Where Leo was awake but slumped over in a reclining chair-bed, draped in the same Dickey coveralls and red plaid shirt that he'd last remembered seeing.

Leo's eyes widened, met his. "How you feelin'?" he asked.

Jeremiah stretched and twisted in a couple directions to relieve his aching joints. "I remember sleeping, I think – but it was restless, like I couldn't get into that deep sleep. It was like a dream. Nurses kept waking me up and asking me like; *Are you resting okay?* What a ridiculous question."

"No dream, brother, no dream," Leo said, humorously. "That really happened. A nurse came in about an hour ago and said that she'd come in later, get some additional blood samples for a few more tests."

"Oh. The one time they didn't wake me, you mean?" Jeremiah sat up in the bed, took his fingers and massaged his head, grabbed the water pitcher on the bed stand and poured himself a cup of water. He drained the liquid in a few gulps, hoping to quench his looming thirst, moisten his thickened tongue. "They should've taken the blood samples while I was asleep. Maybe I wouldn't have felt it."

"Yeah. But they probably needed you awake for that."

"Yeah, of course. Like they haven't gotten enough blood already!" Jeremiah could feel the tremor in his voice, a natural reaction to his fear of needles.

"She's gotta do her job. It's necessary for the diagnosis."

Jeremiah could tell that Leo wanted to divert the conversation for a few moments and engage in a bit of idle chatter. "How'd I get here, Leo? What am I doing here?"

Leo explained that while they were sitting, talking in front of the fireplace yesterday afternoon, Jeremiah had gone to the bathroom, not returning for nearly thirty minutes. He knocked on the bathroom door and called out to Jeremiah, asking if everything was alright. Nothing. "Fortunately, I didn't have to break the lock to the bath because you left it unlocked. I opened up and there you were; passed out, up against the vanity, but breathing fine. I called an ambulance and that's how you ended up you here."

Jeremiah reeled in confusion. "Wow. I don't remember any of that. Hey! Does my wife-."

"I've already called Sue and Arze'. They're both on their way up here. Be patient. It's gonna take them about five hours, something like that, to get here."

Dr. Julius Grant was the general practitioner on call who entered the room; a caramel-skinned brother, German goatee facial hair, and a pronounced eye for fashion with his perfect, black linen bowtie against a periwinkle pin-striped, spread-collared shirt. To Jeremiah, Dr. Grant bore a deep resemblance to Andre 3000 – only in a lab coat.

The physician took a deep, chest-inflating sigh. "Mr. Day, I'll tell you what I think you have, even before the lab results come in. I've seen your symptoms quite a bit recently, and I have an idea what played a part in your contracting this illness. It could be one or a combination of things. But to be positive, I'll need some answers from you."

While Dr. Grant continued his explanation and diagnosis, Jeremiah had walked over to the recliner, allowing the nurse to change his bed linens. "What do you need to know?" he asked, anxious to see whether the doctor would continue speculating or go ahead and confirm a factual diagnosis.

Dr. Grant briefly looked through a paper file and then tapped some notes into an electronic pad. "I think you have what is medically known as *Giardiasis*, specifically, *Giardia lamblia*."

Jeremiah blinked. "What's that, doc?"

"Most people don't use the big, scientific name. They just call it *beaver fever*. It can take up to five days for us to be completely positive of this diagnosis, though."

"Beaver fever?"

"Yes sir. It's an intestinal parasite that attacks the digestive tract. What have you been experiencing?"

"I started feeling sick a couple days ago. My stomach cramped up, and I can't stop burping these nasty smelling burps."

Under his breath, Dr. Grant said, "Sulfuric, I suspect. Your throat has a burning sensation?"

"Yes, that's it." Jeremiah began recounting his symptoms. "And then I kept needing to go to the bathroom. That's when I began feeling like something was really wrong. You know?"

"I understand."

"How could I have gotten this?"

Dr. Grant squeezed his chin, as if in contemplation. "Do you have a pet?"

"No," he quickly replied.

"You don't work in child care, do you?" he asked as he examined Jeremiah's chart on his laptop.

Jeremiah looked over at Leo, who returned a sly grin. "Not unless you count a high school math teacher."

"What about anything you ate, or bad drinking water?"

"Nothing I ate, but on the camping trip we had our fill of fresh drinking water from a lake."

"One time or more than once?" Dr. Grant asked.

"You mean *you* had your fill of fresh drinking water," Leo corrected.

"Hey! I wanted the experience. Surely that wouldn't have caused this."

"Well . . ." Dr. Grant's voiced lowered, "that could have been the culprit. Drinking contaminated water can bring on a multitude of problems. What looks fresh can fool you."

Jeremiah began to realize the foolishness of his act. "I'm not dying, am I doc?"

"No, you're not dying - of this," Dr. Grant replied in his bogus attempt at some medical humor. "Let's wait for the lab results to make a concrete diagnosis of Giardiasis. In the meantime, we'll let the nurse finish her work. You try to eat the light lunch, and get some rest."

"Yeah! The kind of rest where the nurses wake you every thirty minutes." Leo joked.

"You won't be in here long, but you'll need about six weeks for the treatment," Dr. Grant told him.

"Oh my God! Six weeks?"

"While this infection won't be life-threatening for you, yes. You need six weeks or so for your digestive system to equalize. The rest, in combination with the drugs, will be the most effective and successful way for you to get well."

By the end of the doctor's visit, Jeremiah's bed linens had been replaced. Just as the doctor had predicted, his usually huge appetite had been downsized to a few bites of some tasteless strained green beans, applesauce, and sips of beef bouillon.

Close to six hours later, Arze' and Susan had made the long drive into Sault Ste. Marie and the hospital. After spending close to a half hour together in the room, Leo and Susan left the hospital for the cabin to pack their belongings and then to a local hotel, leaving Arze' in the room with Jeremiah. "Hey, honey," she said, "how will we handle the paperwork needed for the closing and mortgage?"

"Listen, don't you worry about that." Jeremiah hoped that Arze's concern would subside with just his assuring tone, but having confidence in a positive outcome was easier said than done.

"I don't see how I can handle everything while you're recuperating."

"I know. But God has a mysterious way of doing things. The finance company has delayed the closing anyway."

Arze' face had a wounded expression on it. "You mean we may lose the house?"

"We won't. If the house is for us, it will close in due time."

"Yeah." Her look relaxed. "I guess you're right."

"I wouldn't have you trying to handle all that business alone. Don't fret about it, Arze'. Nobody's knocking down doors to get into that house. It would take some strong personalities to take up that remodeling project."

"Or crazy folk like us," Arze' replied with a bit of humor.

"We're in no danger of the home being sold out from under us. The closing's been delayed. Not denied."

"I was so worried about you." She began rubbing Jeremiah on the head.

He began to relish the comfort of her touch. "Were you worried to the point where you and Susan will come on the trip with us next time?"

Arze' backed away. "Uh, you can forget that, sweetie," she said. "But I am glad that everything is going to work out. We've got to get you home."

"In a couple days, baby." He sighed, thinking of just how blessed he was that his illness could've been worse, maybe even fatal. "I love you."

"Back at you." Arze' leaned in close to him, and he could feel the cool, herbal breeze flowing from her mouth. The closeness felt better than any meds the doctor could've prescribed, better than any care a nurse would've administered. *"Build your hopes on things eternal,"* she sang, *"hold to God's unchanging hand."*

As she ended the tune, Jeremiah gave her hand an abrupt squeeze and gazed into her almond eyes. He hoped that she would catch the message in his unspoken plea.

She smiled, leaned back in to him and resumed her song. She resumed with a medley, based on a premise of hope. *"On Christ the solid, rock I stand . . ."*

Verse 43 ♫

*Man that is born of a woman is of few days, and full
of trouble. Job 14:1 KJV*

Ultimate dream living existed in one area east, west,
north, or south of Olds. That was the twenty square mile
section of town called Bloomfield Hills.

There, you could locate the pit vipers of the auto
industry; those overstuffed execs that had saved their
financial souls and their multi-million dollar mortgages while
the real workers living in the inner city were scraping and
grinding just to stay afloat with only pennies to their names,
foreclosures on their minds.

Despite the city of Old's sufferings, the communities
of Bloomfield Hills survived because of mortgagees that
didn't depend on the making of cars.

In other words, money was still being made,
mansions were being bought and sold. Renard dreamed of
Bloomfield Hills' living. One day.

For his father Adrian, though, affluence was already
his reality.

690 Taverhill Drive was a six-bed, seven and a half
bath, six thousand square foot estate with custom
landscaping, towering pergolas, and every amenity that an
artist specializing in piping out treble and bass clefs could
afford. During the times when the home was fully occupied,
nearly every square inch would have people congregating
within its walls; parties, recording sessions, and even the
occasional vacation rental for very selective clientele.
Because of Adrian's hectic work and travel schedule, he had
hired a live-in housekeeper over two years ago; a voluptuous
Latin-American chica named Frances, who kept the residence

in top order during and between his stays. "Agua, you want?" she asked in her heavily accented Spanglish.

He followed her into the great room. "No thanks," Renard said, shifting his eyes from off her ample rear when she briefly turned around. He couldn't prove it, but he was positive that Frances was doing more that Adrian's housekeeping. The way she moved in flawless rhythm, it was no way his father could resist putting her music on paper.

"Sentarse aqui'. On couch." She motioned toward a leather sectional that was the center piece of the room, and then walked away.

Moments later, Adrian, with a drink in hand, emerged from the entryway that Renard knew led to the kitchen. He sat on the outer edge of the sectional, placing his glass on a coaster that sat on the floor. "What's up, son? How's Kira? And my soon-to-be grandchild? When should I expect the new addition?"

"Middle of July." Renard sighed, knowing that cordiality equaled wasted time; and frankly, he had more pressing matters to attend to. "You got me traveling way out here. You do realize we had snow last night and the roads were slick, right? We could've met somewhere halfway."

"I don't believe this! You know you didn't have any trouble getting out here. And you're complaining about the travel time to see your own father."

"Uh, okay. We don't visit. We just talk. So yeah. I guess I am complaining."

"Might I remind you that I've wanted some quality time for several weeks? Maybe months. But you're the busy, up-and-coming new writer and music producer. So excuse me!"

"Don't exaggerate."

"Oh, I'm not exaggerating. Look at you. I've been trying to talk to you but you've brushed me off time after time. With you here on my territory, you have less of a chance to run . . . once I tell you what you want to know."

"I wouldn't be so sure-."

"And I think it's going to be the same thing I've been trying to tell you for practically all your life." Adrian stood up, walked over and pulled out the pocket doors from each side of the wall, closing off both entrances to the massive room. He returned to his seat with a troubled look on his face. "This is just for appearances. This really isn't a secret because Frances already knows what I'm about to tell you."

"She does?"

Adrian appeared to be nervous and withdraw, without giving an answer to how much his housekeeper had been privy to. "I'm going to tell you what you've wanted to know, and I need you to listen, carefully," he demanded.

"Why do you think I'm here?"

"No Renard. You have a bad habit of interrupting, making judgments before getting all the info, and speaking out the side of your mouth."

"You got no idea what you're talking about."

"That's a lie. I *know* you. And this ain't going to be easy for you or me. Once you know this, take your time, digest the whole thing before you go off on some kind of a rant."

"Look-."

"No, son. Shut up! You look. And *listen*." Adrian went on, reminding Renard that both he and his mother Terry loved him as a baby, but that he couldn't deal with his mother's drug addiction and lifestyle choices. "I couldn't be with Terry. I wanted to be. But I vowed you wouldn't have to deal with how your mother and I felt about each other. You'd get the best I could afford."

"But this court case that I found online. Is it some kind of hoax?"

"No. This is where it gets complicated." Adrian did his best to explain how someone's name could be changed from their original by court order and agreement between parents.

"So you weren't around when I was born?"

"That's not true. I wasn't around while she was pregnant. Well, not at first. She hid her pregnancy. From everybody."

Renard waved his hand in the air. "Okay, okay. I got that."

"Once I found out that she was pregnant and you were mine, I started hanging around. And I gave her money when she needed it."

"Oh."

"Let me, umm, correct that. I gave her money when she wasn't too proud to turn it down, and when I was pretty sure that she wasn't gonna use it for something stupid."

"Like drugs."

"No. She was clean during her pregnancy. She didn't start using until after you were born. Don't worry. You were no crack baby."

"Mmm."

"Anyway. Your name was changed."

"You all led me to think that Renard was my given name all along."

"We didn't lead you to think a darn thing. We couldn't deceive you with something you'd never known."

"Of course, mom's not around to defend her position."

Adrian shot him a dismayed look. "Dog, son. There's no position to defend."

"Okay, so my name was changed. Why?"

"What dya mean?"

"*Why* was it changed? It had to be a reason."

"I wanted something a little better for you. That's all."

"Got to be more to it than that. Who gave me the first name anyway?"

"That's not really important."

"Why not? Some thought must've been involved when ya'll first decided on a name. And then I guess somebody must not have liked what was chosen, to want to change it."

"Not totally true, son. That's not exactly how things went down. But look, I don't want to revisit that road. I'm not interested in bad-mouthing anyone."

"I don't understand," Renard said. "What could you have to say? Either you had something to do with the first name, or not."

"I can say without any reservation, that I didn't."

"Then it was my mother's decision?"

Adrian sat in silence.

"Then don't say anything." Renard felt that he had seared Adrian's conscious. His father sat still with the look of a wounded animal; and he understood why. A secret had been partially uncovered, a mystery that was supposed to have remained hidden. He imagined that Adrian was probably damning the very invention of the Internet and all of the information that was now available to the public.

Renard ranted with a windfall of cusswords. "I guess you're not going to give me a choice but to think whatever's left to my imagination." He shifted in his seat. "So, *what* was my original name?"

"Son, that name had been erased out of your life before you could even talk. Leave it alone."

"I'll bet that if the shoe was on the other foot, and your parents had changed *your* name, you would've wanted to know what it'd been, wouldn't you?"

Adrian folded his lips under his teeth. He had to force his mouth into relaxing before saying a word. "That depends. I don't know. Actually, no. I would've trusted my parents to do what's best for my well-being. But we live in a different generation and time."

"Easy for you to say that after the fact. So what was my name?"

"I'm only telling you this because I've tried to warn you. Stop going down the road that you're headed with your music."

"My music's got nothing to do with this-."

"Not true. It's the music. The very thing that I've feared for you has become your reality."

"Whatever, old man. The name?"

Adrian drew in the longest deepest breath that any live human could have possibly drawn. It seemed to have taken every inch of that breath for him to say, *"Luciferious."*

Verse 44 ♫

*Thus saith the Lord of Hosts, Consider ye, and call
for the mourning women, that they may come; and send for
cunning women, that they may come. Jeremiah 9:17*

Prior to his untimely illness in the Upper Peninsula,
mountain peaks, wild game and fresh air had been Jeremiah's
friends. Now Jeremiah was back in Olds, resting inside of an
apartment filled with boxes, packing peanuts, wide tape and
permanent ink markers ready to be moved, but at least he was
in familiar surroundings. Arze' prepared him for the brief
financial hit that they would endure because of his illness.
And since he'd only been in his teaching position a few
months, accumulated sick leave wasn't enough to cover five
to six weeks, so they would have to work through close to
four weeks of unpaid leave. This affected their financial
bottom line on the house closing, which Freestar Financial
seemed to have been miraculously aware of before Jeremiah
and Arze' had time to even report it.

Jeremiah, however, refused to be alarmed. "Just keep
the faith," he shared with Arze' during one of her bouts of
uneasiness. "We'll be okay."

He was thankful that his beloved Arze' was there to
take care of him before and after work. As a nurse, she could
give excellent care, but the inescapable effects of Giardiasis
still took a toll on him physically. Jeremiah was twenty-five
to thirty pounds lighter and was experiencing bouts of
extreme fatigue. Eating solid foods seemed out of the
question, so he had to opt for unseasoned prepared baby food
out of the jar. He was in his third day of taking Flagyl three
times a day as prescribed by a local gastroenterologist, and
taking grapefruit seed extract as suggested by Susan
Richter's naturopathic doctor.

It was on Saturday afternoon that he was awakened from a sleep-aid induced nap to hear voices outside of their bedroom. He recognized Pastor Trantham's and Arze's voices, but he couldn't make out the subject of their conversation.

Arze' knocked on the bedroom door. "Rev. Trantham wants to come in for a visit."

Pastor Trantham peeped in. "You decent?" he asked.

Jeremiah sat up by propping a couple pillows against the headboard. "Wow. I feel honored."

"You're my minister of music. But actually, I visit all my members. At least those who let me know that they're sick," he replied with amusement. Pastor Trantham came in and laid his overcoat on a nearby chair. "Brother Day, the church is continually praying for your recovery."

"I'll be fine, Pastor. I'm more concerned more about the music ministry than about me." He took a series of belabored breaths, trying to speak freely above slow, painful phrases. "I just can't allow Renard to take over for what might be six weeks."

"I've already seen what he does when he gets just one week of authority," agreed Pastor Trantham. I can't let our church go back to the problems we've had in the past."

"I know it took over a month to get the music department on track after he dug his claws in them the first time I was out of town." Jeremiah turned his head toward Arze', who was in a corner folding blankets and placing them in a box. He spied her for a while. She didn't seem to be paying attention to the conversation. "I know of one way that we can resolve the situation, but she's not gonna like it. Arze'?"

She snapped her head and eyed Jeremiah without a single blink. "Uh huh?"

"Uh huh nothing. You were doing a fine job playing poker face." Realizing that she'd been listening the entire time, he made his humble plea short and to the point. "Will you?"

"Will I what?"

Jeremiah did a quick glance toward Pastor Trantham, then returned in Arze's direction. "Girl, stop playing! You know what!"

Her eyes had moved from a gaze to a glare, with an unwavering determination on her face. "Pastor, I hate to talk about this in your presence, but Jeremiah already knows what I promised not to do when we moved here. I'll gladly work in our church, but *not* in the music department. Sorry, but it's no reflection on you."

"I would never feel like it was, Sis. Arze'," Pastor Trantham replied. "But dear, we need your help. *God* needs your help. I'm asking – begging – you to use your gift just this once. Please."

It was truly an eternity before Arze' answered the man, but after several grunts and inaudible conversations with herself, she said, "I'll continue Jere's duties to the church for only the time it takes for him to get well. That's all." She leaned in close, closer to Jeremiah until her flaring nostrils burned against his ear and whispered, "You owe me. Big time. But I know we need this income to continue." She backed from off the bed and stood upright.

Jeremiah caught her frozen gaze and winked, hoping to incite a response. She remained emotionless. Embarrassed by the tension in the room, he turned toward Pastor Trantham's comforting face. "She'll do it, Pastor."

"Yes Pastor," Arze' chimed in, "only for you, because your ministry's been good to us," She explained that the regular rehearsal hour needed to be set back about thirty minutes to allow her a bit more time between leaving her regular job and getting to the church.

Jeremiah could feel his angst rising when Arze' began stretching her luck with a second request: during the weeks of his recovery, she could work exclusively with the Voices of Ezekiel, which would give the other choirs a brief sabbatical. She reasoned that her job would be more effective if her concentration was solely on a single choir. "If you can work out those two issues, we can do the job."

Jeremiah was confident that her last appeal would be flat out denied.

"That's an easy fix. God's always timely." Pastor Trantham began gathering his coat and hat. "If I never see another miracle in my lifetime, I'm a witness today. Prayer works. I was doubting whether you would consent to helping out, Sis. Day. But thank you."

Jeremiah squirmed in the bed, nodding in disbelief. *Whatever this chick wants, she gets.*

"Understand something, Pastor," Arze 'insisted, "This is only a temporary situation, so don't get any ideas or get used to this."

"Praise the Lord! So this is what it took to get you?" Pastor Trantham joked. "I'm sorry that God put your husband on his bed of affliction, but now that I know Bro. Jeremiah'll be all right and he will recover, we look forward to your part in the ministry."

Pastor left their apartment with a relieved continence, but no one was as thankful as Jeremiah. With his wife briefly at the helm, his work, his music and his ministry would remain intact.

Verse 45 ♫

*And I will cause the noise of thy songs to cease; and
the sound of thy harps shall be no more. Ezekiel 26:13 KJV*

Luciferious.
It was something in a name. Ever since that day, the
day of Adrian's revelation, the memory of that name had
lulled Renard to sleep, awakened him in the mornings,
followed him at every move like an out-of-body experience.
That name was a bastard twin; separated at or near birth only
to be reunited in adulthood. It had become his haunting, his
hope. He was intent on Luciferious becoming his future; a
resurgence, of a sort, to his former self just to balance out the
life he'd always known. But Renard had come up with a
solution to his dilemma, because he refused to allow the
blemish of his past to become a calamity going forward. Yes.
The name of misfortune would be turned into his fortune. He
would stake his belief in the Ras el-Ain on that.
His eyes were weighted from what resulted in an
entire day at Sound Shocker. Renard clicked the mouse and
transferred the view of the music tracks from his MacBook
over to a 52" monitor that was mounted on the wall. "I hear
something extra on this track," he said to Fredrico. He
stretched out the wave pattern on a synth line that they had
recorded so that the view of it could be easy to repair.
"There. I think it's fixed." The two listened:
Go ahead you religious mongers!
Build your altar to watch it burn
Episcopalian, Lutheran, Presbyterian
Baptists, Methodists and C O G I C
Like your Abraham – call your god. See if he answers

BECAUSE TYRUS ALWAYS ANSWERS ME!

"I think the song fits the bill for what Wretched Killer wants," Fredrico said without a glint of enthusiasm. "It's radical, lyrical. Got a driving beat."

"Aw man. It's over the top! And the best part is that it's anti-religious."

"Yeah," Fredrico replied, "To a fault."

Renard knew the difference between hearing and listening. Listening usually warranted an enthusiastic response, and Fredrico wasn't giving one. "What's got you?" he asked.

"Nothing. Nothing at all."

Renard smacked his lips and waved him off. "Yeah, right. But if you don't want to talk about it, cool."

Fredrico seemed intent with changing the subject and replied with a feeble sounding, "Cool."

It didn't matter what Fredrico's attitude was, Renard was locked into the reality that they needed each other, and the scale wasn't tipped in either one's favor. He wasn't going to be deterred, however, and his producer was going to hear him. That day. "Listen man, I've got a new idea. A business. It can be a load of cash down the line for everybody involved."

"Whatcha got in mind, dude?" Fredrico asked with a wind of indifference.

"I'm set on forming a publishing and music empire, like all the great writers and producers. I've been writing down ideas, developing and formulating them for some time now."

Fredrico leaned back in his chair and rested a cheek against his curled hand. "To do what?"

"You know. To follow in the legacy of the greats. Holland, Dozier, Holland. Jam and Lewis. Gamble and Huff. L.A., Babyface-."

"I get the picture. Why?"

Renard laughed to try to break up the dissonance in the room. *What a ridiculous question.* "Why? You gotta ask why? Even you've gotta admit, we're on a roll. Things are good."

Fredrico nodded as though he was semi-captivated. "Yeah. We haven't lacked for work. Although, I still say that all work ain't good work."

"You sure can put a damper on things with your pessimistic attitude. Point is – things are good, so we ride this train while it's still rolling."

"What you got in mind, Re?"

"I told you. A creative group. We'll incorporate songwriting, artist development, production, concert promotion. The whole gamut."

"Have to hand it to you. When you dream, you dream like big." Fredrico went back to manipulating music tracks. "It's like, you dream colossal."

"Yeah! Publishing. Composing. Artist development. . ." Renard grunted. "The more I say it, the more the idea seems to blossom in my head. And I've already come up with the name."

"I got one," Fredrico chimed in. He lifted his hands and formed a picture frame. "I can see it now! The RFM Group."

"And what would that mean?" he uttered.

"Well, on the surface it means radio frequency music. You know. Like the product we put out will hit the airwaves."

"And of course since the product we put out is music and the music will be on the radio and radios have frequencies, et cetera, et cetera, et cetera," Renard rambled on. He was far from impressed. "You can keep that."

"See, you need to hear me out. Underneath, the RF stands for Renard and Fredrico."

Renard rubbed his chin. "Uh, no brother."

"Whatever."

"How's this? Luciferious and Odyssey of Mind," Renard announced, deciding to spill the name without fanfare.

"Huh?"

"You heard me. *Luciferious*. And the Odyssey of Mind part of the name is incorporated for you and whoever else we would bring into the artistic group. I'm sure we'll need to create an LLC for this," he said, his voice trailing off. "I would be the CEO, of course."

"Have you, like, lost your mind?" Fredrico said between streams of cuss words. "I mean, really? You done fell off, right?"

"What's the problem?"

"Why would I be associated with a group that sounds like Satan is the founder?"

"C'mon, man-."

"Naw, you c'mon! What possessed you to think of that?"

"Not what. Who. And I didn't come up with it. It's something my parents thought of. Well, not the artistic group, but the name."

"Okay now. I never knew your moms, but your dad? *He* ain't thought of no such thing. You know I've gone along, listening to you, watching you create. I ain't gonna front; you're a genius when it comes to music. But honestly bro . . . you take your mind to places that scare me."

"Stop dipping in melodrama."

"I'm not," Fredrico replied. He began swirling a trackball between his fingers, a spare that wasn't connected to anything. It was what he always did when he seemed agitated. "I like my life."

"And I don't? Listen. I've never made it a secret that having an artistic legacy is my end result. I want it. I'll get it. Luciferious is a god-send. The perfect name. And I'll achieve what I've set out to get. With you or without you."

Verse 46 ♫

*Thou shalt not covet thy neighbor's wife. Exodus
20:17a KJV*

Renard watched intently as the person of the hour
seemed to be Arze' Day. She walked into the Voices choir
rehearsal, seeming to be as organized as the fool of a man
that she married. Maybe, even more so; an upgraded, female
version of Jeremiah.

And she was fine. A peach bronze tone to her
flawless skin. Short, brown hair that accentuated her eyes.
Given more time to study her, he might've put her looks
above Tamla, with her fine self. Renard could sketch the
outline of her body despite the oversized polka dotted boy-
shirt she was donning. If he didn't know any better, she was
purposely attempting to lean away from being seductive
when it came to her fashion sense. *C'mon baby* he thought.
Arze' needed to do like the other female musicians he'd seen,
heard and had. Showing more skin wouldn't have hurt her.

By the time the Voices had gathered, the music and
lyric sheets were already laid out. There was a brief
explanation of how she would carry out the rehearsal with the
auxiliary musicians, and then she opened with prayer and a
scripture, and went right into rehearsal.

"Before we get started," she said, "I want each of you
to know that I am doing this only while your minister of
music is recuperating. But I'm sure that we can have a great
time and minister to our people in the process."

Calvin Inman stood up, and without permission
announced, "Well I think that I should say on behalf of the
choir that we're glad to have you, Sister. Whatever you need
during these few weeks or so, just ask."

The rest of the choir happily chorused in agreement. Renard decided not to even pretend to approve that sentiment.

Arze's face glowed with appreciation, and then briefly turned solemn. "Please continue to keep my husband in prayer."

Renard went over to the organ after Arze' gave him marching orders for rehearsal and the upcoming Sunday. He laid the evening's music repertoire on the music stand. He hadn't been asked to teach any of the choral parts or provide music accompaniment for any of the difficult passages. *She must think she has it all covered.*

"My husband has written a song that he's wanted me to sing for a while now. He's calling it *Wonderful Things*. It's describing praise as the essence of our warfare. You can get with that, can't you?"

The singers sounded like a machinelike church congregation with their, "Amen."

"Jere knew that I'd be uncomfortable coming out of the congregation during a service to sing the solo, but I can't win that argument now." Arze' told them.

The Voices seemed to find her comment amusing, but Renard's stomach curled in disgust. He wished that she would stop lying to the people and just told the truth. He regarded her statement as a sly way of letting them know that she liked singing solos.

Arze' adjusted the boom by the piano to a standing height. "I'm sure it wasn't his intention to have me sing it while he was ill, but God has a way of making things happen on His time; Amen?"

It was baffling to see the choir members so cooperative with Arze'. They were doing their best to sing parts in one take and when she asked them to repeat a part, they took correction without backlash. And there were more *Yes Ma'am's* than he'd ever heard come from that group; too much respect for a meddling newcomer, an eternal outsider. He couldn't play the organ correctly without seething over the fact that Trantham had given temporary charge over the music department to that woman - without the benefit of him even being considered. But it was okay, he have his way of avenging Trantham's oversight. And retribution would come hard.

After rehearsal, Arze' gathered up the remaining lyric sheets and music, assembled them in a small stack and placed them in a leather tote. She left the sanctuary, saying goodbye to the few stragglers that hadn't left for their cars. Renard followed her, staying several steps behind. When she had turned the corner to head down the last vacant hall before getting into the vestibule, he called out to her. She turned, appearing somewhat startled. "Hey Bro. Singleton."

Renard caught up to her. "Hey, umm, Arze', isn't it?"

"Yes?"

"You, umm, handle yourself pretty good in a rehearsal."

"Thanks."

He could tell that she was slightly cautious; answering what needed to answered and saying no more. It was no telling what Jeremiah had said to her about him. "Your husband never told me that you played the piano. And sing, too." He wet his lips, making sure that he had her attention. "Wow."

"I appreciate that," she replied without expression.

He could still sense the standoffishness about her. He knew that if he would just test her, that tough, ministry-pretending exterior would falter. After all, she was one more whimpering little biological clock; she just happened to be the wifey of his most hated acquaintance. Aside from his natural disgust in her being married to Jeremiah, he thought she was something to behold. He wished he had gotten to see her in another light at last October's Festival of Lambs.

He moistened his lips again, surveyed his surroundings, checking to see if anyone else was in the near vicinity. He moved in toward her, close enough for anyone to feel that some semblance of personal space was being invaded. But it didn't matter. Her well-being wasn't at the forefront of his mind. He reached up, palmed her breast, pressing her soft flesh.

Arze's eyes widened into an icy gaze. With the arm that wasn't holding her tote, she swung at him with an open-handed cross.

Renard caught her by the wrist just short of connecting with his cheek. He was surprised, yet impressed at her natural strength. "Wow, chick, I didn't see that coming," he said.

Arze' face contorted in a snarl. "Maybe your pregnant wife needs to know how you behave around other women. Yeah! I think I'll consider letting her know you ain't all you seem. What do you think?"

For a fleeting moment, Renard felt a pinch of anxiety at her threat. He stood there; fixed, saying nothing.

"What?" Arze' twisted her head to one side, raised an eyebrow and held a wild, deranged expression. Did I strike a nerve?" she asked.

It was obvious to him that she would probably make good on her proposal, but he couldn't let her know that he actually didn't want that to happen. "Sure. Open up a Pandora's Box. Once my wife knows, your husband will find out, too. And I'm sure you wouldn't want the burden of disproving to your husband what he would think."

"Really? And what's that?"

"That it wasn't *you* making advances to me! Now, what dya think about *that*?"

Arze' grunted under her pursed lips. She flipped him off, turned and began walking away, speaking in an almost indiscernible voice, "I know just how to fix your butt. So help me God."

Verse 47 ♫

Oh that men would praise the Lord for his goodness, and for his wonderful works to the children of men! Psalms 107:8 KJV

Five rehearsals and five Sundays had flown by. Arze' was in the final chapter of her agreement with Pastor Trantham. She had to admit to herself that the work didn't seem like an eternity. The opportunity proved to be a pleasant and beneficial one, enabling her to rekindle her chops and allow Ezekiel to view her contribution to the church as more than the, "wife of our minister of music."

She did have to remind the saints that her commitment, though, was as a substitute, and that she couldn't wait for Jeremiah to return and take his rightful place.

It was mid-February, the second Sunday, and she stepped into the robing room where the majority of the choir was inside, the rest of them were standing in the wings. Sis. Georgia approached her carrying a huge smile on her face and a large bouquet of red roses accented with leather leaf and baby's breath.

"We wanted you to have a small token of our appreciation for your work, Sis. Day," Georgia said as she presented Arze' the flowers. "You've been great. We look forward to the time when we can sing under your guidance again."

Arze' accepted the flowers and thanked them, but thought to herself that Jeremiah should not ever get sick again. It won't be as easy to secure her services the next time. "Thank you, Georgia. Thanks, all of you." As she hugged Georgia, she began to feel tears forming. "Each of you made the task easy and enjoyable. Your minister of music should return to you by choir rehearsal this week. We both appreciate every one of you."

The choir's hugs and well wishes ran right up to the last remaining minutes before the zero hour of worship service time, where Arze' was startled by Renard, who was standing in a side entranceway to the sanctuary. She tensed as he brushed his hands across the stems of the floral bouquet, a snarl on his face as he eyed Arze' from head to toe. "Well, that's special. I guess you feel on top of things, huh?" he asked.

Arze' chose to ignore him, but he refused to move aside. "Renard, I have a job to do. I suggest that you go on to the organ, too, since the service is about to start."

"Sure, babe," he said, but he stood right there, seeming to meet her challenge with head-on determination.

"Look," she replied adamantly, "I ain't your babe, and I don't play games with people. So you need to move."

He crossed his arms and said nothing.

"I'm sure that if we stand here and there's no sound coming from the piano and organ when service starts, that somebody will come around looking for us. Or do you have to feel me up again before you're motivated to play this morning?"

Grinning, Renard stepped aside.

With a tremendous spirit, The Voices of Ezekiel sang from the three verses of *Lift Ev'ry Voice and Sing* up to the selection before Pastor Trantham's sermon.

The gang of musicians had their guitar picks, drum sticks and amplifiers ready, awaiting Arze's signal to begin the song written by her husband. Renard sat at the organ with a disinterested look, as if he could predict the outcome of the song. The choir started out with the chorus.

Arze' looked out into the congregation, realizing that her vantage point was the same one her husband had every Sunday. She felt an air of relief; they seemed to be enjoying the song. Most of the people were clapping and some were even trying to sing along with the choir. She hoped they were in tune with the new composition, not because of the rhythm, but because of the believable message in the lyrics:

> *Don't you know you have power to give God the praise? So praise Him in every way, all your days, don't delay And in all my days I will give him praise for the Wonderful Things he has done. . .*

After the morning service, Arze' had an uneventful exit from the choir stand.

"Sister Day, we hate to see you retreat to your usual position in this church. It was a pleasure," Pastor Trantham said to Arze' in the administrative hall. He passed her a check. "And that other matter?" He winked at her. "The situation will be dealt with."

"I understand, she said. Arze' looked at the check, which turned out to be Jeremiah's regular salary, not the usual amount that's given to substitute musicians. "Thanks so much, Pastor. We both appreciate it."

Pastor Trantham's gestured toward her with a think-nothing-of-it wave. "Not as much as the church did. The people have been blessed by you. No joke. They loved you. But we do look forward to seeing Jeremiah this week."

"He'll be right here, Pastor." Arze' looked at her watch. "Let me get home and check on that husband of mine."

"You do that. I have urgent business to take care of myself before the evening goes away."

Verse 48 ♫

*There is no peace, saith my God, to the wicked. Isaiah
57:21 KJV*

Renard had well cleared sight of Ezekiel's campus
and was miles away when he answered his phone.

"Bro. Singleton?"

The voice on Renard's cell was dispirited, almost
inaudible. "Who's calling?" he asked.

"It's Rev. Trantham. I tried to catch you before you
left the church, but you must've run outta here."

"So you're still there at the church?"

"I probably won't leave here until the afternoon Bible
study is over."

"Oh. Well, you're the Pastor," he said with an
intentional dose of sarcasm.

"I even had Deacon Steele to try locating you but . . .
anyway. I need you to return here so that we can talk about
something important."

Out of anguish, Renard gripped the life out of the
steering wheel. "You sure it can't wait. I mean, I'm already
well away from there and-."

"No." Trantham's voice was insistent. "I need you to
do better than your best to come back here ASAP. This is
urgent and needs your absolute attention."

"Alright, alright. I'll be back there in about twenty.
No, give me thirty minutes."

"See you then." The phone went dead immediately.

Renard made his return trip in less than thirty
minutes, but not before making a stop at Lou's Deli for a hot
pastrami sandwich. He would have been able to discuss
anything with Trantham on an empty stomach. He parked

there at the church, taking a few minutes to digest some of the sandwich before going in.

"Bro. Singleton! You made it." Trantham peered down at his cell phone. "Not bad timing. Have a seat." He motioned to a small, round conference table that was situated in a corner of the office.

Renard sat in a chair, facing him.

Trantham stretched out his arms above the table, reaching across to Renard. His eyes were a signal that he wanted them to grasp hands. Although reluctant, Renard responded.

"Let's pray," Trantham said as he bowed his head. "Lord, we're asking your choicest blessings. We know you are aware of our sins. We also know that you are just and able to forgive if we would just ask. Clean up carnality and make us whole again. These and other blessings we ask in Jesus' name, Amen."

Renard pulled away without giving recognition to the end of the prayer.

"Before I get to what I really called you for, I've got a question." From his jacket pocket, Trantham pulled out a piece of lavender felt.

Renard tried to hide his embarrassment to the preacher's obvious discovery.

"In the midst of doing some study, I needed to check a reference that could only be found in the pulpit Bible, and I found this."

"What is it?" Renard asked.

"I don't really know." Trantham took his time, carefully examining the piece of felt. "This was in the Bible. I know these are music symbols. I've forgotten the little music I learned in middle school," he said, amusingly.

"I hear ya."

"And I know my Greek. This sign is Gamma." He was speaking as though he was trying to answer his own questions. "You ever seen it before?"

"No. I can't say that I have." Renard was stretched in his search for a suitable response. "I tell you what. Are you gonna do anything with it?"

"I don't have need for it. I just thought maybe you'd have some idea what it is."

"No, but if you let me take it, I'll ask around. It's possible that one of the other musicians lost it." Renard was impressed with the velvety precision of his falsehood.

"Funny place to lose it," Trantham replied, but he handed it over.

Renard was shocked at the ease of getting his arcane device returned. "I'll take care of it." Now, he would have to figure out a way to place a new item.

"Sure. Now I don't want to take up any more of your time, because both of us should be drained from working in this morning's service. Can you recall any unpleasant interaction between you and Sister Day this past week?"

Renard was in total shock. He dared not repeat the stream of female-dog names he was calling Arze' at that moment. "No, I don't know of anything out of the ordinary that took place."

"Well that's unfortunate, because Sis. Day brought it to my attention that you made some inappropriate gestures toward her; invaded her personal space. Even fondled her."

"She said that? Are you sure she was talking about me?"

"You're the only Renard Singleton I know. Yes. She specifically identified you as the one who approached her in a sexual manner."

"Absolutely not! She's highly mistaken. I've been nothing but an upright gentleman to her. I welcomed her into the music department for her short stay, and offered my assistance to her."

"Well, that's quite unfortunate-."

"What?"

"That you couldn't see it in yourself to be upfront with me. In this day and time, sexual assault is taken seriously; not just in the church, but anywhere for both men and women. But she didn't want to press charges."

Renard swallowed. "Oh she wanted to go there, did she?"

"Yes." Trantham's voice raised, and his nostrils flared. "It's her prerogative if she knows she's in the right. But you need to listen, because she's just done you a favor."

"What dya mean?"

"If Sister Day were to take this to the measures she can lawfully go, that would mean you'd get arrested, she would have to face public scrutiny, both of your spouses would be aware of what has happened . . . so forth and so on."

Renard grunted.

"So as your employer and her pastor, I've decided to take an employment measure, and with this, she prefers to keep the reasoning behind it under wraps and away from the public. I've discussed this reprimand with the appropriate leadership. I've vowed to keep it silent, and my advice is that you do the same."

Renard breathed deeply to control his annoyance. "And that is?"

"I'm giving you an unpaid leave of absence," Trantham stated resolutely.

Renard leaned forward. "So I'm supposed to take a reprimand because of her lies! This is ridiculous!"

"Kill your arguing, Bro. Singleton, you did it. And I'm doing what I need to do in hopes that you assess your position here, if you want to keep it." Trantham moved in as well, further closing the distance between them. "Better yet, take the time off to assess your life. By all indications, you're in disarray."

"I don't believe this . . ."

"Well, believe it. Would you rather the church find out, the law find out – her husband find out and come after you over his new bride. Believe it brother. This is your best option."

"I guess I have no choice."

"You don't. Take this. By the time this leave is done, her husband will be back and in charge, and you'll be back ready to help get music prepared when I start a new preaching series. True Praise."

Renard was tossed. On the one hand, he didn't need the income; there were streams of income flowing in his direction from orifices that the church would never be privy to. As for Arze', he didn't care about that tramp; there were too many other woman that he would get a positive response from, if he were to approach them. On the other hand, without a church, he couldn't continue his membership in the Society. He *had* to be employed with a church. Tyrus was no-nonsense when it came to the upholding of that edict. So yes, he would take the punishment to preserve his job there at Ezekiel.

And thank you, Trantham. With the knowledge of an upcoming preaching series on Praise, the very thing that Renard was against, it would be a perfect time to launch his rematch of a DOA.

Trantham twisted his head and rubbed his face. "Renard, do you even feel *any* remorse for your wrongdoings?"

"I think the Bible talks about coming into the knowledge of wrong. Then, it becomes easy for someone to come into repentance. And then they can be saved. I'm just paraphrasing. . ."

Trantham nodded.

"Well, as long as *I* don't see it as wrong, it ain't wrong as far as I'm concerned."

Trantham shook his head in obvious disgust. "What an amazing philosophy."

"And fortunately for me, one that works."

Verse 49 ♫

But the Lord is my defense and my God is the rock of my refuge. Psalms 94:22 KJV

The city of Olds and its inhabitants seemed to be in the true summertime mood. A bit of financial stability had come to the city, because many of the automotive plants and their suppliers were at least partially up and running. Some credited Obama government stimuli; some gave value to financiers moving out of their own way. Whatever the reason, the working class went back to work, which made for happier spouses. Happy, working parents treated their children better. Happy children played and interacted with their peers better. Happy families made churchgoing more pleasant.

Whether the citizens admitted it or not, the spread of happiness was God's doing, and it was restoring faith in and to the city. The people's faith even had a direct effect on Jeremiah and Arze', who were admittedly part of the city, having lived there now close to a year.

It was early July 2014 and Jeremiah felt confident that his blessings were outweighing any of his challenges.

Fully recovered from Giardiasis and in great overall health, he completed an enjoyable first year as a teacher at Olds High. Nine and a half months as a married man, he was still in his honeymoon stage, where he and Arze' continued to grow in love and understanding. The anticipation of moving into their home had dwindled somewhat; each day seemed to require another closing document, another file or some random form, but they remained faithful. "We're not going to be defeated when it comes to that house," he had told Arze'. "Closing day will come when it's supposed to come."

Months and Sundays at Ezekiel had been drama - free. Great singing. Anointed preaching. Wonderful fellowship. He had witnessed Family and Friends Day without incident. The Easter presentation went off without a hitch. Women's and Men's Day, well - Renard who? His nemesis was cooperative, and had even made attempts at being helpful. Could it be that a life transformation was in his future?

Jeremiah should not have blinked. Just when he figured that the dog was no longer in the fight, a new crop of troubles – this time, filled with fleas - emerged.

Jeremiah's relatives had always warned him. *Beware.* As long as a snake had a head, he'd be quiet for a time, but the snake was soon destined to raise its head. And attack.

Jeremiah began to witness the resurgence of demon Renard in that same seventh month. It first began as minute, insignificant incidents. Questioning a song here. Intentionally missing a chord progression there. It was an abundance of short-lived circumstances where the average person not acquainted with the opposing parties would say, "Jeremiah, you're just being a baby," or, "Bro. Day, your imagination's running away with you."

On the contrary. Jeremiah had not taken loss of his senses. He had carefully studied the source. And the source was up to no good.

Jeremiah commented during a choir rehearsal that he was at a loss for a fitting invitational song for the upcoming Sunday morning service.

"Why don't you try this," Renard suggested, and he broadcast the title of a song that had no significance to the sermon title, and would be self-serving, highlighting his prowess at the instrument.

He thinks he's slick. Renard's suggestion sounded innocent enough. Jeremiah thought what nerve, to make the suggestion aloud and in the presence of the Voices, so that any reaction Jeremiah displayed would be in full view.

He was proud of himself for having masked his anger toward Renard from the rest of the choir. He might have been wrong, but he felt it wasn't important for the entire music department to know that their two main musicians were in an ongoing battle.

"That's a nice song," Jeremiah replied, although he felt like saying that to sing nothing would be better than Renard's off-base recommendation. "But I think we need a song that speaks more directly to the sinner who stands, indecisive, wanting to accept salvation. Don't you?" he asked.

That silenced Renard for the moment.

Jeremiah was certain that his organist's central purpose was to halt the flow of service; underhanded, devious attempts to latch on to and kill the spiritual joy that Ezekiel had now relished for quite some time. Then, Jeremiah had another thought. Maybe Renard had no clue to what the flow of a service was?

Leo's explanation of the Society and Renard in particular was absolutely correct. Jeremiah was having to endure a spiritual battle. The fight itself might be among carnal, mortal beings, but Heaven was engaged. Jeremiah knew it, and wanted to act accordingly. He was in touch with his feelings, though. He needed to unload some steam off to someone who would understand what he might be going through.

Jeremiah trounced into Pastor Trantham's office. "Renard's got to go!"

Peering over a set of reading glasses that sat on the edge of his nose, Pastor Trantham asked, "What happened now?"

"The better question should be; *what isn't he doing?* It's hard for me to make decisions on our music when I feel like I have to watch this man on every turn."

"Too hard, huh? I understand."

"Not *too* hard, Pastor. Respectfully, I don't think you do understand."

"I do, I do. Really," he said. His composure was always so calm and composed. It was so much of a contrasting personality to the fiery preacher that Jeremiah witnessed during his sermons. "But let me ask you. Which type of demon would you rather fight?"

"What do you mean?"

"Which one? Would you rather have a demon right in your presence, one that you can just about know that they're making themselves known? Or would you rather have a devil that hits you and dodges, and you can never identify them?"

Jeremiah hadn't given it any thought. Some may have wondered whether the prize was worth the contest, but he was resolute. "I guess that's a unique perspective."

"Me," Pastor Trantham went on, "I'd rather have a demon that I can prepare for their attacks, because I've already put a tag on them."

"I guess you're right. When I pray, every time I pray, God shows me that I should be on guard."

"There you go. He's doing what he promised. How we respond is up to us."

"Sorry."

"For what?"

"For coming in like I did. I had to let go of the anger I was feeling. Somehow."

"For what it's worth, apology accepted. But that's what I'm here for. It's my job to make you know that you're being supported, even when the job gets hard. But aside from that," Pastor Trantham continued, "I was needing you to stop in anyway."

"What's up?"

"I'm going to delay my series on True Worship for probably another month. I just got back from the Baptist Congress in Dallas and I'm tired. When I start this series of sermons, I want all my attention given to it. This includes the music."

"Whatever you say." Moments passed and the two sat in silence. Jeremiah came upon an idea that he initially thought was mindless. He already had Pastor Trantham's attention, so he forged ahead, believing that Heaven had laid Inspiration in his lap. "Can I ask you a question?"

"Yes?" Pastor replied.

"What if we ask the singers and musicians to join in a fast for the church and this series of sermons? I mean, we lead worship during the majority of a service, and we need to be spiritually prepared-."

"I think it's a great idea!" Pastor Trantham said. He began to moan in a way that told Jeremiah his excitement was sincere. "You work out the details. In fact, do this for me. Study the Daniel Fast. That's the one I'd like you to do."

"I didn't realize that you'd be on board so fast, Pastor."

"A spiritual cleansing and focus will do the music department much good. There'd be no valid reason to deny going through with it."

"Consider it done, Pastor. We should have time to do a complete fast before the set of sermons start."

"Our people need this, and I want to deliver the series with a refreshed body. But get ready. I want the music to coincide with this preaching in every way."

"Alright Pastor. And I'll set aside the repertoire of music and songs we were gonna use until you give the go ahead."

"I know that something good is bound to come of these sermons."

"Is that right?"

Pastor Trantham nodded. "Oh yes, considering the number of times they've been put aside for other things."

Verse 50 ♫

...In the ninth month that they proclaimed a fast before the Lord to all the people in Jerusalem...   Jeremiah 36:9b

Much to the delight of the congregation, the Youth and Young Adult Choir sang with unbridled energy on that Sunday. After the sermon, Jeremiah was allowed to make a special announcement, in which he set a special meeting for the entire music department.

That Monday evening, close to three hundred men, women and youth met in the old sanctuary around 6:30 for Jeremiah's called meeting. To Jeremiah's knowledge, only two people outside of Arze' - Pastor Trantham and Rev. Knight – knew what the subject matter for the gathering would be.

That evening, someone had failed - in the hottest season of the year - to turn the air conditioning on before the people arrived. So, the cool had to catch up with the heat the crowd had already generated, but that didn't sway Jeremiah's motivation. "I'm really glad that the majority of you decided this meeting was important enough to come out this evening," he said while standing before the crowd. "I don't want to take up much of your time, but I needed us to meet in person so that if there were any questions, each of you would have the chance to get them addressed face to face. Firsthand."

He asked Rev. Knight to pray and Georgia to read a short scripture which came from Daniel 1:12.

After thanking the department again for coming, Jeremiah spoke. "There's a tremendous significance in what Sis. Georgia read. In fact it sums up what this meeting is actually about." He paused, shifting his eyes toward Renard and Tamla, who had entered through the door together, and stood in the back. "What we'd like to declare is a fast. Some of you may have special needs that you need the Lord to give you an answer to, and Pastor has taught us that some things require more than just an altar call or saying a quick prayer before you go to bed. It's not my business to know your needs, but if I'm to be an effective minister of music, I should recognize when the entire department may need renewing, or refreshing."

"What kind of fast?" Georgia asked.

"The same kind of fast that you just read in that scripture. A Daniel fast," Jeremiah replied. "I'd like to start this weekend, if possible. It would be wonderful to have one hundred percent participation. More powerful that way."

"A Daniel fast?" came the question from one of the ladies.

"Yes ma'am. It's where you refrain from meats, sweets, fruits, juice, coffee, tea. It's basically a diet of vegetables and water. And the fast would last for ten days."

There was a slight murmur from a few in the crowd.

Jeremiah snapped his fingers to spark his memory. "Oh and one more thing in addition to the fast itself. Prayer is supposed to go hand in hand with it, so if everyone will join us and devote yourself to some time in prayer as close to noon as possible. On all ten days."

"We've never done anything like this before. I mean, the church has fasted, but not the music department specifically. Include me," Calvin stated. "How will this help the church, though?"

Jeremiah looked over at Pastor Trantham, who stepped forward to address the department. "There's an important event coming up in the life of our church. Not like a special day, but an event. It's spiritual, powerful, it's forcing me to wait until I hear from the Lord on how he wants His plan to be unveiled. Jeremiah has asked me about doing this fast. It will be under my watch. It has my full approval." Smiling, he beckoned for Jeremiah to continue.

"I realize that singing requires a sacrifice, but each of you is a warrior. And like a soldier in an army, you need mental, physical, and especially spiritual renewal. Prayerfully, this ten-day fast will be your answer."

Jeremiah caught the watchful eye of Renard, who had started pacing along the back wall. He turned his attention back onto the remainder of the listening crowd. "There will be some that won't participate. Some may try to convince you that *all this ain't necessary*. But believe me, this is essential for our growth as a department, as a ministry. And you may not see tangible results immediately, but God will reward our efforts, I guarantee." There was no mistake in hoping that Renard heard his comments. It was no telling what his nemesis might say to one of the choir members, trying to convince them that their music minister was out of his mind. "I'm only asking," Jeremiah said, "that you follow your heart as God leads you."

Verse 51 ♫

For rebellion is as the sin of witchcraft, and stubbornness is as iniquity and idolatry. Because thou hast rejected the word of the Lord, he hath also rejected thee from being a king. I Samuel 15:23 KJV

"Follow my heart. That's exactly what I was going to do. I didn't need him to tell me what I was planning to do the whole time," Renard whispered. He yanked on Tamla's arm, and they both left out the same way that they entered.

"So what do you plan to do?" Tamla asked Renard.

"What do you think, girl? No, I'm not doing that fast. Why on earth did you have to ask? You knew what I would say."

"I'm not you, Renard. I don't know what you'd do. Personally, I don't see the harm in the fast. Matter of fact, it may do the choir some good."

Renard looked at her in disbelief, wondering how such a vixen could be so ignorant. "What? Listen to you! You've become one of them."

"Them who? In case you haven't noticed, I'm my own woman, with my own thoughts."

"Oh yeah, you're your own woman," he said slyly. "But capable of your own thoughts? That's debatable."

Tamla eyes widened with an entrancing stare. "I'll tell you what!" With a mix of curse words and derogatory phrases, she told Renard where he could get off.

"Man! I won't insult you in the future. Dog, baby, I'm on your side. I'm only trying to keep you outta things that're ridiculous wastes of time. Chill."

"You chill!"

Renard reached his arm across her shoulders and leaned in close to her." C'mon now. Don't be like that."

"Like what?"

"You know." He gave her a peck on the cheek. "All uptight. Now you know I don't mean you any harm."

"Sure you don't."

"Believe me, baby. Things are good. Breakout artists are contacting my artist group on a daily basis. They're clamoring to be a part of Luciferious and Odyssey of Mind."

"I'll bet." She softened her hard sneer. "Well, you can't be all bad. I hear that you're pulling in the talent."

"Not to mention, the money. I'm just waiting for you, baby."

"What?"

"You didn't know? I *need* you in this artistry venture. With your raw sound, I could start you off singing demos, on to background for some major artist or label, and then on to your solo career."

"It's just one problem with that."

"What?"

"I sing Gospel!"

"You're just not gonna let that go, are you? Girl, there's no life in that religious bull-."

"You need to watch yourself."

"Like you live what you sing. All you need is a taste of this," he said, pulling out a wad of hundred dollar bills from his pants pocket. "Remember. I know you-." Renard felt his cell vibrating, and he stopped to check the message:

HONEY! YOU NEED TO COME HOME. MY WATER BROKE!!

"We're gonna have to continue this conversation another time," he told Tamla as he rushed to start his car.

Verse 52 ♫

Delight thyself also in the Lord; and he shall give thee the desires of thine heart. Psalms 37:4 KJV

"Give us, I don't know, maybe a couple hours to get ready?" Jeremiah asked on his cell while kindly brushing Arze' off to another part of their apartment. He couldn't stay focused on the call with her continuously asking who he was speaking with.

The voice at the other end of the phone replied, "Sure Mr. Day. How about 10:30?"

"We'll be right there," Jeremiah said. He turned to Arze', who had moved a few feet away, an excited look on her face. "Baby, get ready to leave here. We're taking a trip," he told her.

When Jeremiah and Arze' entered the offices of Nichols & Satterfield, Attorneys at Law, Darren Satterfield met them at the door without allowing the office receptionist to voice her usual greeting. "You ready to get a house today?" he asked.

They were more than ready. Jeremiah and Arze' had counted close to eight months of searching, praying, arguing, and reapplying. It had been a long, arduous road to home ownership, but their test was about to be a testimony.

"Has Peonie made it yet?" Jeremiah asked. Mrs. Peonie Taylor was the realtor the Day's had secured for their home search and purchase. No doubt, she was happy to see that day, too.

"Not yet," Tara Nichols replied. She was hurrying toward them, a stack of papers in her hand.

The office receptionist stood up from her desk, holding a receiver against her ear. "Mrs. Taylor should be here any moment. She's on the phone, letting me know that she's running a bit behind."

Jeremiah felt his phone vibrating, and looked at the text. "She just sent me the same message," Jeremiah said, quietly. "Seems like everyone will be in place."

Atty. Nichols escorted them into one of the conference rooms where a long table, eight chairs and a couple computers were some of the fixtures. "Here everyone, have a seat," she said. "Relax. I have a little more work assembling your mortgage package, and I'll be right back in.

"I guess it's going to come off today, honey," Arze' whispered.

By then, the realtor had arrived and had been seated at the conference table.

"Pinch me, because I don't believe it myself," Jeremiah said to Arze'. "But we shouldn't be surprised. We're saved."

"And the race isn't given to the swift or to the strong-," Atty. Nichols interrupted. She sat down at the conference table and neatly placed two stacks of paper in between the three of them.

"Now you know we can finish Ecclesiastes, don't you, attorney?" Jeremiah asked confidently.

"C'mon you two." Atty. Nichols pulled a set of pens from her suit jacket. "Let's get these papers signed."

To see the glow on Arze' face was worth more than anything Jeremiah believed he would ever own. Sure. He wanted to be able to claim 57 Central Avenue as theirs. He would take on a feeling of completeness, a man conquering his territory.

But it was Arze' who summed up the event. As she began to sign the seemingly endless mountain of papers, she wailed with a smile, "We've endured this to the end."

Verse 53 ♫

And it shall come to pass, when many evils and troubles are befallen them, that this song shall testify against them as a witness; Deuteronomy 31:21 KJV

"You think something's wrong, Kira? They told us that the baby's due date is July 24th. What's happening?" Renard asked as they made their way to Old's Mercy Hospital.

Kira was in the back seat, wrapped in a thick, cotton robe and twisting in obvious agony. "I don't know," she managed to mumble.

Renard swiped the beads of perspiration on his forehead. "Too soon. It's too soon."

It had only been a week ago that Kira, who was in her thirty-second week, went to get a pre-natal check-up with Dr. Haddad, her OB-GYN. On that day, the doctor examined the baby's vitals and recorded its movements with the ultra-sound. Dr. Haddad had assured them, "Everything's in order, you're coming along fine."

During that same visit, Kira kept worrying Renard, asking if he wanted to know the sex of the baby. "Oh no," he told her. "I can wait until the baby's arrival."

To be honest, yes. He wanted to find out that day, but Kira didn't, and the doctor was going to honor the mother's wishes. All that Renard could do was shrug his shoulders. "It's up to you, babe," he replied in hesitation.

Secretly, he wanted a boy. His reasons were selfish for desiring a male child, although he lied to Kira, saying that the gender didn't matter. She didn't need to know just yet how he intended to cash in on Luciferious; branding the name that had been kept so long from him.

He hadn't spoken with Adrian in six months; the day he was informed of his birth name. Renard knew that he would soon have to communicate with his father on some level, and patch up their relationship. After all, on some date in July, there would be three living generations of Singleton men, making Adrian a grandfather.

He looked over at Kira with her fully developing baby-bump. He couldn't help it. At that moment, Renard vowed that whatever they decided to call the baby, he would be proud to give the history behind how they settled on what to call him. Or her.

A small team of healthcare professionals were waiting at the door when they arrived at the hospital. While they attended to Kira, Renard kept insisting on getting answers to her condition.

One of the nurses, a thin, chocolate woman who appeared to be in her early forties, turned to him. He could tell by her annoyed expression that he had better back away and allow them to do their job. "Your wife is going to be fine," the nurse assured.

"What about our baby?"

"Honey, we will take care of the mother. We *will* take care of the baby."

Once Kira was settled into a private room, Renard was allowed to enter. He touched Kira on the shoulder.

She turned, looked up at him and smiled. "Hey honey."

"Hey. Is everything alright?"

"Oh yeah." She paused for a breath. The baby has decided to come early, that's all."

"That's all? You act like it's nothing."

"The baby is a person with a mind of its own."

"If you say so."

"Honey, I worry about you."

You should be thinking about yourself, he thought. Shocked that the subject of conversation turned so rapidly, he asked, "What's happening to me?"

"I've tried to stay out of your way and not say anything, but this path you're on makes me afraid."

Path? Yes, he was busy. Between a job, his music, and other personal endeavors, he had quite a bit going on. Admittedly, he kept a huge part of his daily activities from her, purposely. Not wanting to assume where she was going with her questioning, he asked, "Of what?"

"That's the bad part. I don't know enough about what you're doing to tell you what not to do. I think your music is suffering."

"No way," he rebutted. "It's better than ever before. You're right. You don't know-."

"And this Luciferious kick you're on? What good can come of it?"

Oh. This is where she's going. "It's not a big deal. It just the name of the LLC. Nothing to worry about. I promise. You need to concentrate on resting when you can."

"I guess you're right. The next contraction is sure to be on its way very soon." She turned away from him and buried her face into the pillow.

About an hour and two or three contractions later, Dr. Haddad and his nurse came into the room to give Kira a brief exam. "It won't be long," Dr. Haddad said to her. He motioned for Renard to follow him outside of the room.

"What's going on, doctor?" Renard asked.

"Oh nothing that can't be handled quite easily," he replied. "The nurse had already explained to Mrs. Singleton about the timetable for a baby being full-term, and I wanted to tell you personally. Calm down. I sense the tension in your voice. There's nothing to worry about."

"What makes you think something's going on with me?"

Dr. Haddad formed a compassionate smile. "Uh, let's see. Medical degree. Longtime hospital resident. Should I go on?"

"I get it, doc."

"Look. Kira's well into her third trimester. Lots of mothers have babies in their thirty-sixth week. The chances of the newborn being perfectly healthy are well into ninety percent. The lungs are developed by now."

"But I thought full-term is th-."

"Thirty-nine weeks. But Mr. Singleton, no science is exact, especially this one. A full-term baby must be given the same kind of professional care as a preemie. I'm here and will be here until Kira delivers."

"Thank you doctor."

"No thanks needed. What I need you to do is stay calm and be reassuring to your wife and the future mother of your baby that everything's going to be fine. I need all concerned to help her focus on knowing that she and the baby will come through this fine and healthy."

"I can do that."

"I got word that a relative of yours has arrived. I think they're in the hospital chapel. And you know . . ."

"Thanks. What's that?"

"Prayer can't hurt."

Are you kidding me? Prayer? You were doing fine until you said that, doc.

The hospital's chapel was on the first floor near the D elevators. Renard did his best not to pay attention to the vivid stained glass windows radiating against the dark paneling on the walls. Even more evident was the cross centered on the front wall behind the rostrum. He walked down the aisle and recognized the back of Adrian's bowed head. "I know you ain't praying."

Adrian looked up at Renard. His face had a penitent expression. "Kira's mom called me to let me know my daughter-in-law was about to have my grand," he said softly.

"That's what they're telling me."

"Yeah? Well it's something that you should've been doing. You know, calling me."

"Everything's happened so fast. But I'm glad you're here. Really." Renard hoped that his father could sense his sincerity.

"And it's nothing you can do about it," Adrian replied. He looked around. "So, why are you in here? I can take care of myself. You should be with Kira."

"It's easy to say that I'll be in the room while our baby's being born. Now, I'm not sure. Don't know if I can get through it."

"Man you better get in there. That's what Kira's expecting outta you."

Dr. Haddad came into the room, washed his hands and donned gloves before examining Kira, whose legs had been propped up under a bed sheet. "Cervix is looking good. This baby is on the way," he said. "Daddy, you need to follow the nurse so that you can get into some scrubs ASAP."

Renard left as they prepared Kira to be rolled into the delivery room. By that time, Kira's mother and father, Adrian, Terry and Val McClure, and Fredrico Knight had come to be well-wishers for the new arrival.

A laborious hour passed, but Renard survived the delivery.

Kira was still being attended to, but she was okay and in good spirit.

And *he* had made it. Gershon Tobias, 5 lbs. 11 oz., had survived the journey. Dr. Haddad walked up and congratulated Renard, and spent a couple minutes with the entire welcoming party. He leaned in to Renard and whispered, "Mr. Singleton, may I speak with you, privately?"

Renard wasn't alarmed at the doctor's request. Dr. Haddad kept a broad smile as the two walked a ways down the hall. "Stick your chest in, daddy. You're about to burst."

"It's that obvious, huh?"

"Oh yes." Then, Dr. Haddad's expression changed gear. "There's something I need from you. But don't be alarmed."

It was always unnerving to Renard how, when a person warns another not to be alarmed, that it never fails to happen anyway. "What's going on, doc?"

"We need some blood. For the baby. That's all."

"Oh. That's nothing."

"We couldn't ask the mom, since she's trying to replenish herself."

"Of course. But why does the baby need it in the first place?"

"Well, he has a slight anemia. We need the extra cc's for red blood cell stabilization."

"Say no more, doctor. Tell me where I need to go."

"If you'll follow me to the nurse's station and they can take care of you from there."

Dr. Haddad was right. Renard chest was about to burst. "Anything for my son," he bragged.

As the nurse prepped a vein to draw his blood, Renard's phone vibrated with a text from Freestar:

LIGHT A CIGAR FOR ME – WEVE ALL FOUND OUT YOU HAVE A BABY BOY! The message was followed by a series of ludicrous emoticons.

Renard responded: THANKS!

His cell buzzed again: MORE GREAT NEWS. THE DAY MORTGAGE FILE IS COMPLETE. RED FLAGS ON PRE-CLOSING CHECKLIST HAVE ALL BEEN SATISFIED. SUPERVISOR HAS GIVEN APPROVAL IN YOUR ABSENCE. THE AGENCY HAS ATTACHED ITS SIGNATURE. DOCS SENT TO THEIR ATTY. CONGRATULATIONS! THEY HAVE FINALLY CLOSED!

As the nurse loosened the tourniquet and began preparing to take the blood sample, he relaxed in the chair, refusing to look at the needle being inserted into his arm, seething over the thought that Jeremiah and Arze' had received their wish; 57 Central Avenue had become their reality. He relished the fact that he had strung the couple along, burying them in red tape and paperwork for over six months. *And the Days never found out that I was responsible.* He knew that his cheeky maneuvering to delay their purchase would eventually come to a halt, allowing them to get their contemptible little closing date. "What the heck, I still won," he said aloud.

Verse 54 ♫

But draw near hither, ye sons of the sorceress, the
seed of the adulterer and the whore. Isaiah 57:3 KJV

Renard was genuinely concerned about Kira's health, and didn't want her trying to entertain the visitors that had now been at the hospital for several hours. She wasn't going to have it otherwise.

So, the entire crowd of friends, relatives and acquaintances packed into her room with armloads of flowers, candy, balloons and, of course, baby gifts too numerous to name.

And although Renard had to rush Kira to the hospital the evening before, he didn't forget to load his pocket with Nub Connecticut 358's; the chosen cigar of the Society's Gamma chapter. "Have one on me," Renard said, smiling as he passed out the stogies to the men.

"Say the baby's name again," Fredrico demanded. "I want to make sure that I know his name when he becomes famous."

"Yeah, just like his daddy," Renard said as he stuck an unlit cigar into his mouth. "Gershon. Gershon Tobias."

"That's a beautiful name," Val said as she help Kira adjust her bed position and then poured her some water from a pitcher.

Kira had propped up into the bed, just shook her head and pursed her lips in Renard's general direction. "Now I know I won't be able to do anything with him now." When she said that, the entire room filled with laughter.

As the proud couple fielded one questions or suggestion after another, Dr. Haddad slowly opened the door and poked his head in. The grin on his face would make someone believe that he'd just become a father. "Congrats again to the couple. I hate to disturb your good time everybody. Please, carry on, but I need to see you, Mr. Singleton, if you don't mind."

Renard had to put down a small baby gift from one hand and a newborn diaper from the other; he had been busy cracking a joke about baby-changing responsibilities. "Sure doc." He followed Dr. Haddad out into the hall.

"Mr. Singleton, I really didn't want to interrupt your celebration, but it was somewhat urgent that I talk to you. Alone."

Renard sensed a bit of apprehension in the doctor's tone. "Is the baby alright?"

"Oh yes, the baby is fine. We are feeding him with some extra nutrient intravenously. It's fortified with iron. I really want to put a few more ounces on him before he goes home. But he's going to be fine."

"What is it, then?" Renard asked.

"Well, this is in regards to your blood draw. You know, for the baby?"

Renard noticed that Dr. Haddad's smiling and grinning had completely dissipated. He had a *delicate conversation* look on his face. "Doc! Gershon . . . is he really okay?"

"Yes, yes. It's you, sir."

"Me?"

"Ye-yes. You see, by law, whenever a healthcare facility takes blood for the purposes of donation, they are required to test all samples for any communicable diseases, sexually transmitted diseases, and so forth. . ."

Renard's body began to cringe with tension. "I have an STD?"

Dr. Haddad shook his head and began to sigh as if he still had not found the words to convey his findings. "No, not that." He paused. "In addition to those screenings, we conduct DNA and paternity tests, particularly when the child is in need of blood, marrow. This is for genetic purposes, and ultimately to find out the type of the donor."

"Yes?"

"We do it to prevent what we call hemolytic disease."

"Simply put?"

"We don't want to make the mistake of putting blood into any recipient that's not compatible with their own?"

"What *exactly* are you trying to tell me, doctor?"

Dr. Haddad curling the edge of his stethoscope between his fingers. "We typed the baby's blood. It's AB. We know that Mrs. Singleton's blood is B. That's fine."

"And *my* blood?"

"Your blood is O positive."

"So-."

"So it is a zero percent chance that you're the father."

"Huh?" he shouted. People in the hallway turned in their direction. "Not the fa-."

"Please understand that there's a delicacy in this situation. This is the reason why we needed to talk outside of the room."

Not the father. "Oh. I understand, doctor. But, how can that be?"

"I'm sorry, Mr. Singleton. It is one hundred percent, scientifically impossible that you're the father."

Okay. Renard needed time; space to resolve himself to the fact that his current dreams of survivorship and legacy had been shattered. He stood there, boiling in a mental state of confusion. His heart had been excavated, and the hole that was left could not be filled with well-wishes or rhetoric coming from a Society membership book.

Without informing anyone else of his whereabouts, he walked out of the hospital into the sunlight, in wonderment, questioning even why he would want his name attached to the baby. Now, the only need for another paternity test would be for scientific protocol and to establish the proper last name for little Gershon. But Renard didn't need a paternity test for his peace of mind. He already knew who the father was. The only question was how it did happen if everyone involved took precaution?

"Dude, you can't just haul off without telling someone where you're going. You've got more than a wife to see after," Adrian scolded after searching inside of the hospital to no avail and finding Renard sitting out in the hospital courtyard.

"Kira's got plenty company." Renard yanked a rose up from its root and began plucking pedals from the flower one by one.

"But your son is lying there in the maternity wing, attached to a couple hospital instruments, waiting to be held or touched by someone."

Renard wasn't going to ogle and goo-goo any baby that wasn't his. Kira was still weak from the delivery, and was still entertaining visitors, so she could go.

Terry, the father who didn't know, wasn't visiting the baby by himself because – well – he didn't know.

"Have you been listening?" Renard asked in a flurry of intentional anger. "I'm not the father of a child that I thought was all mine for these last eight months," Renard told Adrian. "The baby has only been in the world a few hours. He won't die from neglect right now."

"I hear you. But you really don't act like a man who's just found out that his wife was cheating on him. You just don't."

"Well, in a way, she didn't."

"What do you mean by - *In a way, she didn't? -* Didn't what? Cheat? What do you call it, then?"

"I don't know how to tell you, dad. It's really complicated." No matter how he spun the story to his father, Adrian would be sickened by the thought of husbands passing their wives around. Renard regarding his father as one who lived and thought liberally, freely. But he wasn't *that* liberal.

Renard had to think of how he would explain two men's willing exchange of spouses during a Tyrus Society celebration. It wasn't just their willingness, though. The *girls* did play a role, too. Kira was the only one that got pregnant and had a baby. And, to tell the truth, Renard would've considered the tables evenly played if Val had gotten pregnant with his baby. He didn't care whose womb his legacy had come out of. His main problem was that he had no legacy, no heir to speak of.

"Son, you need to go upstairs and talk to you wife."

Returning inside the hospital was an emotional and physical impossibility just then, knowing that everyone who'd meant anything to Renard were congregated in Kira's room at the present. And some of the same persons he felt like *killing* were situated in that same room.

Verse 55 ♫

Stand in the gate of the Lord's house, and proclaim there this word... Jeremiah 7:2a KJV

It was a hot, late-July on a Saturday afternoon. Jeremiah and Arze' had gone shopping in Bloomfield Hills at Hillside Furniture, and they were inside the store quietly having a disagreement over traditional versus contemporary living room styles for their new home. During that time, Pastor Trantham texted Jeremiah, wanting him to call when it was convenient.

He needed the air to settle between him and Arze', so he called the pastor back immediately. "You should be out and about yourself Pastor," he said.

"Don't you worry yourself over me my friend. Contrary to popular belief, Ezekiel Baptist doesn't take up all my time. And I wasn't expecting you to call me back this quick," Pastor Trantham said.

"I needed to get away from that woman," Jeremiah replied while giving Arze' a playful face. "There's a fight going on and I'm not winning."

"Well, ya'll work that out. I won't be long. I wanted to let you know that I'm ready to start the series on worship."

"Alright, that's great."

"I know. It's been a long, long time coming. It's time now. Let's start the series on True Worship."

"Now? You sure?" Jeremiah couldn't constrain himself from laughing. "Really, I'm not trying to be funny."

"Yes you are, Bro. Jeremiah," Pastor Trantham replied.

"Okay, maybe I'm trying to be a little funny. The choir is ready to pull out the special music that we've prepared."

"Go ahead and get it ready. First Sunday in August. That's when we'll begin."

"How long will it run?"

"Close to eight weeks."

"Wow."

"I know. But eight weeks is what the Lord wants me to do. Our people suffer because they don't have the knowledge. When we're done, they'll have a full understanding of what praise and worship really is."

"Alright now!"

"The first sermon is *This Word*. I won't change it unless the Lord tells me different."

"This isn't like you, Pastor."

"What?"

"Giving me advance notice on what you're preaching. I'm not used to this much strategizing."

"I don't want to leave anything to chance. Our worship is tremendously important, and I want all involved in the service – ministers, deacons, ushers and especially the music - to be on their best. So now you know. You have two weeks. Plan your music accordingly."

Verse 56 ♫

What city is like Tyrus, like the destroyed in the midst of the sea? Ezekiel 27:32b KJV

Renard was slow in leaving the choir stand after the evening's rehearsal, which was an intentional move on his part.

Kira wouldn't expect him home that soon. He'd made a habit of staying out late and coming home at unusual hours, even according to his standards. Some evenings, he'd taken up with Tamla, who would lend him her ear and, on a few occasions, her bedroom company. He knew that he'd taken advantage of her starvation for a man's attention.

Maybe she would bare him a baby. No.

Tamla made it clear that her reasoning for wanting him was strictly sex. His was an act of revenge.

Sure, both the Singleton's and the McClure's have resolved themselves to the knowledge that Gershon was Terry's son. And the four of them – Renard, Terry, Kira and Val - were going through the emotions that accompany unforeseen knowledge. To Renard, however, it was more than DNA. Kira had let him down. Above that, a major part of the empire he was creating would be left unfulfilled. He didn't know whether he could live in the same castle with a woman and a child that he did not father. In the meantime, the heat from Tamla's body was proving to be an elixir while he sorted through that part of his life.

Now his power in Tyrus was another story. He was feeling invincible, and the Edicts confirmed it:

The amount of energy exerted over time can take you to pinnacles never imagined. You have been armed with the Universal Language, the ability to infiltrate and transcend cultures, races, and ideals. Mortals dare not listen to you, but they must listen to your possession. They cannot help but be transfixed on five lines, four spaces and the mathematical formulas that are composed on this grid of melodic and harmonic display. Put the power in the air and the mortal will worship you, the composer, while setting aside the composition. Lacrima. AΩ

Renard could time the preacher's movements perfectly and move accordingly, because Trantham had interrupted the rehearsal again, summoning Jeremiah to his office for yet another one of their secretive meetings.

Once he was confident that Jeremiah had gone into the administrative wing, Renard stepped into the pulpit, this time to plant one of his most prized possessions of the Society: his Teardrop Pin. His Tyrus brothers may think that he'd lost his sanity by placing his 14 carat gold, diamond crusted Society of Tyrus pendant in a book that he would never own and would never have a desire to read, but Renard wasn't leaving his next spell to chance. This DOA was going to work, and since Trantham found the felt insignia - his arcane device - before, he felt inclined to deposit the ultimate symbol of his membership. The brotherhood had already labeled him a renegade, one who operated off the grid, so why not? There was nothing to lose, everything to gain as Jeremiah admittedly won a battle last December, but he was determined to win the war. He willed that, one day, Tyrus would recognize his ultimate sacrifice, and seal his immortality.

He sighed, opened the book, and fastened the pendant into the distressed leather on the back, inside cover. "There." He smiled to himself. "Lacrima."

Renard was driving home, deciding not to wait until he arrived before calling Terry from his cell. "I want you to know that my employer is planning something big. Really big."

"What? For Freestar?"

"Naw, man," Renard replied, wondering how Terry could ever think that he was referencing his day job. "The church. And he's being secretive about it, but I know it's for this coming Sunday. There's been several meetings with Jeremiah. And there's been more prepping for this music than any other time that I've known."

"Oh really?"

"Yeah. I wanted you to know that I'm doing it. I'm going for another DOA. I'm gonna make this one work."

"C'mon, man. Let's not go down this route again."

"Look, you just don't get it, do you? Really. You don't listen."

"What!?"

"The national DOA was embarrassing for me. And I need redemption. So screw protocol, and screw whether it's approved by the national officers."

"Renard! Doggone, it's already June! In just two months, Auerbach will announce the next national DOA for this year. Man, exercise patience."

"I've got something to prove, and I don't wanna wait. I ain't gonna wait!"

"Kira said something's wrong with you . . ."

"What dya mean by that? Kira? You been talking to her?"

After a long pause, Terry said, "Well, she's gotta talk to somebody. She thinks you may need to see somebody –

professional. And it's not only her. Everybody's talking about how irrational you are."

"Like who?"

"Everybody. Olufemi. Bacchus . . . everybody. Look. Do I have to name? So Kira came to me, worried. She thinks you're losing it-."

Renard swore. "Kira came to you? I don't think I want to hear any more about how my wife has taken to you or confides in you. I guess I had it coming. It's *your* seed that she carried around for nine months. The child's yours, now your legacy in Tyrus is sealed. Serves me right."

"Hey, you had my wife, too! So don't go putting a guilt trip on me! We both got what we wanted-."

"No I didn't get what I wanted!" No, he didn't. He still wondered how his legacy would come into being. "I'm not crazy. Tell anyone who asks that I'm not losing it. And from now on, let me handle my wife's concerns. I'm done with you tonight."

"Okay Renard. No harm done."

Renard didn't immediately speak into the receiver.

"Renard?"

"My name's *Luciferious.*"

Verse 57 ♫

And the four angels were loosed, which were
prepared for an hour, and a day, and a month, and a year,
for to slay the third part of men. Revelation 9:15 KJV

The weather on August 3rd proved to be dismal;
cloudy with an impending threat of thunderstorms. Jeremiah
was happy to be in the refuge of Ezekiel, where it was not
only dry and warm, but the air held an inexplicable electricity
that morning. The saints were buzzing about, in a hurry to get
inside the sanctuary. The choir was in full attendance,
already arrayed in their robes with not a single singer
carrying on some wayward, unholy conversation.

It was certain that the word had gotten out. Pastor had
hinted to a few of his inner circle, Jeremiah included, that he
would begin a unique series of sermons, and he told them not
to tell it. But someone did. Praise. Worship. Those two words
loomed on practically every choir member's lips that
morning, and they didn't happen to have picked those words
out of the clear sky. So if the singers knew what Pastor
Trantham was about to preach, the rest of the congregation
knew. Jeremiah's experience taught him that choir members
were the world's worst at keeping secrets.

Before Jeremiah entered the robing room, he kissed
Arze', who waved to the Voices before taking her usual spot
in the sanctuary.

Rev. Knight followed in the room behind Jeremiah. "I
can't put my finger on it," he said, "but there's a strange
energy in this place today. God's on the move. The
intercessors mentioned it as we spent time praying in the
auditorium this morning."

"I feel the same way, Reverend. I woke up this
morning with that feeling. And Arze' brought it up on the

drive here. She starting singing, *Welcome Into This Place*. I almost pulled the car over to the side of the road to just shout."

Rev. Knight shook his head in praise. "Amen! Let's pray with the choir, get ready, and go on in."

In the worship service, everything that was scheduled to be completed leading up to the sermon, had been accomplished. Then, it was time for the Word.

Pastor Trantham opened the pulpit Bible. "You heard Rev. Knight read from the Book of Jeremiah. I want to emphasize some of the words from a portion of that same Scripture." He read, "Stand in the gate of the Lord's house, and proclaim there this Word . . ." He closed the Bible, refreshed the screen on his computer pad and declared, "On this morning, I'm standing at this gate, Ezekiel, to proclaim this Word. "This," he lifted his computer pad and then his Bible, "is the only book where we receive the Word of God. So the title of my sermon today is This Word. Repeat after me. This Word."

The congregation responded in chorus with the sermon title.

Pastor Trantham continued, "Now John tells us, *In the beginning was the Word, and the Word was with God . . .*" He went on for twenty more minutes to unveil how the Bible was inspired, prophesied and corrected. His preaching started out as instruction, but evolved into an evangelistic drive as he neared his end:

"So when I enter into the Lord's gates, I'll enter with thanksgiving, with praise. Saints I'll enter with this Word. Look at your neighbor and say to them, *This Word.*"

The congregation responded.

"C'mon! Do it now. Lift up your Bibles and say *This Word*!"

All over the sanctuary, Bibles of all types, computer pads and phones were up in the air. "This Word!" could be heard loudly.

"Knowing and holding onto the concepts of this Word is part of worship, which makes this the first of my series on *True Worship*. For us to worship in the House of the Lord, the first thing we must do is enter in! God beckons to you to enter in. His House is the haven of worship. Think of the many songs that commands us; ENTER. So, with *this Word*, I'll praise! With *this Word*, I'll thank Him! With *this Word*, I'll stand on His promises! With *this Word, I WILL WORSHIP!"*

While Pastor Trantham had worked himself into the drive of his sermon; wiping sweat, grabbing his microphone, shouting a spiritual truth, and then waiting for the Amens. The congregation fell in rhythm, shouting responses. Jeremiah had been listening, enjoying the sermon and making the Hammond organ squall.

Pastor Trantham was into the very last sentences of his sermon; toning down his delivery, inviting everyone to the altar prayer and the unsaved to accept Christ and His plan of salvation. Jeremiah arranged the drawbar registry on the organ and began to play, allowing the Leslie speakers to send a chorus of flutes throughout the sanctuary.

Jeremiah began to hear a progression of off-patterned, dissonant chords whose volumes enveloped the organ's soft harmonics. He knew those chords, recalling college professors who were steeped in music theory coupled with the psychology of religion, who warned him that certain progressions stirred beings from the underworld, and had no place in Christian worship. It was Renard who, in addition to his apostate piano playing, had a turbulent expression on his face. His eye were eerily aglow, like a camera that can't correct the red eye. He sat there, smirking, pretending that he didn't see choir members motioning to him that his playing was out of order.

Jeremiah, beginning to feel a strange case of Déjà vu from about eight months prior, came eye to eye with Renard, and twisted his face as if to tell him, "What in the world are you doing?"

Renard acted contrary to Jeremiah's expression, even increasing his volume as he continued to play.

Jeremiah widened his eyes, and turned his head to one side, getting Renard's attention again. "Stop!" he mouthed in a silent yell.

Renard's boisterous playing continued. By this time, Pastor Trantham had turned around to Jeremiah, who responded by hunching his shoulders, confused as to what to do next.

With ministers looking around, choir members uneasy, and the auxiliary musicians gone silent, Jeremiah knew that something needed to happen quickly, for the atmosphere was out of control. Unconsciously, Jeremiah lunged his body forward. His lips fell against his microphone, and he demanded, "Satan! Get behind me!" The climate inside the sanctuary calmed. Jeremiah leaned back; not out of embarrassment, but trying to reason what heartfelt place his spiritual energy came from.

Pastor Trantham stood up from his chair and hurried over to the piano where Renard's unyielding performance had ceased. At the same time and without any cue that Jeremiah had seen, Rev. Knight followed Pastor Trantham, who was already hovered over Renard.

All eyes were in the direction of the choir stand, with the exception of a few saints who were either moaning, praying, or sleeping. Curiosity had even overtaken Jeremiah, who had stopped his band of flutes from whistling in the air. All the while, two handwritten notes had made their way to the organ, but Jeremiah set them down without reading them right away.

It seemed as though Renard tried to raise up, but a force seemed to prevent him from moving. Not a soul was holding him down. No one had touched him. Not right then.

As soon as Rev. Knight was in a position that Pastor Trantham seemed satisfied with, the chief shepherd pressed his fingertips to Renard's head and his associate touched Renard's shoulder.

It all happened in a second. A split second.

The concert piano bench, which was in perfect condition until then, collapsed, splintered in innumerable pieces. Renard fell on top of it, and collapsed on top of it, unconscious.

"Oh my God!" Jeremiah shouted, not realizing that his microphone was still on.

Choir members within plain view of what had occurred began to scream and shout. Georgia Fisher fainted in the first row of the choir stand. Calvin Inman tried to quiet a small group of the singers who were lost in the excitement of it all. Pockets of people in the sanctuary began to grab jackets, purses and other belongings as they headed for the exit doors. The noise from the frenzy filled the air as though the commotion had consumed the sound system.

Pastor Trantham walked over to the rostrum, reached down at his belt clip to activate his lavalier mike. "Ezekiel! Hush!" he demanded. "Ushers, get up and take your posts!" He pointed out above the congregation. "Stand at the doors!"

Pastor Trantham's voice put the people under control. He knelt down and began to pray an audible prayer while Rev. Knight fell on his face and commenced to pray in a Heavenly language.

Jeremiah didn't remember unfolding the paper that Georgia had passed to him, and he was confident that he received the note folded. In fact, he knew that at no time did he unfold that note. But there it was. Sitting upright and opened for his viewing. The other note, the one that Renard had supposedly written, was missing; nowhere to be found.

PLAY AND SING COVER ME was what the scribbling on the note said.

He didn't know why. She'd never sent a note requesting a particular song. Ever. Believing it to be a sign, Jeremiah did just that, undergirding the prayers with his playing and light singing:

> *Let me feel your righteous Power*
> *Encircle me, Lord this Hour*
> *Wet me with your Latter Rain*
> *Cover Me, My Lord, again...*

In the midst of his playing, singing and listening to the prayers coming from the two ministers, Jeremiah stopped. *I can see them.*

There they were. It wasn't an apparition or shadows. It definitely was not a figment of his imagination. They were there. *Angels.* Heavenly bodies drifting over and throughout the congregation, occasionally descending on one person or another, touching; moving to the next person, interacting with the same manner of touch.

God is real. Jeremiah felt the blessing, and was honored to have been able to see the angelic host in the fle... - for himself. Then, in that moment, the Spirit spoke, telling him that the angels were traveling about, performing in their duties, but he was shirking his. He had been instructed to play...

Jeremiah obeyed and began to play, singing:

> *Cover me. Cover me.*
> *With your Holy Spirit, Lord, cover me.*

It had been an hour, maybe longer, since the Lord manifested Himself there at Ezekiel. Renard had since been removed from the sanctuary and wheel chaired out to the nurses' station. There was no need for an ambulance. He wasn't ill. At least, not physically.

A couple of the deacons, Bro. Steele leading the way, revived Sis. Georgia, having her to remain in the choir stand, sipping on a cup of water.

Jeremiah looked over at Rev. Knight, who looked back with a smile and nod. *He saw the angels, too.* Jeremiah wasn't surprised, though. Rev. Knight was just spiritually constructed like that.

The congregation began to file out of the sanctuary; Pastor Trantham had ordered the ushers away from the exits, allowing people to leave at their will. Their departure, though, was in a most unusual fashion.

Everyone left in a hush. Everyone. In total and complete silence, like each had been hit with a stun gun. Would they remember what had actually hit them?

Jeremiah looked out into the sanctuary, wondering if anyone else had witnessed the move of God in the same manner. Did they see the angels, too? Would they be able to tell their story with the same details that he had seen?

Verse 58 ♫

And thou shalt come unto the priests the Levites, and unto the judge that shall be in those days, and inquire; and they shall shew thee the sentence of judgment: Deuteronomy 17:9 KJV

There was a calm inside of Pastor Trantham's office. He was busy removing his dress shirt and putting on a light jacket to keep from catching cold. He slumped into his desk. "What a service. That . . . was a service."

"*This Word.* Wow! I'm almost afraid of what might happen from the rest of this series you've started," Jeremiah replied. "God showed up and showed out."

"It was more than that-."

"You're right. That's the best way I can explain it. I mean *I could see angels in the sanctuary*."

"You had to be in tune what was happening, or you'd miss it. Those who had their minds on God, they could see, and witness-."

Jeremiah nodded his head in agreement. "When you said, 'ya'll smell what I smell?' Many of the choir members were looking around, dumbfounded – okay. I was laughing to myself. They missed it."

"That's the truth," Pastor Trantham said, agreeing.

"That let me know that I still have some teaching to do. Choir members need to know when they call on God to show up, you need to be aware when he does."

"In all my days of preaching . . . no. In all my years of being a Christian, I have never seen such an event."

"Me either."

"Whoever says God doesn't reveal himself in this day and time, is a liar," Pastor Trantham said.

"Thing about it is; if Renard hadn't done all that craziness, God probably would've shown up sooner in the service."

"You might be right, but that won't happen again, I promise."

"I don't know, Pastor. I can't make that promise."

"Actually, what I mean is that it won't happen again with the same person," Pastor Trantham replied. "Bro. Jeremiah, I have given Renard all the chances that I believe I'm supposed to give him."

"Yeah. He really messed over the music yesterday-."

"I'm not talking about the music, although he has done that, also," Pastor Trantham said. "He's shown me nothing that says he loves the Lord or desires to accept Him as Savior. I've done all I'm supposed to do. I can't make him come to Christ, but I am definitely going to fire him. We can't use him in this music department any longer."

"Oh my goodness, Pastor. It's about time."

"I know you've wanted to get rid of him at least in the last few months."

"Longer than that."

"I understand, but I had to come to the decision after every opportunity has exhausted itself. And we've come to that."

"No problem, Pastor. You're the leader and I may not agree with each decision you make, but I'll always respect your position. When are you gonna do it?"

"I have a state Baptist minister's meeting to attend in Flint over the next two days. I want to release him in person."

"Okay."

"I didn't want to go out of town right after some heated argument; I know when I talk to him, it won't be so pleasant."

Jeremiah looked down at his cell, which was ringing. "Speak of the devil." He pressed a button which muted the ringer. "I'm going to stay clear of him until then. I'm not even going to take his call."

"Whatever suits you. I'll call Bro. Renard and talk to him on Wednesday."

"Will do, Pastor."

"And until I actually talk to him, keep this to yourself, Bro. Jeremiah."

Verse 59 ♫

*But the wicked shall be cut off from the earth, and the
transgressors shall be rooted out of it. Proverbs 2:22 KJV*

It began to thunder before Renard's meeting with
Trantham had ended. By the time he reached the house, it
was a full-fledged storm; rain, lightening, wind. The works.

He parked his car in the driveway and sat for minutes
on end. Time went by unnoticed, unattended.

Ras el-Ain. You've failed me.

He cranked the car and opened the garage by remote,
pulled in. Instead of going into the house by way of the
utility-slash-washroom door that led into the rest of the
house, he stepped out of the garage, completely aware that
he'd left the garage open, the keys in the ignition and his cell
in the seat of the car. With no umbrella, hat or overcoat, he
turned the corner of the house and walked up to the front
entrance.

In the storm, Renard stood there on the landing;
dripping, motionless, mortified in thought. *Ras el-Ain. You
failed me.*

"Honey! What are you doing?" It was Kira, draped in
a heavy bathrobe and house slippers. "Oh my God, what's
wrong with you? I thought I heard the garage door, that
maybe it shorted out and opened accidently, until I saw your
car in there?"

"Yeah."

"Renard?" She pulled him by his suitcoat through the
front door. "You've lost your mind, standing in the rain. You
might as well kiss this suit goodbye." She closed the door
behind him.

Renard said nothing. Standing there, he felt like he was in a dream; the space appeared foggy, as though the acid in the rain had glossed his eyes over. "You doing okay?" he asked.

Ignoring, or possibly not hearing, his question, she hurried down the hall. "I'll be back. You stand right there."

Actually, he didn't feel like he could go anywhere.

Kira, returned, carrying several bath towels; a couple of them were placed at Renard's feet. He took one towel and began patting himself dry, suitcoat and all.

"Here. Take this one. Just take off your clothes and pile them on top of those towels." She pointed to the one dry towel that remained. "Wrap yourself so you won't get a cold."

"Okay."

All you had to do was knock on the utility door, Renard . . . wait. You had your keys." Her voice trailed off. She stood there with a contemplative expression on her face. "Renard. Why did you come to the front door?"

He nodded his head as if to say, "I don't know."

Kira shook her head. "I don't get it. Maybe it's a man thing."

Renard grunted. *No Kira. Ras el-Ain failed me.*

"You want something to eat?" she asked. "Mama cooked this weekend, and since it's just her at the house, she brought half of it. You know she never learned how to cook for one or two people." She laughed faintly.

"Yeah."

"I wish I could get more than one word answers. Something not go right at church?"

"No. everything went fine." He almost felt like he needed to lean against the wall to steady himself. That lie gave him a slight stomach cramp. "I'm just not feeling well."

"I can see that, but walking and standing in the rain doesn't help any. Are you hungry or something?"

"No," he said, remembering that he'd had a partial sandwich earlier. "I just want to lay down."

"Alright honey. Get a shower first."

"Umm hmm."

"And honey?" Kira touched his arm just as he was headed up to the bathroom.

"Yeah?"

"I know that we haven't been on the best of terms since . . . since . . . you know."

Renard just stared.

"I want you to know that we'll get through this. I love you."

"I know, Kira. I love you, too." The baby. Yet another reminder of an incident that ultimately was his fault.

Everything that had happened. It was all. His. Fault.

Finale

A true witness delivereth souls: but a deceitful witness speaketh lies. Proverbs 14:25 KJV

Kira came into the guest bedroom where Renard had slept last evening. "How'd you sleep?" she asked, but didn't appear to have expected an answer. She handed him two Tylenol, waited for him to place them into his mouth, and then placed a large glass of orange juice in his hand. Drink all of it," she demanded.

"Is there any gin in this?" he asked as he began sipping the juice.

"Oh, jokes today. You must be feeling better."

Renard was thankful that she didn't place specifics on her question. His body was better, not that it was ailing in the first place. But his heart was just as weighty as the day before. "Girl please. I'm fine. What'd you think?"

"Renard. Seriously? You were standing in the rain yesterday, and it didn't look like you were trying to get into the house. What was I supposed to think?"

"I had so much on my mind, Kira, stop worrying. I'm cool."

Well you slept really well last night, even snored up something. That's why I'm glad you were in a separate room. You would've gotten on my nerves!"

"Whatever."

"You had some phone calls, but I didn't want to disturb you. Fredrico called, left a message."

"What did it say?"

"Something about one of your artists wanting to renege on a contract? Hey. You handle your business."

He didn't have the mind to be surprised. "Okay."

"And Terry called. And Pastor Trantham. They just left their numbers."

"You didn't speak with Terry personally?" Renard meant to be sarcastic.

"Kira stood in the doorway, a toasty brown silhouette with a shaky smile on her face. Part of him didn't want to be apologetic. Didn't she realize that he was quietly carrying his burden, too? And then, he inwardly answered his own question. "I'm sorry."

She said with a nervous tinge in her voice, "It's alright." She sighed. "What about today? You going into work?"

Renard straightened up in the bed. He couldn't shake the myriad of feelings that had evolved over a long course of time. He had to understand his motives, his consequences and resolve to live with the decisions that he made. Or, *die with them.* At that point in his life, either option looked pretty inviting. "Yeah, honey. I'm going."

"Well, I'm going to drive over to moms this morning. I'll be back by the time you should be coming home, unless you're working late."

"What about the baby?"

"Gershon is four and a half weeks old, Renard. His immunity is building up, so that short ride won't hurt him in the least. His grandma says so."

"She should know," he replied. *And I should care?* "Nothing on my plate should have me at the office past four o'clock or so." He was so proud of himself, concocting that answer on the fly. It wasn't a lie per se, then, it wasn't the truth, either. The truth was, he had plans, but he didn't want her to know. "I may beat ya'll getting back to the house."

Kira smiled. "That's a bet." She slowly closed the door, leaving him in the room.

When Renard opened the bath door after a shower, he was startled by Kira, who was in an overcoat, car keys in hand. "I'm headed out baby." She leaned in.

He took Kira in his arms, and they locked in an embracing kiss.

"It's been a while since we've had that kind of passion," she said.

"I know. Things have been . . . you know."

Kira lowered her eyes. "I know. See you at home."

DaCapo al Fine ♫♪♪

Idolaters, and all liars, shall have their part in the lake *which burneth with* fire *and brimstone. Revelation 21:8b*

Kira was out the door and backing out of the driveway when the phone rang. Renard looked at the caller ID. Fredrico. After the fifth ring, he cussed at the air, realizing that either he or Kira had turned the answering machine off. No, he would not pick up. The last thing he wanted to hear was how some fool music artist wannabe was going to sue Luciferious & Odyssey of Mind, LLC in order to back out of an agreement. No idiot would back out on him in business. Nobody.

Ten minutes later, Renard headed to Chase Bank, to do some banking business.

"I'd like to cash this counter check, please."

"Sure, sir," the teller replied. Her eyes widened one second, narrowed the next. "Can you swipe your card, sir? For ID."

"Sure," Renard said. He pulled out his bank card, and ran it through the machine at the counter.

The teller's expression let him know that his credentials checked out. She asked, "Does it matter about the denominations?"

"No, it doesn't matter."

After a manager signed off on the transaction and the teller secured the money from another location, Renard was escorted to a private room. "Here is your twenty-five thousand dollars in various denominations, Mr. Singleton. Please, if you would allow me, I'm going to count it out to you. Then, if you would count it to double-check the amount."

She counted it, and then he counted it back. The amount was confirmed. He walked out of the bank, cash in a brand new zippered bank bag. He returned home.

He checked the caller ID, which revealed four other callers had been missed. Oh well.

He took the bank bag of cash, went to his office and sat at his desk. He looked at the glass clock given to him by Freestar Financial for his years of service. 9:20am.

He slumped into his office chair, turned on the back massager which had been fitted in the seat. As the mechanical fingers rolled up and down his spine, he began to contemplate:

The Society of Tyrus was not all that he had summed it up to be. There had been many great times, but lately, he had dug up flaws in its dictates. Or was it that he didn't follow its dictates to the letter?

No matter how hard he tried, he would always be reminded that Gershon was the child of a seed that wasn't his own. He would be raising *Terry's* offspring and legacy. There was only one thing that could correct this: *If Terry would allow him to have sex with his wife, Val until she got pregnant by him – and if she would give him a boy child.* Then the child would need to live in his domain, enjoying the fruits of his labor. There, the balances would be righted, and Renard's legacy would be secure.

But that was too many ifs.

The phone rang again. This time, it was Freestar. He didn't pick up.

Then, he thought about an ultimate question. Was the god of Jeremiah what he was adamant to proclaim? Renard didn't know, didn't care to know, and likely, wouldn't have opportunity to know for certain. He was proud of Jeremiah, Trantham, and all of Ezekiel. That were bold enough to stand for something.

Renard stood up, threw his hip against one of the desk drawers, reached back and swept his forearm forward across the contents on the desktop. Sheet music, cookies, files and his personal copies of The Edicts of Tyrus Society and the Codified Manual of Tyrus went in every direction.

He looked down at the floor, at the mess he had created. Tearfully, he brushed aside cookie crumbs and ripped files, lifted the book of Edicts and read a passage for what would probably be his last time:

Musical patterns unveil melodies. These risings and fallings of naturals, sharps and flats are the display life. They do, however, initiate a more intricate series of countermelodies; they are real-life fugues, much like the way personal situations show a revelation. But mortals must be watchful! The fugues could reveal something more powerful in the end than the beginning. So which is better; the fugue of life or the countermelody of death? Contemplation and decision is yours. AΩ

Renard palmed both manuals and left the office.

He went into the master bath and opened the toiletry cabinet. He looked around and over the colognes and brushes, to find a prescription bottle of Hydrocodone and Kira's Misoprostol. He put them in his pocket, left the bathroom and went downstairs. He went to the liquor cabinet and yanked up his favorite, Jim Beam Black.

He grabbed his car keys. With the pills, liquor, bank bag and the two manuals in hand, he went into the garage by way of the utility door, where he located a roll of toilet paper and some duct tape.

He locked the utility door and bolted the garage door. He got a ladder and unplugged the automatic door opener. 10:00 am. With Kira believing him to be at work, he was in no danger of her returning in the next few hours. He was confident that he wouldn't be disturbed. To his surprise, he wasn't nervous or wavering, for the certainty of his impending decision might lessen.

He was ready and it was time.

With the tailpipe stuffed and secured, he cranked the car engine and revved the accelerator. He rose out of the driver's seat, walked to a corner of the garage, where he took gas can and poured about a cup of the gas onto the cash, inside the bank bag and onto his two membership books. He zipped up the bag, and took those three items over to another corner of the garage, where a metal trash can sat. It had been used one time to make a six-liquor punch for a Tyrus Society mixer. The container was empty, except for some dried peels that had been left in the bottom. He placed the books and the cash in the can, took a lighter from his pocket and lit what he had now considered unneeded – unwanted, trash. He stared as the flames rose higher and fumes consumed the space.

Then he took a handful of pills from each bottle, chasing them with the whiskey.

He flopped into the driver's seat and closed the door. In what seemed to be a short amount of time, he could feel the effects of the meds. In his delirium, he rattled off just about anything that came to mind. Allegory. Mixolydian. Christian. *Jeremiah*. Ras el-Ain. Lacrima. *Ezekiel Baptist*. Vivace. *Luciferious*. Death. Festival of Lambs. He sighed, "Oh my."

This door handle seems distant.

Too weak to kick.

Oh no. No turning back. Ras el-Ain failed me.

Can't breathe. Can't see. Can't think. No choking or mental grasp for a reversal of his destiny. He would just sleep. Was Salvation to bypass him?

Too late.

Renard just might get his place in the Ras el-Ain of Fire.

♫FINE♫♫

Neglect not the gift that is in thee, which was given thee by prophesy, with the laying on of the hands of the presbytery. I Timothy 4:14 KJV

It continued to be a regular incident for Pastor Trantham and Jeremiah to meet. The two realized that for Ezekiel to grow spiritually it would take teaching from pulpit and music from the choirstand working in concert and not against each other, as they finally realized that Renard was trying to do.

At one of their meetings, Arze' was included in the conversation, and was occasionally from then on; she had increased her involvement in the music department after Renard's death. When Pastor Trantham questioned Jeremiah about the notoriety that he was receiving from the entire city of Olds because of his work at the church, he replied, "I don't measure greatness. It'd make me no better than Renard was."

"For a long time, we suffered from an internal rot. The music can influence church members in peculiar ways. They will fake excitement. Choir members will sing songs they don't believe in. Musicians and music ministers get thrills out of commotion, and cause pastors to instigate it all," Pastor Trantham said.

Arze' gazed at Jeremiah with clear, confident eyes. "You remained steadfast when a lot around you was corrupt. You were faithful. At the right moment, God worked through you and Pastor Trantham to do a housecleaning. It took time. God's time. Some got deathly sick. Some moved on to other churches. Some lost possessions. Many were exposed in their lusts. At least one has even passed on."

"He will continue to nurture you and guide you, but I guarantee he won't forsake you, Jeremiah," Pastor Trantham declared in agreement with Arze'.

Jeremiah looked out the window of Pastor Trantham's office into the afternoon sunlight. "I imagine there's more work for me to do."

"And you'll run across a new set of pitfalls and temptations. Just keep the faith, please," Pastor Trantham begged.

Jeremiah understood. "I'll continue praying that God shows me all that's needed to keep hell out of the choir stand."

Pastor Trantham reached over, and the three of them clasped hands. "Just do one main thing," he replied. "Keep hell out by keeping God in."

♫ The End ♪

Footnotes:

Please take the time to study the accompanying Holy Scriptures quoted at the beginning of each chapter inside the novel. Careful consideration was given to ensure that Bible passages were included that not only corresponded to the events of that chapter, but give insight to God's Word and bless the reader in some way.

Each reader must understand that The Society of Tyrus is, for the purposes of this book, an organization under creative license of the author, Titus Pollard. It is not, under any circumstance, meant to emulate any organization which exists in real life. It must be understood, however, that any Geographic coordinates and many of the terms used are historically authentic. The Society's membership manuals are a work of fiction. Happy Reading!

GLOSSARY OF TERMS AND HISTORY

Of

THE SOCIETY OF TYRUS

Secret Symbol: The symbol is a purple teardrop outlined in black with an eighth note in its center. For the purpose of the *Society of Tyrus,* The teardrop is used freely within the organization, and used in public without explanation to those not in the membership.

Ras el-Ain: this is Tyre's (Phoenician) water supply and the natural source from which the membership believes the Society's wisdom is derived. Tyre, historically, was a principal port city, a main source for the shipping and fishing industry of Greece.

Lacrima: Is the secret code word used throughout the Society.

Cadmus: Phoenician alphabet named for the son of a Tyrian king. This is the basis for which most PanHellenic/Greek organizations derive and utilize the Greek alphabet.

Purple/Lavender: this is the principal color for use in the Society.

Ezekiel 28th Chapter: The basis for the antagonist's arcane devices and the premise from which this story is derived. Please do not study the Bible as merely a historic work, but the basis for which Christianity establishes its belief. *This includes me – I am a Christian - I am proud to declare!*

33° 16' 15" North & 35° 11' 46" East: These are the actual geographical coordinates of the city of Tyre. For the Society's purpose, these coordinate numbers are used in secret meetings, membership challenges, and to commit their deceased to the afterworld.

Conclave & Refectory: the annual meeting of the Society of Tyrus where nation-wide "confusion of church services" are planned.

Festival of Lambs: an autumn celebratory dinner which can involve a ritualized exchange of spouses for sexual pleasure.

Edicts of Tyrus Society & Codified Manual of Tyrus: These are the two secret publications for which the Society references their history, carries on daily operations and holds their membership to standard. Each member is required to study these manuals regularly and commit certain portions to memory.

Murex: Biologically, this is a tropical predatory snail from which its secretions produce the color purple. In the Society, it is the lowest degree of membership after induction.

Degrees of Membership: taken from names associated with scientific organisms and Biblical characters

> Murex "snail"
> Asaph
> Chenaniah
> David

Musical Modes: used by the Society interchangeably to conjure their power:
> Mixolydian
> Phrygian
> Dorian
> HypoMixolydian
> Locrian
> Aeolian
> Ionian

READER'S GROUP QUESTIONS FOR

HELL IN THE CHOIRSTAND

The author based this book on the background scripture of Ezekiel the 28th chapter. Discuss with your group why you believe he did, what symbols and terms you find in this scripture that relate to terms and phrases in the novel itself.

Ezekiel 28:18 speaks of an illuminated one who has defiled sanctuaries. Do you feel that this scripture relates to the novel in any way?

The author infused a 'satanic book' inside the novel. Has it in any way helped you with the storyline and / or the understanding of Renard's personality?

One of the author's intentions was to show how music can influence a Christian culture. Did you see that in the novel?

Do you believe that the Spiritual realm responds to the actions of the mortal realm?

Luciferious, Arze', Jeremiah, Micah, Daniel and Gershon were all intentionally named to represent their personalities. Did you see how?

How do you feel about musicians who play in church and have secular gigs as well?

The lyrics inside the novel are original tunes written by the author. Can you see their significance?

www.ingramcontent.com/pod-product-compliance
Lightning Source LLC
Chambersburg PA
CBHW061942170626
46813CB00006B/2505